DRAGONS WAKE III

SON OF FERUS

KENNETH MENZIES

JaCol Publishing Inc.

FIRST PRINTING
February 2021

JaCol Publishing Inc.
195 Murica Aisle
Irvine, CA 92614
818-510-2898
Editor-in-Chief: Randall Andrews
Managing Editor: Alison Summers
www.jacolpublishing.com

ISBN: 978-1-946675-60-6

Cover Art by Christina Myvrold

DEDICATION

I'd like to thank JaCol Publishing for believing in my work, to Writers World Boot camp and other members for keeping us on track. I'd like to thank Christina P. Myrvold for her work on the cover, and my editor Randall Andrews.

CONTENTS

1

I stared at the gravestone of 'everyone's friend;' aware of death's different flavors; all of them bitter. Three of them were around. My best friend, John's body lay cold and lifeless beneath the stone with those appropriate words. I'd never see him again this side of eternity; my only mortal ally. My new assistant, Keith fidgeted beside me; an example of another flavor of death. A machine chopped him to pieces and a windfall of chaos magic gave him a reprieve and immortality as well. Despite it or perhaps because, he insisted on remaining dead to his life before then. I didn't understand dying while living but respected his choice. The third flavor of death would greet me out of the clear night sky. My wife, Vedi, a chaos witch, faked her death more than a year before and fled to the void; a virtual death. I wanted her back and because of what I've been through, the void seemed reachable and I doubted if death frightened me anymore.

Keith interrupted the silence, "It's night and it's pretty cold for early fall in California. Couldn't this visit have waited until morning?"

"I'm not just here for John. Notice the night sky?"

"Got it, you're going to talk to Vedi. She can talk to you from the void through clear night skies. Okay, but why am I here? Only you hear her voice. No offense, but I've never met either her or John. I'm just here, it seems."

I activated the weather app on my phone and handed it to him. He pushed his hair out of his eyes and puzzled over it. "What am I supposed to be seeing?"

"What does it tell you the weather should be?"

"Wait. It says it's cloudy and yet it's clear. Now I'm confused."

"Alexandra convinced her husband that he owes me a few clear nights. You're here because I knew this would be his first installment."

"What do you need me to do?"

"If anyone happens upon me talking to Vedi, it won't look like I'm talking to myself."

"Ah, okay. I get it. Sounds like an easy job."

I stepped past John's grave marker to concentrate on the void. Keith amended himself. "Just try not to get too mushy. I don't want to pretend we're an item."

I knew he meant well, but that last sentence threw me off. I thought he had a boyfriend just before he got flayed but he hadn't shown much of an interest in either gender since. However, he expressed a sincere aversion to being seen as gay. Another thing for me to not understand about him, I guessed, and worked to resume concentrating on the stars.

"Aiden?"

Her voice jumped into my head. It hadn't usually come on so fast. Normally I would have to try for a few moments.

"I'm here Vedi. Your voice inside my thoughts is more pleasant than any through my ears since you've left."

"My sweet dragon."

I waited for her to add something to that. I sensed her use of the word dragon had a purpose beyond just being what I am and a word to attach her love to. Yes, I'm a dragon. One usually in human form; so much that I consider it my native form. She usually called me her boy or even her monster more than her dragon. *Why so coy?*

"Is Nix nearby?"

"Yes, as the goddess of the void she's always nearby."

As a dragon of order, I can read sincerity. It's like a lie-detector. Vedi, of course, knows this. She knows better than to lie to me. Unless—she finds advantage in it, and she's as brilliant as any wizard I know in such regard. Calling me her dragon meant she wanted me to pay close attention to what she was about to lie about.

"Relax, Aiden. I want you to rest easy for the next few weeks."

She didn't. My nature won't allow me to pretend I believe what I don't as that would be a lie. I could only manage a meaningless prompt. "Why?"

"It's important that you be well-rested before the coming war in Olympus."

Oddly, that was true, even though she didn't want me to rest, at least not easy.

"How can I do that, Vedi?"

"Read a book, perhaps? There was this one rare piece of fiction I had up until five days before our wedding. I regret not finishing it."

It wasn't fiction and she didn't particularly regret not finishing it. *What was I supposed to do with this?*

"What was this book called? Who wrote it?"

"I don't know who wrote it. It was quite a good piece of work."

She did know who wrote it, personally, and she wasn't lying about her opinion of it.

"And, you can't tell me how to find it? What good is that to me?"

"Oh, if only I had John make a record of the sale. If only. It would be quite the read for you."

I turned to Keith. He held a flashlight to a gravestone when he noticed my stare. "What? Why are you looking at me all of a sudden?"

"Vedi, I think you've given me enough to go on."

"Aiden, so sorry not to talk longer but I do need to go."

Our conversation ended with her telling me the truth. That gave me a mixed feeling; happy she told the truth but not that she had to go.

Keith returned my stare. "What?"

Lightning flashed across the sky. The world blinked blue. More lightning branched like a mighty tree. I learned enough meteorology in high school to know my weather-controlling friend's pushing away clouds for me didn't cause that. The muffled thunder followed by a hiss told me the rest.

I patted Keith's back. "Run to the car."

"What the heck is going on?"

"I don't know, but I'd rather find out back at the hotel."

The blue lightning continued. Stranger than the sound and color, the intensity fooled my peripheral vision into thinking glowing blue nets repeatedly fell on us. The hissing behind the muffled thunder accumulated into eardrum-piercing pain.

We reached the car and the blue lightning ended when we got there.

"Okay, Aiden. What were you about to tell me before the sky turned into a graphics glitch?"

I started the engine and hurried our exit onto the street. "Your job's about to become more challenging."

"Not as a lightning rod, I hope."

"Tomorrow we need to search through John's old records of my business."

"What in blue blazes are we looking for?"

I ignored his word play. "Records of the sale of a rare non-fiction book. Something's in that book that gods don't want us to see."

2

Back at the hotel, Keith opened his laptop. John's records of my possessions were thorough and in digital form. He scanned all receipts except for a few relevant to Vedi. Those he noted were in a self-storage unit in the south end of San Jose. By simple elimination, the record of the book sale had to be there. "Good work, Keith. We'll get some rest tonight and tackle things in the morning."

"But why not go get it now?"

"I'm a dragon of order. I can't even pass through an open door without some kind of invitation or sign of welcome. Sneaking into that storage facility at night would add some broken laws on top. I can't do that either."

"No offense boss, we don't know what's in this book, but if it's something your wife doesn't want Nix to know about, it must be awfully important. Are you really unable to break in?"

"Dragons are the result of magical contracts that we can't break. We can't cheat it. It's self-enforcing."

Keith held a curtain aside. "What about that blue hissing lightning? What if whatever caused that gets to it before us?"

"I can only hope not."

"You could send me right now."

"No, Keith, not even that. I can't tell you to and if you get caught and thrown in jail, you might tip someone off and you won't be able to help me sift through whatever's there."

"I'm not going to sleep well tonight."

"You suspect so. That may not turn out to be true."

"So, you're heading back to your house for the night?"

"No, actually, Keith, I know you too well to do that under current circumstances. There are two beds here and I'm going to take advantage of that."

"You don't trust me."

"Not to head out after that record on your own? Yep. In most things I do trust you, but not this sort. Remember how Gregor captured you?"

"Which time?"

"Both. Now let's get some sleep, or at least try, shall we?"

I texted a magic expert, Alexandra Saint-George, about the blue lightning just before turning in. She gave me a quick response. "Puzzling. I've never seen or heard of blue lightning. I'll get back to you."

There were people more knowledgeable on the subject than her, but not ones likely to be on Earth. Besides, she was Athena's chief researcher. If she hadn't seen or heard of something before, it's likely the Olympians hadn't either and that frightened me.

I TIMED the next day's arrival at the storage facility for right when they opened the gate, in case anyone followed us. I counted four people, ourselves, the manager and one security guard. A raven perched at the end of my unit's row and cawed when we turned down it.

Keith noticed. "I could almost swear that bird's trying to intimidate us."

"I've seen better intimidators in my short time."

The bird cawed again and then again as we walked down the row. It rose into the air and its caws continued coming. A shorter time between each until it started to resemble a car alarm. Keith waited for a response from me. We both knew something was up.

I gave him a response. "Let's get the record."

Blue electric arcs like the lightning from the night before radiated from the bird's wings. The arcs danced along the unit roofs. They branched to the ground.

I grabbed Keith's shoulder to tell him to hold up. He pushed my hand away. "We need that record, boss."

Smoke poured out the structural seems of the units only to be sucked back in. A cacophony of the crunching and whining of inanimate objects under stress competed with our voices.

Keith yelled and ran for the unit. "I think things are imploding."

I ran after him. "Let me get the record. You, get out of here."

He didn't stop. He reached the door and unlocked it just before it warped in. The blue arcs danced across him and he followed the door inside.

I grabbed a corner post and reached after him. Amidst all the material moving to the unit's center a piece of metal pushed outward and into my hand; the door. Keith yelled, "it's in my way. Pull it out."

I wanted to pull him out, not the door. The door was the only thing I could reach. The post bent a couple of inches in and I still couldn't reach him.

"Keith, grab the door. I'll pull you out with it."

He ignored me and reached for a metal box. The door continued warping as I held it. It pinched my hand. A black ball of air appeared in the center of things. Metal and cardboard squeezed into it and vanished. It made no sense.

"Keith, we need to go. Grab the door."

He held the metal box in one hand and reached toward the ball with his other.

"No, Keith, no."

His hand made contact and I feared to lose my second assistant in as many weeks. His hand disappeared into it and I didn't want to watch. Metal fragments of storage units clashed about me and I realized the opposite of my expectations happened. Keith and I lay amidst the remnants of the units across from mine. The implosions had stopped and blown us back.

I ran at the raven, but it vanished as in a likely teleport. Keith remained on the ground holding the box he risked it all for. “What was that?”

“Hopefully Alexandra can tell us something soon.”

He opened the box. “Well, we should soon know more about what Vedi wanted you to find.”

“You sure you grabbed the right one?”

He pulled out a bill of sale. “I’ve got very good eyes. I had those before the Grey Wolf came along.”

“Okay then, Good Eyes, does it tell us who bought the book and where to find them?”

He read the slip to himself and rubbed his forehead. “Wow.”

“Wow? Wow what?”

He handed me the slip. “I think Athena has it.”

3

According to the slip the book had been bought by one Marcus Harmon. Keith and I knew the man. He owned a bookstore in Chicago and for some reason we weren't sure of, Athena employed him. I say for some reason because understanding Athena's reasoning in things is like a hamster comprehending Einstein's reasoning.

"Marcus bought it? So, Keith, you think he acquired it for Athena?"

"It would explain why she's so interested in maintaining a bookstore. She could be using him as a collector."

"Let's get to the car."

"Is that it then?"

"No. We should get out of this place before the police arrive and ask questions."

Once in the car, we had Marcus on speakerphone and gave him the date of sale for reference.

"Here it is."

A high pitched sneeze led to a trumpeting.

"Bless you," said Keith.

"Thank you, blessed child. That old file drawer needs dusting."

"You kept the book in a file drawer?" I asked.

"No, silly. I wouldn't do that. I sold the book to a man named William Scott. He's an old white man with white hair and a rich man's watch."

"Do you have an address or a phone number, anything we can find him with?"

"Yes. He picked that book up at the store, but he's had me ship books to him since then. I think he's still alive. The last book was sent to him last May."

"Text me the address."

"You want me to pick you up at the airport?"

"He's in Chicago?"

"About an hour's drive from the airport."

"Yeah. I'll let you know once my flights set up. Thanks, Marcus."

"So, we're off to see that book?"

I tossed him the phone. "Not we. Arrange two flights; one for me and one for you."

"You want us in separate planes?"

"I'm going to Chicago. You're going back to Slovenia."

"But I thought you wanted me to straighten out records and stuff here in San Jose."

"All the ones not in your laptop imploded at that storage place, and besides, I'm not trusting your decision-making under stress right now."

He turned a shoulder. "I got the record of the sale. Would you rather we not have gotten it?"

"Things turned out well just now but as a general rule I need to know you can control yourself and not fly into danger's way."

"Flying into danger's way, that's your job, right?"

"Yes, and you won't be able to do your job if you get yourself sucked into a little ball or something."

He lowered his head. "You're right, boss, I need to be more careful."

I patted his shoulder. "You forced my hand back there. All turned out well this time and I don't know why. So, I'm not pushing my luck if I can help it."

"So, what am I supposed to do in Slovenia?"

"Have you finished John's inventory of my horde?"

"No. That's at least a year's work."

"Yeah."

Marcus picked me up in an ancient Mazda. He had to put the driver's seat all the way back to fit his well-fed frame behind the wheel. He pushed the passenger door open for me.

"So, man, what do you want to do about this book?"

"Get it back."

"Good. I told him over the phone that you wished to buy it from him. You brought cash, right?"

"That depends on what he wants for it."

I pulled a thumb drive out of my luggage. Marcus' eyes widened peering at it. "Are you ---"

"If he asks for more than a couple thousand, I've got some crypto-currency."

"How much?"

"Half a million worth."

Marcus squealed. "I'm an armored car today."

"I know it seems silly but it's either he accepts under a few thousand or I jump to this. I wasn't going to get a suitcase full of money or get my bank involved."

"You want this book bad."

"Just drive, Mr. Brinks."

William Scott's house embraced all who were allowed through his security gate with wings as large as small mansions. Marcus' car pulled up like an ugly puppy to the mother it didn't deserve. Another creature approached; a raven.

It could have been any raven but I took no chance. I stepped out of the car. “Marcus, drive off until I call you back.”

“Why?”

“There may be trouble here.”

“You’re not going to hurt my customer, are you?”

“Marcus, just drive. You know me.”

He answered with confusion, “Yeah I do,” and drove off.

A woman in a short dress, a domestic I guessed, met me at the door and led me to a large sitting room. A thin elderly man waved her off like he might shoo an animal. “You’re Mr. Ferris?”

“Yes. I’d like to buy back my wife’s book from you. Did Marcus tell you which one I mean?”

“Yes. Yes he did. That’s an interesting piece. There are some complex drawings in it. They look quite technical and yet with ancient symbols; Sumerian, I’m told.”

“You still have it?”

He pushed himself up out of his chair before he answered. “You seem quite anxious to get it back.”

He read people well. I needed to be careful. “Do you have it?”

“Yes, yes, I do, but based on how much you seem to want it back I have to assume my suspicions were right about it.”

“Suspicions?”

I hoped he’d feel silly sharing any wild theories he had.

“It’s a magic tome of some sort. It may have instructions on how to open a portal to another world.”

I tried not to respond. A moment of silence ended with dreaded words.

“Young man, I don’t want to sell it. I sense it’s too valuable.”

As a dragon of order, I couldn’t take it from him. He had to sell it to me.

What could I do?

A large floor-to-ceiling window shattered. A loud hiss forced our hands to our ears. Blue lightning arcs enveloped the curtains until they disintegrated into bits too small to explain where the rest of them went. The raven hovered and cawed one long caw.

I jumped at it. My leap crossed the twenty or so feet to where it flapped only to leave me empty-handed. The bird blinked away and reappeared across the room.

The blue arcs fingered along the old man's shelves and furnishings. The old man stumbled to a trunk and swung it open. Arcs jumped inside and across a book. I guessed that was it. It started to follow the same fate as the curtains. I rushed over and grasped it. The arcs dropped once I held it.

The raven cawed once more and vanished. Dust fell on the ravished remnants of the room. The old man lay across the chest. "What happened?"

"When you give into greed Mr. Scott, you walk amongst dragons."

His hand trembled. "I don't want the cursed thing anymore. Take it from me and go."

I pushed his fingers around the thumb drive. "Half a million for your trouble."

He shook his head. "But I was just giving the thing to you."

"You're an honest man, if a bit foolish. Take my payment."

4

The damage to the book might have caused it to fall apart if not for the restorative magic in my touch. As it were, the book still had holes in it.

I touched the old man's shoulder to see if he had been injured. He hadn't. I also could tell he didn't want me around anymore. My payment may have insulted him or perhaps he needed to forget the trauma of the destruction. Whatever, I needed to leave. My nature compelled me. Marcus picked me up halfway down the driveway and took me to his bookshop.

The book's lack of physical integrity demanded I found a table before opening it. The drawings were familiar to me; like ones I once saw in Vedi's notes about the void, chaos, and portals. Only the Sumerian text made these different. I also saw other drawings; a fat wingless dragon and faces. I knew two of them. Two wizards, I wish I never knew, Harold the Dread and his former apprentice Dogan. I didn't know the other faces; two women and one man.

After the drawings came page after page of Sumerian. Marcus' finger landed on a page. "Alexandra can read that. You want me to call her? We could do a skype."

I hesitated. Vedi didn't want Nix to know about this. She may not want Athena to know either, and bringing in her chief researcher could make that difficult.

I flipped through the remaining pages. The last one had Vedi's printing in English.

The first few lines identified the book as her great grandfather, Dakk's, journal. Most of the rest was magic jargon beyond my vocabulary. Even if I knew what they meant, a large hole in the page would have left me guessing the intended message.

The last line I understood. That is up to where a second hole cut it off. It read, "He's discovered me. He will kill Aiden and me if I don't throw him off. I will fake my death before Harold—"

I noticed Marcus had been reading over my shoulder.

"I don't like the sound of that," he said.

"She faked her death to save me, but from what?"

"I don't know much about your past, but my eyes see someone named Harold."

I closed the book. "Marcus, I need to ask a big favor of you."

"Okay, but remember I'm a book guy. I'm not likely to be able to do anything about whoever that Harold is."

"My wife, Vedi, is in the void. Gabe and Alexandra already know this."

He opened his eyes wider. "And I'm sure there's a good reason why I wasn't told."

"The less you know, the less your risks. I'm sorry Marcus to bring you into this at all—"

"Don't be sorry. A man in need is a friend indeed. Ooh boy, what am I getting myself into?"

"Okay. My wife directed me to this book for some reason and she didn't want Nix, one of Athena's allies, to know about it. I'm guessing Athena shouldn't be told either."

He took a deep breath and waited on me to continue.

"I'm asking you to keep this a secret for me. Don't tell Athena, Alexandra, Gabe, or anyone else in Athena's service."

"I can do that."

"Will you?"

My question probably irritated him, but I had to ask it. I needed an answer I could read the sincerity of.

"Yes. Don't doubt me, Dragon. I may be a fool, but I'm loyal to my friends."

His level of commitment exceeded my expectations.

"Thank you, bookman."

My attempt at levity earned half a smile.

"So, what are you going to do?"

"You've read the same words I did. She wanted me to find this now because she's worried about what Harold may be up to."

"You know this Harold?"

"Too well. He's a powerful wizard. He trained me as a child only to betray me as I entered adulthood. Not to mention he's a war criminal."

"What do you think she wants you to do about this war criminal?"

"Find him."

"He doesn't sound like the sort Olympus would tolerate wandering around on Earth."

"That will be another secret I'll need you to keep for me."

"He's here on Earth?"

"No, that I'm leaving Earth to find him."

"You make that sound bad. How bad is that?"

"It's pretty bad. It will be a huge risk for reasons you're best off not knowing."

The fewer who knew I was my father's son the better and Marcus definitely fell into the not needing to know category. Nothing in my life is more important than protecting my father from the knowledge of the child he promised to never have. Even my marriage. Vedi knew this going in. She wouldn't have sent me on a trail putting it at risk if more than just us wasn't critically involved.

"The way you say 'risk' frightens the hell out of me. Mama, forgive my language, but really. Does it have to be you? Can't you send someone else?"

"Only I can know enough to know what to look for without knowing what I shouldn't."

"You're scaring me."

"Me too."

5

No matter how important Vedi could convince me it was, my leaving Earth had to include precautions to ensure that my father and I didn't meet. Just the smell of me would probably be enough for him to know. That knowledge would most likely destroy him. A promise made by a dragon of order can be a harsh thing.

I needed a particular child of Galinthius to help me. He went by the name Thumper. The Children of Galinthius are the Olympians' enforcers. They look like giant housecats. The CoG, as they are often called for short, would not approve of me leaving Earth. Thumper, though, may help me considering he knows what could be at stake and he's gone rogue with me before. He could probably make sure my father and I didn't meet. The plan had one problem. He stopped talking to me after I put his job in jeopardy. I needed a go-between.

With Marcus already well burdened with secrets to keep, I left him and returned to Milpitas. I could find someone there already awash in my secrets. My brother-in-law and the stupidest warlock on Earth, Hunter Asta. Due to some odd sibling connection with my wife he knew about her circumstances and too many other things. His lack of wit both helped and hurt our cause. The Olympians tolerated him because they thought him too stupid to cause much trouble.

That made him handy at times; a hole in their vision whenever I needed one. I needed one then.

I found Hunter at a street corner of two four-lane roads in the Alum Rock area of San Jose. I caught him in the midst of his favorite hobby. He held a panhandler's bike by its crossbar. Knowing Hunter's supernatural strength and stupid meanness, I had no doubt what caused a clunking noise. The bike fell out of Hunter's hand, bent and useless.

I resisted the temptation to knock him senseless. Instead, I picked the bike up and grasped the bent crossbar.

"My bike. My bike. It's all I have left," cried the panhandler.

I knew he lied about it being all he had left. I sensed he had quite a bit more than his desperate for money act put on. It still was, in fact, his bike and as a dragon of order, I could respect that. I allowed my restorative magic to mend it. Another magic about me I had no control of, my aura, cleaned it for him as well.

Tears washed paths down the dirt on the panhandler's face. "Who are you?"

"Someone who respects people's property."

I glared at Hunter. He showed no repentance. "Yeah, yeah. Why are you stalking me?"

The panhandler grabbed my arm. "What should I do?"

"You're a deceiver, but it makes you a living. I can't tell you what to do but I'd advise you to seek a more honest living if you can."

He got on his bike and rode away. I doubted he'd change. Hunter wasn't about to either. "Not, 'go and sin no more,' Aiden? There may be hope for you yet."

"You know, Hunter, some of the apparent homeless really are in desperate straits. You do your eternal soul no favors by tormenting them."

"You may have somehow managed to marry my sister but you're not going to change me. Why are you out here?"

"I needed to find you."

He set down the sidewalk and I walked along.

"Why? Vedi coming back?"

"Not yet, and I fear something could delay her indefinitely."

"Why tell me?"

"I need to find Harold and I need Thumper's help."

"Okay, but I still don't see where this involves me?"

"Thumper's angry at me and I can't contact him."

He laughed. "So?"

"Aren't you still helping him round up John's killer's?"

"That's done. I've got a collection of gold teeth to show for it. Want to see them? I haven't had them framed yet."

I winced. "I don't want to know any more about that than I need to; just that you got them."

"Yeah, you're disgusted, just like Thumper."

"You offended him? Oh, wait. Why do I ask? Of course, you did. I hoped all this time had changed you somehow."

"You're not changing me, dragon, and Thumper doesn't talk to me either. I'm afraid I can't get him for you. He don't like me."

I stopped and pulled my phone out.

"I wish I could help you help Vedi, but I can't." He walked on.

I was down to desperate plans. I called my contact with the CoG, Zeke. Unlike Thumper, I couldn't let him know I was planning to leave Earth. He'd have me arrested and Olympus would likely exile me to some distant and lonely rock in space. I hoped I might be able to get Zeke to arrange a meeting between Thumper and me without him knowing why. I figured I had a better chance of getting struck by lightning in a cave, as in not good. I still had to try.

"Howdy, son, what's going on?"

Zeke calling me "son" meant he was happy to hear from me.

"Zeke, I'd like to speak with Thumper about the terrorists he helped me with."

Of course, I didn't lie. I can't. I did want to talk to him about that, just not before some other things. Hunter mumbled something in the distance about biting him. Zeke's tone changed. "Kid, you and Thumper find yourselves enough trouble on your own without teaming up. I don't think I want to set that up."

Pain pierced my ears. The muffled thunder must have hidden

amidst the road noises. The dreaded caw defied pin-pointing amongst dozens of cars on a pothole infested highway. The only sound I knew the origin of came from my mouth. I cried out.

"What the Hell's happening, son?"

"Got to hang up now, Zeke."

My head ached. The hiss of the blue-lightning's thunder accounted for some of it. The rest came from concentration. My sensitive dragon ears told me the direction of the caw.

A car's tires exploded, and it careened across the path of other cars. Mechanical mayhem ensued. The raven flew over and along the median. Its blue lightning fingered out like fishing nets over the road. More tires popped and windows shattered.

I jumped over the lanes at it and it vanished, only to reappear over where I started. *Whatever causes it to leave?* I jumped back and it vanished again. That time, not reappearing. I caught my breath and got back to my phone when a male voice spoke inside my head.

"Don't call Zeke. He doesn't need to know you found me, or rather I found you."

6

I looked around. Thumper hunched his shoulders. The roadside ditch's depression hid his frame from the highway. I moved and placed my ankle against his side. "You've got a better place for us to talk?"

He answered as he always speaks, inside my head. *"West hills should do."*

He teleported us. The sights and sound of the chaotic road ceased. Evergreen peace enveloped us. I gave my head a knock to end the residual ringing. "So, you say you found me. That's extremely convenient for me."

"I wouldn't be too fast to say that."

"Convenience for me has so often meant I was being manipulated or maneuvered into someone else's schemes."

"Well, in this case, it started with you, rather than some manipulative Olympian."

"You knew I wanted to see you?"

"You asked Alexandra to find out about the blue lightning for you. She's still not sure but thinks it's potentially dangerous enough that I should look for the culprit.—Well, it is."

"And that brought you to me?"

He gestured in the direction of the San Mateo Valley below us. Smoke rose from where we'd been.

"This was the worst. No persons have been hurt so far, but I fear this may be the time that changes. The first incident you reported had no associated damage. The storage lot was the first damage, then the Scott mansion, now this. The destruction is bad enough without getting progressively worse, especially if people start dying."

"Are those the only incidents?"

"Yes, dragon of order, and so far, you're the only common thread."

"You know I'm not responsible."

"I know. I know who you are. I know whose son you are."

"Okay, so what brought you to me is that this raven seems to be stalking me?"

"Yes, this raven. Whatever it is. Whatever it's up to. So far you're the only lead."

I moved to get a better view of the dust-plume that had been passible highway a few minutes ago. "I need you, Thumper."

"To protect you?"

"To protect my father."

"Your father? How can this affect him? What do you know about this raven thing you haven't told me?"

"Probably nothing you don't already know."

"I don't see what this has to do with your father then."

I needed a reason for him to want to help me and it couldn't have anything to do with Vedi still being alive and in the void. I had to keep that from him. I, also, of course, couldn't lie.

"Remember about my former teacher, Harold?"

"Yes. He tricked you into marrying a chaos witch so you could lift a transformation curse from him."

"I discovered something recently about something else he may have gotten up to and it needs my personal attention."

"You need to find him?"

"Yes."

The big cat's ears drew back. *"No."*

"It has to do with unfinished projects in Dakk's journal."

I couldn't tell him all my reasons. That one I hoped would be enough.

"If someone has to go stop a forbidden magical experiment, that's to be done by the Children of Galinthius or perhaps some Olympians or their proxies, but definitely not by you. Especially not by you leaving Earth."

"It's tied to the plot to usurp Zeus. Who can we trust to want the right results?"

"You can pass on what you know to me and I'll do it."

I didn't exactly have him where I wanted him but at least he had come on board. I introduced some finesse. "Thumper, you know I can't lie, correct?"

"Yes. It can be most inconvenient for you and I can attest, for anyone working with you at times."

"I recently discovered that my wife discovered things going on that got us marked for death and that's why she's gone."

"And you want revenge? Not a good enough reason to risk destroying your father."

"I can't tell you I don't want revenge, but I can tell you there are other things that need doing that must be done by me."

"Things that I can't do?"

"Things that I must do."

"I don't understand. You know there are other dragons, especially off Earth? I can find Harold and whatever he may be up to, if I can't deal with it alone, I can gather whatever abilities or talents I need and none of them need to be you."

The finesse only played out so far. I needed to try and force the rest. I let my eyes glow and sprouted wings for emphasis. "I cannot tell you precisely why it must be me, but it must be. Whatever Harold was up to, it involves not only the Cabal to replace Zeus, not only more chaos than the Children of Galinthius should ever want to see, but it also involves me and my family in such a way that I must deal with Harold. Do not doubt my word."

His white hair rose in a ridge along his back. *"Dragon, I'm worried about your emotions in this."*

"I worry about that too and I can assure you my reasoning is not thus far tainted."

"It would be less of a risk to your father if I found Harold and brought him to you."

I could tell he lacked confidence in what he just said.

"That would be a greater risk to you and if I lost you, I would be unable to do anything at that point. Our greater cause would be lost."

His chin met his chest. *"I hate this. What do you want me to do?"*

"I'm going to use the portal in that Georgia basement. I need you to keep track of my father and me to make sure we don't cross paths."

"You'll need me to first make sure I know where your father is. Once I do, I'll come back to you and you can walk through then. From there I'll be doing a bit of jumping back and forth to keep tabs; on your father and you; and still on this raven thing. I'll be very busy."

"I'll be near the portal in Georgia."

One more task remained for the setup. I needed someone to welcome me into the basement. Poor Marcus would have another secret to keep. I was becoming someone perhaps best not to know.

7

Marcus wrung out his handkerchief. "Who knew north Georgia could be hot in September—Me."

Keith jumped around. "I'm not feeling it. It's like I'm numb to sunshine or something."

I could tell this aggravated Marcus. He projected his irritation into a paper fan. I feared if we waited much longer, Marcus' restraint would run out, his irritation with Keith would generalize and I might have to leave the basement before I could use the portal.

"I've located your father. You're clear."

I grasped the torch pendant. "Thanks, Thumper."

Keith's motions stopped. "We're going in?"

I patted Marcus' shoulder. "Thank you so much, sir. You should be back in air-conditioning soon now."

"Halleluiah. Thank you, sir dragon."

Keith threw on his backpack and waited by the portal.

"You're taking that pack through? That seems a bit to pack for just popping through long enough just see what's on the other side and then come back."

"I figured you didn't have me fly all the way here just to take notes."

"I didn't bring you here to stay long on the other side of this either."

"Stop worrying about me, boss. I packed some things you might want where you're going. You know, from your horde. Once we're there you can decide what if any of it you want to keep with you. I'll return with the rest."

"Ah yes, doing your job—Marcus, wait no more than half an hour. He should be back by then."

Marcus glared at Keith. "Don't doddle. I have a date with the motel shower and some ice-cold AC. You're not going to make me late."

I put a hand on Keith's back. "Let's go."

We stepped through. Concrete gave way to stone. Possums, rabbits, raccoons, and other normal woodland critters occupied cages that lined the walls. One large cage held a black bear.

"Nothing magical or bazaar about these animals," said Keith.

"I don't feel compelled to leave this place. That means it either belongs to nobody or someone who somehow knows about me and wants me here?"

Keith whispered, "Harold?"

"All these animals seem to have a brand on them. It looks like 'DS'. Could it be something else in say Greek texts?"

Keith shined a flashlight around the room. "All fauna native to the Georgia mountains."

"You think all these critters just happened into that basement and through the portal?"

"Maybe a couple with the help of the raccoons but not all these."

"You seem to know more about Georgia fauna than Greek."

"My family vacationed there more than a few times."

Footsteps approached from the other side of the wall. I held up my hand. Keith held a finger to his lips. I debated if I should play it safe and send Keith back, or keep him until we figured more out. A click followed by a drag preceded a push against the arch of my foot.

"Go back now, Keith."

My words became a farce by the time I said them. Nets wound

around both of us and lifted us. The ropes seemed to be hemp except I could tear hemp ropes like paper. These resisted me. Keith could do nothing. I made progress with a combination of gripping, twisting, and patience. My binds unraveled and returned me to the floor.

A man's voice came through a peephole. "Min eower byldan."

"What?"

"Min eower byldan."

"Keith, you okay?"

"Yeah, except I can't get down."

"Min eower byldan. Loc eow?"

"Does any of that make sense to you, Keith?"

"No."

"Do you speak English?"

"Seriously, boss? On another world?"

The man cleared his throat. "Your decision to pass through that portal was most unfortunate."

I muttered to Keith, "they're apparently collecting more than Georgia's fauna."

A tiny window lifted. "That's magically reinforced rope. Of those I'm expecting, only two possible individuals should come through the portal and be able to snap it."

"You're expecting people to come through this portal?"

"And break those ropes? Only two. The great-grandson of Dakk or a lawful dragon of order that has been trapped on Earth for some reason."

What the man knew disturbed me and what he didn't comforted me. He didn't know who the 'lawful dragon' is or enough of my circumstances to risk exposing me to my father.

"Who told you to expect us?"

"There would be no point in telling you that. I doubt you would believe me."

"You might be surprised."

He cleared his throat again. "I'm Lord Darius Suunt, the lord of this county. You are in my castle's gatehouse. My questions matter most here."

“Okay then, if I answer your questions could I ask some of my own?”

“If you tell me why you've come here, I might be able to help you."

"I'm looking for a man who came through this portal about nine months ago."

I could see his hand rub his chin. Somehow deception rode the gesture.

"What do you seek him for?"

"He had something to do with an attack on my wife."

He opened the door. He was a large man. He grinned and I could tell his expression satisfied him. He was one to choose the emotions he projected rather than allow real ones to be expressed. He pulled a scroll out of his coat.

"I have a piece of paper here instructing me as to what must be done with anyone who comes through that portal into my castle's gatehouse."

"I hope for your sake it doesn't involve violence."

"I am to keep you on my castle lands as a serf until or unless the throne of Olympus orders me to do otherwise."

"Do you think you can enforce that on me?"

"You're not Dakk's great-grandson, so yes, in a way at least. In a way that matters."

"You think I'm weaker than Hunter?""No. I know you must be that lawful dragon of order. Therefore, the seal on this scroll and the words it contains will be all the enforcement I need. You're not going to defy an edict from the throne of Olympus, are you?"

What sort of trap did I walk into?

8

Two men in gambeson followed him. He shouted an order. "Of heer akan reach."

They grabbed Keith's net and signaled to someone above. A string of clanks lowered and released him.

"And who is this who came with you, dragon?"

"My assistant."

Lord Suunt rubbed his chin. He walked a circle around Keith. "I never thought a dragon would have a bearer."

"May I see that writ from the throne of Olympus you say binds me to you?"

He handed it to me without looking. I confirmed Zeus's seal. The script consisted of characters I recognized from English. The language, I couldn't understand. I suspected the same language he spoke to his men in. I handed it back. "Have you read this yourself?"

"Of course, I have. I am literate in six languages."

"And it says that I must be your serf just because I passed through this portal?"

He took a long breath. "I suppose your servant can remain in your service as you serve me. I can't imagine what a dragon's servant could possibly do for me—And, yes, that's what it says."

"Is this true, boss?"

"I'm afraid it is unless he's misunderstood the writ."

"Dragon, I may not be as strong as you or highly skilled in magic, but do not doubt my education."

So much confidence at a time when I sorely hoped for doubt. I caught Keith's eye and looked him toward the portal. The laws of Olympus forbade me to ask him to escape. I hoped for it. Only Earth laws bound him. He could go but unwanted confidence infested both Lord Suunt and Keith.

Lord Suunt held me in an inescapable hold of law and Keith whispered away my hope. "What am I on a world without you, noble dragon?"

"Free," I answered. He shook his head, 'no,' and I recognized the truth even if I didn't understand it.

Lord Suunt lead us outside and through a fog. We moved across a castle courtyard where he introduced us to a man in a brown robe.

"Lewin, this is Aiden and his bearer. Aiden, this is my physician. I'm sending him up the pass today to inspect the village there, and you and your bearer will serve as his escort."

Lewin half bowed. "Sir."

"Lewin speaks English quite well. When you return, I want you to stay with him. He's got some beds to spare. Now, I must attend to other business. Lewin, take good care of my new serfs."

Lewin half bowed to the departing lord and opened the door behind him. We entered a wooden structure that contrasted from all the stone around it. "Come in and sit while I pack. Do you have a lantern?"

Keith reached into his pack. "A flashlight."

He threw a leather satchel onto a desk, opened various drawers and cabinet doors and threw things together. "A flashlight, you say. Well, be sure not to let the guards see that you have one of those or they'll take it away. It should prove handy for us."

I signaled for Keith to close it. "A lot of things seem to have come through that portal, much more than I'd expect to have."

His hands shook. "There will be plenty of time for us to talk on the path up the pass. For now, let me concentrate on making sure I pack the right medicines."

Keith tried to speak. I caught his mouth. "We'll wait quietly until you're ready."

"I'm almost ready. I just need to find my journal."

He squatted and fumbled about under his desk. "We'll be on our way soon and we need to be. The sun will be dipping beneath the mountains in less than an hour."

He stood holding a leather-bound book and dropped it into his pack. He raised a finger and rushed into another room. He spoke with a man, returned for a bowl of bread, and carried it back to him. "He should be okay for the next two days. Let's be on our way."

"A sick man?" I asked.

"Yes. He's been having trouble with his legs lately and complaining about the smell of the castle. Some time to rest in my house should do him good."

I caught Keith's stare and I waved his idea off. "Let the physician do his job."

Lewin overheard. "Are you a physician too?"

"No."

They let us out the gates into a narrow mountain pass. The path he chose started a switchback and we rose above the castle. If not for the fog I imagined I might be able to see the valley beyond the castle.

"Lewin, how do you know where the sun is in this sky?"

He reached into his robe and pulled out a watch on the end of a chain.

"Where'd that come from?"

"The court of Toth did not lack for machines. Nothing like what I'd guess you're used to, but time-keeping pieces and a few fancy crossbows, most definitely."

"Toth. I've heard of him from—" I stopped myself.

"From somebody, I'm sure."

I couldn't tell if he suspected anything or if he only meant to let it go.

"So, you were part of Toth's court?"

"That's why I know English. It's also why I'm one of the better physicians in this land."

"Are you a free man?"

"Lord Suunt doesn't believe in free men. He even oppresses himself."

"I've worked on behest of the Olympians. I don't understand why they would give him this kind of power."

"The power to make an Olympian's cohort into his serf?"

"I was free up until just a short while ago today."

"The first day seems to always be a shock."

9

Keith and I spent the second day in a place called Fife, a village of about a dozen families clinging to a ledge. Lewin tested water samples from a stream. He used what seemed to be chemistry. Keith, meanwhile, took advantage of the villagers' ignorance of English. "This place smells."

"You mean of lavender and pine?"

"Not that. The manure of some animal."

"I did catch that just before my aura took care of it for me."

He held his nose. "Must be nice."

"You think this could be a good time for me to see what you brought in your backpack?"

"No."

"No?"

He pointed me at the path I walked, and then flicked his fingers in a gesture toward a villager. Paving stones lay clear of dirt and dust only where I had passed along. A woman stared at me in fear.

"I don't think they know what you are, but they're guessing you're not human."

"Hopefully they don't have a clue."

Lewin found no problems with the water supply and after a few medical visits, he led us back down. Two days from the start of the trip we returned to the castle gates. The guards yelled at each other and then at us before opening them.

"Did we do something wrong?" I asked Lewin.

"No. There's been a burglar, it seems."

"Someone burgled a castle?"

"Yes. Imagine that. We'll be wise to avoid Lord Suunt if we can. He must be ready to kill someone."

I placed a firm hand on Keith's shoulder. "Let's try to lay low."

He gave me a thin smile. A glint in his eye told me I dissuaded him of some reckless thought.

The fog helped us reach Lewin's house without being seen. I made sure to close the door after us. "What sort of thief must it take to sneak into a castle and steal something?"

Lewin didn't answer. Instead, he walked into the next room. "I wonder where Horus went? I hope it's because he's feeling better."

"Horus? Is he the patient you had here when we left?"

"Yes."

Someone pounded the door. "Lewin, eow mid ongehiones ic pro."

Lewin rushed to his door. "Lord Suunt."

Lord Suunt ducked through the doorway. He studied me and glared at Lewin. "The gem of Suunt has been stolen and your patient Horus has left with it. What do have to say to us about this?"

"Horus couldn't have stolen it. He can barely walk most of the time."

"Well, he's gone along with my gem. Did you have anything to do with this?"

"No, Lord Suunt."

Lord Suunt looked at me. "Do you think he tells the truth?"

"Yes."

"You hear that Lewin. This lawful dragon believes you. If you turn out to be lying, I will send him after you. You don't want to have lied to a lawful dragon, even more than you don't want to have lied to me. Now leave us for now. The dragon and I have something to discuss."

Keith started out with Lewin before Suunt's arm blocked him. "Not you. You stay."

"What have we to discuss?" I asked him.

"Whatever I please, dragon. Whatever I please."

"Be careful, Lord Suunt, for the day will come when you won't own me."

He paused before laughing and then putting his face in mine. "Then I'll be dead, and you won't be able to do a thing to me. Until then you're mine to command. You're my dragon."

"Okay, then beyond the obvious, have you anything else you wish to discuss, Lord Suunt?"

He stepped back and spread his shoulders. "Yes. I'm ordering you to look for the thieves in the interior of the mountains. If you find them, make an example of them and return my gem to me."

"If I find them? What if I don't?"

He smiled at Keith and rubbed his chin. "Well—no. No need for that sort of motivation. You're a lawful dragon and I own you. If I think you've looked long enough I'll send a messenger to fetch you."

I patted Keith's back. "Secure the pack and let's be on our way. We have been assigned a task by our master."

Lord Suunt walked us to the gate. Guards again were yelling at each other. Lord Suunt spoke in stern words and they held the gate open for us. Lord Suunt cleared his throat. "Dragon, it appears Lewin has run out claiming he needs to attend to Horus's medical needs. I am adding to your task. Catch Lewin and bring him back."

I nodded. He pointed up the path we last travelled. "When you catch him, don't punish him. A skilled physician like him is very hard to come by. I will deal with him once he's returned."

"That's the path we took back here. The burglar couldn't have travelled it without us seeing him."

"The other path is for carts. It's wider but it's also longer. They almost assuredly took that one."

"Then I should follow it?"

"And assure they'll beat you there? Take the footpath and catch up to them. Now get going."

The path offered little options for human traffic other than to follow it from end to end. We knew we'd be on it for the first half day. Keith managed a couple of miles before he complained. "This is something, isn't it?"

"I really hoped you'd left me and returned through the portal."

"If you hadn't become a slave I probably would have."

"A serf isn't exactly a slave."

"If you can say that, it must be true, but I'm not sure how. That jerk says he owns you."

"Okay. A semantic argument will tire me right now. How about you explain to me why my becoming a ... err, losing my freedom made a difference in you not to go back."

"My death and return to life made me like some actor who forgot to leave the stage on cue and somehow stayed there through later scenes. If anyone noticed me, it would only be to note I shouldn't be there."

"You have a part now. I gave you one."

"Exactly. Managing your horde gave me a part to play in life again. That means if I returned with you stuck here, I'd be nothing again."

"My horde would be there."

"Without you, your horde is just a stage in need of clearing. I'd just be one of the objects there to clear; the one with the least purpose or meaning."

"Keith, you need to get a life beyond me, you know."

"And, you need to get out of this, boss."

10

I thought of taking wing or even complete dragon form and then thought better of it. Keith's mind found the same questions only a few minutes after mine.

"Lord Suunt knows you're a dragon. Why don't we skip this climbing?"

"My form, even my wings are distinct to the kind of dragon I am. Not that I expect these villagers to know much dragon lore, but it's a chance I'm not going to take."

"So many restrictions."

"Yeah, tell me about it. You want me to carry the pack this time? You deserve a break from it."

"Nah, I don't seem to get tired or sore, no matter what. That Gray Wolf really did a number on me."

"Someone did a number on that bridge ahead."

A place where the path's ledge got interrupted by a sheer section of cliff used to have a bridge. Only posts and bits of boards on both ends remained.

"We sure could use some wings right now."

A trail of loose dirt ran down the cliff.

"I think I see how the bridge was taken out."

My eyes followed the trail on the cliff-face up to another ledge. I could make out a couple posts and railing.

"Keith, if you can cling to my back, I can get us up to what I think is the cart path."

"I think I can climb it myself. I've rock-climbed a few times in my life."

"Okay. In that case, hand me the backpack and you lead. I haven't rock-climbed before. You can show me how it's done."

He led and I learned. He also took longer than I think I could have kluged it with my dragon strength. At least Keith's way, I caused less erosion. We also made less noise. That last part mattered as a cart passed by on its way to the village. A couple of men's voices commented on the broken bridge below. They seemed happy about it. The language barrier left me uncertain as to if they rejoiced at the bridge's fate or that they didn't have to deal with it. Whatever the case, they didn't notice us.

They vanished around a bend by the time we reached the cart path.

Kieth glanced up the path. "You think anyone we're looking for is with that cart?"

"Most likely, and someone's got a complex plan in motion."

"What makes you say that?"

"Lewin took the footpath just a few minutes before we left on it, and he probably crossed that bridge, or else we would have caught him. That means the bridge was taken out only recently and by someone who came from the village."

"An accomplice?"

"Most likely."

"They could have had a distance runner run ahead?"

"Occam's razor favors the accomplice from town, I think."

We reached the town and people lied with their actions. They made themselves busy with tasks most of them wouldn't have attended to right then if they didn't want to deceive me. They wanted me to think nothing unusual had recently happened.

I moved in the direction I sensed created the most discomfort. I came to where two paths left the town on the other side. One climbed higher into the mountain. The other descended into the fog. Two villagers swept their thresholds nearby. I pointed up into the mountain. "Lewin go this way?"

They knew Lewin's name at least. One of them pretended not to notice my attempt to communicate. The other nodded toward the higher path. He lied.

"Which way?" asked Keith.

"We wait."

"Wait? Why?"

"They don't know what I am, you've noted. It frightens them. We wait."

"What for?"

They moved inside their houses and shut their doors.

"That."

I walked down into the fog.

"You wanted to freak them out?"

"No. I didn't want to make it obvious to them that I knew when they lied. Never surrender an advantage if you don't have to."

"Is that from Sun Tzu?"

"No, Harold the Dread."

The path brought us to a cart. Hoofprints led off through the mud to a small barn. Beyond it, lamplight flickered through a house's window. The light showed the back of Lewin's robe.

"The cart and Lewin all together. This could be a short errand."

"How do you get inside?"

"Be polite."

I knocked on the door. "Lewin, may I come in?"

"If you promise not to disturb my patient."

"I will do my best."

He opened the door.

One man, I presumed to be Horus, lay in a bed near the window. Two other men sat at a table and eyed me. Lewin spoke calmly to them and they eased some at my presence.

"These two men brought Horus here? Why?"

Lewin carried a bottle to Horus. "He believes the castle's musty air is the reason he's ill."

"What does all your medical training tell you about his condition."

"Not as much as I'd like. I expected him to improve while I was away, but he's gotten worse. He can't walk at all now."

I felt Keith's expectant stare. I muttered. "Give the physician a bit more time."

"What is that?" asked Lewin.

"I have faith in your science, Lewin."

"As flattering as that may be, dragon, I fear my faith is waning."

"The villagers all seemed willing to lie for you. Do they know something about what's going on that I should?"

"They know that you work for Lord Suunt and they most probably assume as one of his thugs. I'm the only one of his serfs who help them. The rest are trouble when they come."

"He has sent me to bring you back and deal with the thief, so I guess I am one of his thugs."

"I'm sorry to hear that."

"As a lawful dragon bound by a writ from Olympus, I must do what he says, but he can't dictate my every move. I'll do my best to help and not hurt."

"I am most appreciative for your sentiment for whatever it's worth."

My next question had little to do with that sentiment.

"Only one cart left the castle. Do you know anything about the thief?"

"No. I can't say that I do."

He lied.

11

I whispered to Keith. "Stand in the doorway."

He did as I asked. I noted where all the other possible exits might be; three windows.

"Only three groups traveled between the castle and Fife, Keith and me, you Lewin, and those who traveled with the cart. Where was the thief who stole the Suunt gem?"

Lewin grimaced. He didn't lie well if there could be such a thing. He looked away and rushed to his patient. "Horus?"

Horus's eyes rolled back. I detected no deception in that. Lewin felt his pulse. "Horus, don't leave us."

I rushed over, knelt across from him and placed my hands on his chest. No warmth left my hand. Lewin pushed my hand away. "Are you trying to kill him so I can go back with you sooner?"

My hand ended up just below the ribs on his side. My fingers involuntarily spread apart and got warm. They turned hot and I put both hands on the spot.

"What are you doing?"

"He's healing him," said Keith.

This bit of healing burned my hands. Whatever I fixed must have been major. "Horus was very sick."

"So, you put him out of his misery? Is that what you dragons do?"

Horus lurched into a seated position. His eyes returned to normal. Lewin exchanged words with him then bowed. "My apologies, dragon, but what else was I supposed to think? What sort of dragon heals?"

"There are many things about me people are best off not known. I need you to promise me not to tell Lord Suunt I did this."

"I certainly won't. I don't think Horus will either. As for those two, I doubt they fully realize what happened and they're unlikely to ever be speaking to Lord Suunt."

He spoke the truth. The implication encouraged me. "That reminds me, you told me before you didn't know anything about where the thief might have gone."

"Yes, I did."

"Well, something tells me at the very least, no one in this room is the thief."

It was a guess and more importantly one his honesty or lack thereof would advance my investigation.

"Yes, absolutely," he said with full sincerity.

"However, I strongly suspect that the thief did travel with that cart at least as far as Fife and you lied to me to protect him."

Lewin studied the floor. "What are you going to do to me?"

"I'm going to help you as much as I can and still do what Lord Sunnt has asked of me."

"What can you do? Horus could just get sick again if he returns to the castle."

"Lord Suunt demanded I recover two things, you and his family gem. He never asked for Horus back. I'm guessing he's given up on him recovering."

"Oh, thank you, noble dragon."

"I ask something in return though."

"Name it."

"Don't lie to me."

"But I can't betray a good man to Lord Suunt's rath."

"So, this thief is a good man? How can a thief be a good man?"

He shook. “Please, noble dragon, I am merely human. I don’t share the thief’s belief that he helps his family by stealing, even from a man like Lord Suunt, but I can forgive him for believing so.”

Such is the human condition that they believe a good man can steal from another. It sickened me. “How great must his family’s need be to justify taking away what another family cherishes?”

“His family live in caves near Port Poe, having to move from one to another to stay ahead of the patrols and brigands.”

“They are that desperate?”

“Yes, dragon, I won’t lie to you anymore.”

Another feeling joined the twisting of my stomach. This discomfort rested a little higher. “I need to pursue him. I have no choice in that.”

Thumper’s voice jumped into my head. *“Finally, I found you. You wandered in a direction I hadn’t expected.”*

Lewin wrung his hands. I tapped them gently. “I need to step outside to think some.”

He nodded.

“Okay, Thumper, I’m away from others. We can speak freely.”

“I only need to check-in and tell you so far is so good.”

“Things aren’t good here.”

“How so?”

“Zeus put his seal on a writ to the local noble here making anyone who walks through that portal his serf until Olympus tells him otherwise.”

“Does he know you’re a dragon who has been known to work for Athena?”

“Only that I’m a dragon. Someone told him to expect either me or Hunter. In Hunter’s case, he knows who he is, basically.”

“Well, you’re the one who so confidently believed you should use that portal.”

“I may not be so confident now. Why would Zeus want such a thing?”

“It doesn’t sound like him but most of his decisions in the last few centuries have been those of others who talked him into them.”

"Like Apollo."

"And Enki, Poseidon, Hades, and Athena."

"Someone set a trap for me."

"Uh-hum, at the risk of repeating my father's fatal mistake, only with a dragon instead of a god, is there something I can do to help?"

"Do you know the geography around here?"

"Yes, of course."

"Could you teleport some people places?"

"As long as it doesn't involve breaking any Olympian laws or CoG policies, yes. Just keep in mind that I need to go check on your father regularly and I can't guarantee the timing of that."

"For now anyway, that will be a great help. If it will save you some time, there's a fork back at Fife that I took the low path from to get here. You can expect me to have moved in whatever direction the high path will take me."

"The interior of the mountains? Good thing you're cold resistant. I'd tell you not to get lost, since most who attempt to travel very far that way do, but you got me to find you."

"I'm grateful to be working with you again."

"Don't assume too much, dragon. I just know that whoever would manipulate Zeus into trapping you is both powerful and untrustworthy, and that has my hackles up. I haven't forgiven you. Helping you just seems a good way to tweak whoever that is."

12

Thumper left me for Earth and the third thing he tracked, the raven. I returned to the cabin.

"Lewin, does Horus have family somewhere not under Suunt's control?"

"Yes. His daughter and her husband are freemen, but they live in Three Lakes and that's the other side of Suunt's castle."

"Within the next few days, I'll have the means to get him there that skips all the space in between."

"Harold?"

"Who did you say?"

"Suunt's wizard, Harold. He's very good at teleportation. Most wizards can't do it at all or if so, only with portals. Forgive me if I guessed wrong. It just seemed unlikely there'd be another means in the area."

A wizard named Harold who is noted for his mastery of teleportation magic could be no one else but Harold the Dread. I had to contain myself. "I have another means."

"So, you'll move him to be with his daughter within the next few days? What about me?"

"I'll need a translator when I set out after the thief. Are you able to travel?"

"My body is able, but my heart won't be in it."

I muttered, "no weakness."

"What did you say, dragon?"

"I'm not sure myself, but just as you overlook the thief's thievery, I overlook your sympathy for him."

Lewin opened his mouth and stopped. I patted his shoulder. "What I said would probably have required you to lie or say things you think unwise."

"Then you understand?"

"I'm trying, but in the meantime, I have no choice but to pursue this man. The very law of Olympus requires it of me."

He sighed. I gave him one more pat. "We'll rest the night here and set out in the morning. Be sure to dress for the high road from Fife."

"As you wish, but we only have four beds."

"You've got a nice rug. Keith can use that. I'll take the open floor."

Lewin pointed. "You can use mine. I'll take the floor."

"I don't think you understand, Lewin. I'm a dragon. I prefer a hard surface from time to time."

"Forgive me, dragon, but you're confusing. You're unrelenting one moment and generous the next."

"I assure you as I assure myself, it's all somehow consistent. Just don't ask me to always explain it."

I SAVED my questions about Harold for the next morning as we set out.

"So, you say Lord Suunt has a wizard working for him?"

"Oh yes. He's been accumulating a lot of power in just the last year."

"Like a wizard?"

"And now a dragon. I wouldn't be surprised if he has his eyes on the imperial throne."

"Do you have any idea why the throne of Olympus would favor him with the writ he uses to keep me as his serf?"

"I'll tell you what I think if you can promise me not to tell Lord Suunt."

"Promises are harsh on my kind, but I also can't lie, and I can assure you I won't tell him if he doesn't ask me what you think."

"I don't envy your condition, dragon."

"Nor should you."

He cocked his head and shook his hands for a moment. "Alright. I don't exactly see what I have to lose having lost all my freedom. If you want to know, I'll tell you. Your assurance that you won't volunteer it to him should suffice."

"Yes. Why do you think they gave him the writ?"

"The portal used to connect to Dakk's library. I'm told it's not far from here."

"And the library's end-point got moved to Suunt Castle? Why?"

"There was a representative of the Olympians who spent some time in the library. Before he left he had some spell-casters move the end-point from the library to Suunt Castle. I think he trusted Lord Suunt because they were similar men."

"In what way?"

"Now, this is just my conjecture and not exactly an objective observation."

"I respect your conjecture. Please continue."

"While in Toth's court, I've seen a few of the gods before and several other Olympians. Some looked like men and woman and some looked like big cats, but none looked like this one. He had a large braided beard and ruddy skin and he carried an ax."

"Lord Suunt didn't have a braided beard the last time I saw him, though I guess his skin could be described as ruddy. I never saw him wield a weapon."

"He's between beards and no, he doesn't braid them, but he does let them grow long like this one's from Olympus. There was something else between them I couldn't quite place, but I sensed it."

Keith gave a nervous laugh. "Good thing Lewin wasn't trying to give a police report from where we come from. Sounds bigoted."

"Against hipsters?"

"Ruddy skin?"

Lewin shook a finger. "The Suunt's are unusual amongst the noble families of the empire for their ruddy skin. It's a mystery where they came from."

I glared at Keith. "Now, Lewin, this Olympian you say had a large braided beard and ruddy skin?"

"Yes. Now that is an objective observation."

"My dragon lore combined with my own experience with the Olympians tells me this representative isn't really an Olympian."

"Oh, but he is. He had their authority behind him."

"He has worked his way into their court from the outside and become Zeus's primary advisor. He is the god Enki."

"You say you know him from your dragon lore. Is he a dragon god?"

"No. He's the god who killed the greatest and the mother of all dragons. This trap I'm in was his idea. That means I'm in his sights."

13

The high path became only a worn trail defined by where one could walk. All other places required climbing. Some of the walking bordered on climbing. In one place, Lewin cut his hand on a rock. His hand became a mess of blood and dirt.

"As soon as we reach a stream or some snow I'll need to wash this to avoid infection," he said.

I grabbed his arm. "I'd rather not take unnecessary risks."

"You're going to heal the wound? That should help a bit but I still need to wash it."

I slid my hand down to his. The dirt fell off, my aura cleaned his arm, and warmth from my hand healed the cut. Lewin studied his hand. "Thank you, noble dragon, and for the cleaning too."

"That part's an aura. It happens to whatever I touch."

"Then make a note not to touch the Suunt gem when and if we find it."

"Is there valuable dirt on it?"

"No. It's been bathed in chemicals chosen for their bad smell and irritation to the skin."

"To keep it from being stolen?"

"To keep it from being ingested or otherwise placed inside someone's body."

"To be stolen," said Keith.

"Oh no, young man. The Suunt gem has magic on it that will take effect on anyone who takes it into their body. It will make the person god-like, but it will also progressively drive them insane. It's very dangerous."

From a man who has seen a few gods, Lewin's choice of words and their sincerity alarmed me. "Why not destroy it?"

"The family has kept it as a weapon of last resort for generations. Lord Suunt could force himself to swallow it in a moment of dire need but in no other time. If you touch it, dragon, you'll make it easy for anyone to use at any time, so you must not."

"I understand and I'll heed your warning."

"It's very important that you do, dragon."

"I can't imagine Olympus being okay with a mortal family owning such a thing."

"I'm not sure they know about it."

"Boss?"

"Keith, do you know something about magical artifacts like this that could be helpful to us?"

"Well, not about the artifact in specific, but yes."

"What would that be?"

"It's magical."

"I meant, do you know something we don't already know."

"I brought the diviner kit."

"Good man. We might be able to find it with that."

"We should be able to track it at least."

We stopped long enough to get out the plastic contraption Zeke gave me. We had to let its pointer find Keith and me first. A wipe of a runed cloth made the pointer ignore us and find the next most powerful thing nearby. Magic fields are like magnetic fields in that they weaken over distance from the source. The third source's field noticeably fought with our own fields before we applied the runed cloth.

"Whatever the diviner's pointing at is either very powerful or practically right on top of us."

Lewin nodded to the diviner. "You can find the gem with that thing?"

"Well, right now, it's either pointed at the gem or something else possessed of a lot of magic."

"There's a saying about these mountains, dragon. There are no straight lines."

"Is the man we're tracking knowledgeable of dragonlore?"

"No. He's trained in counting money. He doesn't know much else."

"Between that and the fog, I think I have an opportunity to belie that saying, but I need you to head back to the cabin where Horus is and wait for us to return."

"You're not going to breath fire on my friend, are you?"

"No, only catch up with him. Now, hurry along and don't look back. Your life could depend on you not seeing certain things."

He almost fell as he fast-walked away.

"His life could depend on not seeing certain things? A bit dramatic, boss?"

"If he became a loose end, he'd have to be relocated at least. His life, as he knew it, would be over."

"I understand that."

"Okay, Keith. You know how to ride my dragon form. Try not to be clumsy this time. That fall down the slope could be a long one."

"You need me to grab the gem if we find it?"

"Yes, exactly and that's your sole job. I need your hands on that gem. Thus you must do nothing else but that. Understand?"

"Yeesh, do you think I'm compulsive or something?"

"Just promise me you'll concentrate on the gem and leave any targets of opportunity up to me."

"I promise."

"Good."

I took on my half-bus sized dragon form and Keith climbed on my back. Once he had both arms around my neck I launched from the mountainside. I climbed close to the slope.

"Ouch!"

A branch-end whipped across my back. Keith received the worst of it.

I started to speak. "Ach." Then I remembered I hadn't learned to do that in dragon form.

"Yeah, yeah. I heal almost instantly and good thing—by the way, I still remember the pain when this stuff happens."

We flew over the crest of the ridge and down the other side. My dragon sight found a man two switchbacks past a ravine. I dove to where I could approach him from below.

"Are we sure that's him?"

He carried a pack on his back and a sack on his belt. I made a guess. I let the slope just below the man stop my flight and bucked Keith to the path. He made up for previous times not following directions well. The surprise made it easy for him to pull the sack from the man. I transformed back to human form and bound up to the path.

My motions must have seemed unnatural enough to frighten the man. He abandoned the sack and ran.

"There's definitely a stinky gem in here, boss."

"I guessed right then."

"What about the thief?"

"You can't keep up with me and I can't let that gem out of my sight until it's returned to Lord Suunt."

"He gets away then?"

"Let's walk back. I can't guarantee my aura won't clean the thing if it's close enough for you to ride."

14

We hiked along the trail until Keith lost sight of the ground in the darkness and stumbled. I yanked him out of a fall over a cliff. "And now we rest until sun-up."

Keith shivered. "Can you give me a gentle shove in a direction, not toward down? I'll feel out a spot to lie down."

"Do you have a coat or a blanket in that backpack of yours?"

"I packed it for you. What do you think?"

"Yeah, I still don't know why you didn't run through the portal back to Georgia when you had the chance."

"Then there's no point in my re-explaining it, is there?"

"It's pretty cold up here. I know it probably can't kill you, but it could still be uncomfortable."

"I'll manage. I just don't understand why we didn't fly back. We'd be where we're going by now."

"Can I find you two some shelter or is it your intent to camp out in the elements?"

Keith and I spoke in unison. "Thumper?"

"Yes, it's me, though I'm beginning to wonder why. You two may be as foolish as the gods who got my father killed."

"You mean besides my decision to hike and not fly to where I'm going?"

"No. I do mean your decision to hike. I told you your father is nowhere near and still you choose to take caution to such an extreme that you'll stumble around in fog and darkness on a cliff's edge. How does one turn caution into foolishness?"

"As I was about to explain to Keith, we walked in order to give you time to find us before we returned to the cabin you last found us at."

"And why did you want this?"

"We recovered Lord Suunt's gem and I think the powers that be should know about it."

"Magic artifact?"

"Yes, and apparently able to make its user god-like. The writ requires I return it to him, but I suspect if the Children of Galinthius or Athena or many others knew about it, they wouldn't want him to have it."

"So, you're in fact being somewhat wise in this. I'm relieved."

"Who are you going to report it to?"

"As you and I are both too well aware of, with a cabal plotting to take over in Olympus, it's hard to know who we should trust."

"May I suggest Oliver."

"That choice seems good to me as well. I'll present the information to him when I can. In the meantime, can I move you two somewhere warm and dry?"

"Yes, but before we get there, we should discuss another matter I need your help with."

"And that would be?"

"There's a man at the cabin who the physician worries will become terribly ill if he has to return to the castle. I want you to take Keith, myself, the physician, and his patient to a place called Three Lakes."

"They're at the cabin you were last at. I noted them on the way to finding you here. Is that where you want me to take you now, that cabin?"

"Yes."

"And then to Three Lakes tonight as well?"

"Yes."

"You'll have to introduce us. Try not to frighten them."

"Take us to just outside the front step."

"You've got it."

A lit window flashed.

"I'll be right back with the other."

I knocked on the cabin door. Keith appeared behind me. "I did not expect that."

"Lewin, we're back. May we come in?"

The door opened. A hand thrust a lamp through. Lewin's voice followed. "Ah yes, noble dragon and his assistant and what is this?"

"A Child of Galinthius is here to help us."

Lewin swung the door wide. He held his free hand over his mouth. "Oh my—You look just like Rumbler, but that can't be. Oh, how tragic that was."

"This is his son. He goes by Thumper."

"Like your father, you prefer a nickname. I am honored."

"How does he know so much about my father?"

"Thumper, Lewin was in Toth's court. Apparently, it dealt with many Olympians and Children of Galinthius."

"Tell him our plan and let's get this over with. I don't need to make friends with former members of Toth's court."

"Lewin, is Horus doing well?"

"Yes."

"Good. Then he needs to pack whatever he wants to take from here to Three Lakes. We're leaving tonight."

"Am I to stay here until you return to take me back to Lord Suunt?"

"No. I need you to translate for me when we set out to find Horus's family."

"The laws of Olympus will allow you to take me so far away?"

"Lord Suunt told me to retrieve you and his gem. He didn't tell me how."

"Dare I ask what happened to the thief?"

"He got away but the gem didn't."

Lewin half-bowed. "Generous of you, noble dragon. I only wish your mercy could mean more to ease the suffering of him and his family."

"He's a brave fool."

"The best kind."

Lewin's half-smile suggested he understood my inner struggle. Thumper didn't. *"All fools are deadly to those who help them."*

THUMPER MOVED us outside a boarding house in the city of Three Lakes. Lewin tried to thank him. "Thankyou noble son of Rumbler. I must once again tell you how much I feel for your loss. Such a tragedy."

Thumper glared at me. *"Trying to save fools like him."*

"Have I offended him?" Lewin asked.

"It's a tough subject."

Thumper vanished. His voice remained. *"Oh, I probably should tell you. Harold's in town."*

15

Lewin paid the boarding house. Keith presented him with an ancient silver coin from his pack. Lewin pushed it back. "It's the least I can do. Keep your silver."

Keith pocketed it. "As you wish but I'm curious. Could I buy things with that coin?"

"For the silver. Such is the nature of coins from other realms."

Keith showed me the coin. "You see, Aiden, I thought you might get use from these even if they are Etruscan."

"Good packing there, Keith. Too bad you're not back at my lair to find more."

"You think we'll need more? I packed twenty."

He misunderstood. I let it go. We took to our beds.

When my companions seemed asleep, I got up. My whole reason for coming through the portal and becoming a serf was close. I couldn't sleep and set out to find Harold.

I walked dark streets and listened. The sounds people make in their sleep accompanied the creaking of wood. Rats scurried and cats prowled. Pre-electric towns don't see much human traffic at night. Only my footsteps clopped the cobblestone.

I used my dragon sight sparingly in case anyone might peek out a window and see purple glowing eyes. I saw enough to find the part of town I guessed a wizard like Harold might reside. Taller and cleaner buildings with rooms for wealthy boarders was the place.

I muttered to myself, "Shall we peer in every bedroom window?"

One light flickered through a pane. Of the few people who might feel a need for light this evening, Harold would be one. Could I have been lucky? In just four blocks of such buildings I only needed a little. Pages brushed and a book closed. The odds increased. My heart beat against my sternum.

I spotted a useful pillar and leaped onto it. I calmed my breath and listened to the air. I was alone and with a view into the window. The lamp illuminated a face. Harold blew it out. I found him and cherished the luck. I watched his shadow drop into bed.

My mind raced to keep up with my heart. Fifteen feet away lay the man who played with our lives and then gave Vedi cause to banish herself to the void. I couldn't enter his room, but I could scream. Could I ever scream. With all the pain his betrayal caused me, I could scream, and unlike other's screams, mine could bring the stones and beams of his dwelling down on him. My scream could kill.

I rubbed my face and felt the air. My mind caught up and found my heart conflicted. I couldn't scream. The town would hear my father in it. Besides, I couldn't accept the collateral damage; not without an effort to avoid it. I returned to the boarding house and ducked into bed.

Why did I go in the night in the first place? Did I hope to find him wandering the streets? Thumper suggested I was a fool. Perhaps he was right.

With the morning, I decided to wait until we returned Horus to his family. I needed time.

Horus surprised his daughter as she worked a well. She screamed in anger. At first, I questioned if my perception had been corrupted by the night before, but it wasn't. She beat his chest. Horus held her arms and winced with the blows. She yelled at him.

"Lewin, what's going on?"

"Horus left just before her wedding without an explanation."

"Why would he do that?"

"Like so many of Lord Suunt's serfs, he sold himself into his service to pay off severe debts. I'm guessing he didn't want her to know where he went for fear she might try to visit him. Lord Suunt is not kind to visitors, to say the least."

She grew tired of pounding his chest and fell on it in tears. Her emotions had swung to joy.

"Did you hear what he said to her to change her mood?"

Lewin grinned and nodded. "Nothing."

Horus introduced me to his daughter and her husband. They hugged me.

"Who do they think I am?"

"An angel."

"Better than the devil."

"That's a curious thing to say, dragon."

"I want you to stay with Horus for a time. I have something I need to do that won't require a translator. When I'm done with that, I'll come back for you."

Lewin frowned. "I understand. I'll be here."

I patted Keith's back and we walked back to where I last saw Harold. The daylight shone off white stones. A shadow looked like a streak on the pillar I mounted the night before. My internal confusion must have caused me not to notice I damaged it.

"This is the place. I found it last night."

"How are we going to get in?"

"As usual, that's a bit of a challenge for me."

"Last time you said, 'be polite'. That worked then."

"It's worth a try. At least before doing something more desperate."

I walked up to the front door of the building and knocked. If Harold met me there, I'd never get in. Someone I guessed to be a domestic of some sort answered. "Vilk?"

Our clothes had to look odd to him. He noticed them. I answered him before he had too much time to judge. "Harold, we wish to see Harold."

I rushed all the words other than Harold's name since I didn't expect him to understand them. I felt Keith's hand on my shoulder. "We should have taken Lewin with us."

The man stepped aside, and I stepped in. Keith followed. "How do you know you're welcome to enter?"

"Because I can. If I wasn't welcome, I literally couldn't."

I pointed at the stairwell. "Harold?"

The man led us up the stairs and down a hall to a door. He knocked and got no answer. He opened the door a crack at first and then swung it open. I braced for the confrontation that didn't come. A well-furnished room lacked an occupant.

"Where's Harold?"

The man shrugged. Out the window, I saw the scrape I made on the pillar. Unlike the shrugging man, I knew at least why he left, if not how.

"Foolish of me."

16

A breeze cooled my face and led my eyes to the curtains. Not much had pulled them aside; the breeze and something else, but nothing as large as a man. I snatched a white hair from the drape.

I recognized it and sniffed it to be sure.

Keith touched it. "That's an odd length for a man's hair."

"And it would be an odd scent too. That's because it's not a man's hair—in the sense that you mean."

"Now you've got me confused."

"I'm not sure I can believe he'd take that form."

I leaned out the window. Another hair like the first rested on the ledge.

"Take what form, boss?"

"I'll explain later. Please use caution in your efforts to follow me. Remember, only I need to get where I'm going."

I sprung out onto the ledge and ran along it. I travelled the direction Harold must have gone to leave the two hairs where I found them. I reached a rooftop and a long-haired white house cat waited for me at its peak. He scampered away. A chase began.

My size and compulsion not to damage things worked against me. The tiny cat floated between light steps. I bounded between repairs of roof tiles. He didn't drop to the ground until we reached the city gates.

I hit the ground and swam through startled travelers. I pointed at the cat to explain my rush to the guards. I gained ground over the next thirty yards and almost caught him. He found the open window of a hovel just in time to escape my grasp.

"I can't believe this," I yelled. The snooty professorial voice I learned to hate came from inside. "A mighty dragon stopped by a flimsy hut?"

"Harold, you can't stay in there forever."

"I only need to stay in here for the rest of my life. After that wouldn't matter much to me, now would it?"

"What happens if the owner of this place lets me in?"

"That, my boy, would be me, and I aim to stay alive."

"This little shack is yours?"

"Acquired just for this purpose, Son of Order."

"So, you knew I was coming? Who tipped you off?"

"No one. I knew you'd eventually discover I had something to do with Vedi's banishing herself, and then you'd come for me."

"Where are your co-conspirators? How'd you let them hang you out to dry?"

He laughed. "Co-conspirators? My only co-conspirators were Vedi and her mother."

I didn't believe my own senses. He told the truth. "Vedi conspired with you?"

"I think I may have confused you. Weeks before your wedding I discovered Vedi and her mother had been trying to reproduce some of Dakk's work. I decided to help them."

"You helped them with chaos magic? You betrayed me twice over."

"Well, Aiden, I had a choice. I could either turn them in, which would not have gone well for Vedi, or I could agree to help them. I hoped to protect your best interests. I thought I could dissuade them from doing anything especially serious."

"'Looking after my best interests' rings hollow coming from your mouth."

"You know I don't plan to live very long in this hut. I only want to live long enough to explain. After that, I will let you come in and I will be at your mercy."

"Okay. Explain how this led to Vedi feeling she had to fake her death and then going to the void."

"Ah, so you know where she went. Such an awful shame. I'll have you know I tried to talk her out of it."

"What?"

"After you removed the curse from me and discovered I had gotten you and Vedi together with a charm spell, you disowned me and told me to never see you or Vedi again."

"And lied to me when you told me you'd do that."

"I intended to do as I said. I took the portal to Dakk's library in order to leave Earth as you required of me, but ..."

"But what could have seemed enough reason to break your word. Not much, I'd guess."

"There was another portal at the library and decades of being trapped in a cat's body still influenced my judgment, and a good thing too."

"Okay. You had to find out where it went."

"Exactly. It went to someplace in Olympus, and there I overheard some Olympians talking about you and Vedi. They were enraged with Zeus for not stopping your wedding and they planned to kill you two before the consequences become irreversible."

"And so, like you did when you manipulated us before, decided what would be best for us, that Vedi should make me believe she's dead and go into the void."

"No. Not that you might have liked my plan either, but at least Vedi would still be around."

"Then what happened wasn't your plan? What was your plan?"

"I suggested she divorce you."

"And she didn't like that one."

"Yes. She hated it."

"Why wasn't I told about this?"

"I knew you wouldn't divorce her and you couldn't have pulled off the deception involved in either plan."

"So, faking her death and going to the void was her plan."

"One she preferred to divorce. She could have divorced you and continued as if it hadn't happened. It would have broken the ritual magic the Olympians feared so much, but she told me she couldn't do that to you. Anybody else it could work with, but she insisted it wouldn't work with you."

"So, the fault lies with my nature?"

"The fault lies with her love for you; much more than anything achievable through a charm spell. I warned her she was unlikely to ever be able to return from the void, but she insisted. It was a chance better than death."

I fell against the hut.

"There. I've explained. You have my permission to enter. I will accept whatever fate you wish to bring."

"Give me a moment."

"I am so sorry about Vedi. So, so sorry."

I punched the ground. "She's coming back; back to Earth. Too bad I'm not."

17

The door swung open. His silver robe wrapped his ankles as he knelt beside me. “What’s this?”

He spent most of my life in the cursed form of a fluffy white housecat. His clean-shaven human form had only stood long enough before me for me to have discovered his treachery and send him away. I studied his face. “Olympus gave Suunt a writ making anyone who passes through that portal his property.”

“You don’t have to tell me about that. I’m his property as well and for the same reason. Why don’t you come on in? I’ve got a couple chairs.”

I accepted his invitation. “So, Harold, you’re trapped again, and this time I’m trapped with you.”

“We were a great team back then. I could never hope to have a better puppet for my spell-casting.”

“I was a puppet for more than that.”

He patted the back of my hand. “Now, now, let’s not think angry thoughts at a time like this.”

“How am I supposed to feel? I have become property and I can’t return to Earth.”

“You say Vedi will return? Is that just wishful thinking?”

"Are you working with the Olympians who plotted to kill us?"

"No, of course not."

"Vedi's status is critical information that Athena has warned me not to let other Olympians or the Children of Galinthius know. I know you've made sacrifices for Vedi and me but I need to know you will keep what I tell you between us."

"Yes, yes I will. Now please tell me."

"Vedi speaks to me through clear night skies."

"That's wonderful, considering."

"Nix is with her and plans to send her back after the war in Olympus ends."

"War in Olympus?"

"The war hasn't started yet, and currently I'm not sure how it will since I dissuaded Apollo from helping the Cabal, but Enki, who advises the Cabal, seems to have it out for me."

Harold held his finger as if testing the direction of the wind. "Thus, the writ and Lord Suunt knowing you would come."

"He expected either me or Hunter."

"You must have arrived three days ago."

"Yes."

"That explains my being rushed out of the castle on a meaningless mission to this place, but why after that, did he send you here too?"

"He didn't. He sent me further up into the mountains."

"The opposite direction, so how'd you find me and how'd you get here without passing back through his castle?"

"I got help from a Child of Galinthius. He'll be checking up on me from time to time. He's trying to make sure I don't run into my father."

"Well, at least that's good news about Vedi. So, she found Nix, the goddess of chaos, did she? Seemed a crazy and unlikely objective to me. I'm impressed, if not a tad terrified."

"I thought she wanted me to find you, but now I don't know that I didn't just tragically misunderstand her intentions."

"Well, my boy, we all make our beds and have to lay in them."

"That's not much comfort."

"And it wasn't intended to be. I went to work for your wife's great grandfather, knowing he intended to tear existence apart, I killed innocent people in support of his cause, and then when I had a chance for redemption, what did I do?"

"You tried pretty hard. You just couldn't wait for someone else to lift that transformation curse from you. If I wasn't a dragon of order, I could see myself giving in to despair like that, but you did it to me and I am what I am."

"You are way too kind, Aiden. By bringing you and Vedi together in marriage I tore at the fabric of the universe. I cannot hold a candle to that great grandfather of Vedi's, but my character seemed indelibly stained by his chaos. So much so that without even intending to, I fed it."

"And you take me, the son of order, down with you."

"Oh no, no, no, Aiden. Don't feel down. I am the one who deserves no comforting. You have a bright hope still on your horizon. Only I am the one who is doomed."

"What hope?"

"Back near Suunt Castle, I have a school full of hopeless students. The irony is rich."

"Irony?"

He cocked his head. "Did you read the writ?"

"I don't know the language, but I saw the seal and Suunt told me what it said. He didn't lie."

"I doubt he read it all to you."

"There did seem to be a bit more than I would have expected to translate only into what he told me."

"When do you expect that Child of Galinthius to return?"

"In a day or two. Why?"

"The students in that school come from Hunter's coven. Lord Suunt sent someone to lure them here."

"That doesn't sound good for Lord Suunt if the CoG finds out about that."

"More importantly for you, the writ has a condition in it that forbids Lord Suunt from encouraging passage through the portal. His doing it nullifies his benefits from it."

"Then you're telling me I'm free to go back."

He slapped my back. "As soon as we confront Lord Suunt with his crimes against Olympus."

"And he'll just let us go?"

"Essentially, but we'll need to plan that carefully, of course."

"Yes, of course, but I'm confused about something, Harold."

"What is that?"

"Didn't he know you knew?"

"He did, but he also knows who I am. All he has to do is expose me and I would be the hated war criminal that I am amongst the people that justly hate me."

"And he may still live to tell."

"That doesn't matter to me now. It will be your choice to either let me return with you or face things here. As we first started here, I am at your mercy."

"You're resigned to death?"

"Is that what you understood me to say? No. I'm resigned to helping that chaos-affiliated wife of yours. I seem to be doomed to have one foot submerged in the muck of oblivion, no matter how hard I try. I may as well go with it and help Vedi get her husband back while I'm at it."

18

Without his family gem, Lord Darius Suunt took precautions. He had his castle's portcullis lowered at night instead of counting on his guards alone to protect him.

At that portcullis is where the morning sun shined on him and three of his guards. He called to the guards atop the gatehouse to raise the portcullis. They answered back and repeated his command to each other. A mechanism clanked but only once. Silence followed; no voices; only silence.

"Tay birstig zay," he yelled.

Lord Suunt's anger increased. "Tay birstig zay."

A voice, hunter's, came from the other gatehouse. "The field trip's over. Now get through the portal."

Another Californian voice answered him. "It's cool here, Hunter. I wanna stay."

Lord Suunt gave hand signals to his men. I ran out the door of Lewin's house to cut them off. "That warlock in there is angry enough to tear your men to pieces. Don't give him that opportunity."

Hunter's yelling seemed to emphasize my point. "You're walking through or I'm dragging you through leaving a bloody trail where your nose scrapes the ground."

I could tell Hunter enjoyed the chance to threaten a coven member dumber than himself. Lord Suunt stayed his men. "Very well then, dragon, deal with him for me and get back my serfs."

The end of his authority over me didn't end my reflexive impulse to honor his command. Lord Suunt's ownership of people, as much as I hated it, as unjust and tyrannical a thing, it bound my dragon nature for a time. I didn't answer him as most would have or should have. "I ask you to reconsider your order, sir."

"You what? Go kill the great-grandson of Dakk. Do it now."

So many times I wanted to do that. "I can't."

My hand shook. I thought of myself a coward.

"You must. I own you."

Harold came to my side and whispered, "Sorry to be slow with this, my boy."

"Harold?" said Lord Suunt.

"Yes, Lord Suunt. You see the reason the dragon can't do what you ask is that your authority is null and void."

"Have you cast some charm of deception on my dragon, sorcerer?"

Harold displayed the writ. "No. In fact, I read him all of the writ. The one that became null and void the moment you encouraged creatures from the other side of this portal to come through."

He shook a finger. "The caged animals and those useless students of yours were brought through, but the dragon and you came through of your own accord."

Harold read from the write, "all powers and benefits will be forfeit."

"But the dragon still struggles to resist my command. He merely begged me to rescind it."

I pointed at him. "Don't mistake my hesitation for a lack of conviction."

Harold tore the writ in half. "You, Lord Suunt, have made this paper not worth the space it occupies."

He tore it two more times and it ignited into flames. I breathed easier. My leash fell from me. The paper held no magic power. Nonetheless, I needed to see it destroyed. “I’m not following that last order. You had no authority over me to give it.”

Lord Suunt recognized the pouch hanging from Keith’s belt. “Then you must at least honor this dragon. Give me the Suunt Gem. Nothing in that writ takes it from me. It is mine. You must give it to me.”

I didn’t want to have to fight a god-like Lord Suunt and hoped someone had a plan for this. Like the panhandler’s bike. I had to respect his property. I turned to Keith. He nodded and ran for the gatehouse.

Lord Suunt signaled his guards to give chase. “You can’t protect a thief, can you, dragon?”

The guards tackled Keith. His backpack reached the gatehouse gate without him. One of them caught the gem’s pouch by a drawstring. Another caught Keith by his arms. A blade landed next to his neck.

“Don’t hurt him. You’ve got your gem back.”

“You’re right, dragon. I do. Now one more thing you must do. Leave my castle, now.”

I looked to Harold. He shrugged. “There’s nothing fast about my incantations.”

“Is this how this ends? We leave him with god-like power?”

Lord Suunt jumped to the guard with the pouch and held out his hand. “Get a move on, dragon. I’ll deal with you after whichever of your allies are foolish enough to stay.”

“Let’s get to the portal,” I said.

I’d always been close to an exit when made unwelcome. The compulsion to leave hurt like a hot poker to the back of my head. I struggled through those short trips to keep a semblance of calm. This trip would be an entire middle-class American home in length. I ran and hoped I’d be followed.

The pain, though, didn’t come. I stopped. Lord Suunt cried out. “Where did it go?”

Not only did the pouch disappear but his guard with it. Lord Suunt and I exchanged confused stares until I realized what happened; why I had no overwhelming compulsion to leave and he lost his Suunt Gem.

"The Children of Galinthius, Lord Suunt, they've confiscated your castle and especially your family gem."

He fell to his knees and screamed into the ground. "I am destroyed. My family is ended."

"Well, there's going to be a trial before that's decided."

I whispered back to Thumper, "what about the rest of his serfs?"

"There's a gold dragon in the capital who's been looking for a reason to free them. This should do."

I helped Keith to his feet. He wiped the blood from already healed scrapes and bruises. I brushed him off. "Collect all my stuff from the ground and go on ahead of me, will you?"

I walked back to Harold and grabbed him by the shoulders. "You're a brave man, willing to face justice for all you've done wrong."

"Yes. I am at your mercy."

I hugged him and left him for the gatehouse. I threw open the door and yelled back. "Blast you, Harold. You'll cause more trouble here than you will with me. I can't leave you."

He caught up and we passed through the portal together. I braced for the hot basement air and got cool incense instead. Tinted windows of a New York city skyline. An odd figure sat with his back to us. A young man's voice came from a black canine-like head. "Sorry to move the portal while you were away, Aiden, but Enki has finally done it. He's taken over Olympus. I hope for our sakes that you managed to bring us back some help."

19

The figure touched his head. The animal head vanished. I recognized him. Siet had let his dark hair grow to his shoulders since last I saw his native form. His silhouette grinned. His aqua eyes glistened. "Since I am the one individual whose sincerity, you can't read, I thought it the least respect I could show you, Son of Order, to greet you in my real form. At least that much will be a sincerity you can recognize."

Though I couldn't read his sincerity, as he said, I noted his projection of glee and its contrast with the first news he greeted us with.

"I didn't go where I went to recruit, but I did happen to return with the wizard Harold."

"I see that."

Harold backed toward the portal. "Aiden, how is it that you're working with the destroyer of worlds?"

"The same way it is that I have brought you, Harold the Dread, back to Earth with me."

Siet held out his hand. "Destroyer of Worlds, the Dread, we are not these titles anymore, are we, Harold? Besides, we have more important matters to consider before we share the stories of each other's redemptions."

Harold scoffed. "Redemption? Aiden, Minerva killed Siet."

I pulled Harold over. "Enough, for now. We'll catch you up later on that. Siet, please continue with the matters you consider most important."

Siet walked around the chair. "While you were away, dragon, the cabal made their move."

"Without Apollo?"

"Thanks to you, they did it without him."

"But how can they claim any legitimacy without him?"

"Enki, Poseidon, and Hades convinced Zeus to seek out a teacher of great wisdom who lives on the edge of existence. This puts him on a long journey and in his absence, Enki serves as his proxy. Such a pathetically simple play for power. Dare I say crude."

"What of Athena and Apollo?"

"Zeus ordered Athena to accompany him. Apollo has been missing since he last spoke to you. All the other Olympian gods are deferential to Enki and his backers, Poseidon and Hades."

About then I wanted to know why he projected glee. "Then we're alone. We have no allies in Olympus. The Cabal can do anything it wants, yet you're grinning with a twinkling eye like you just killed Osiris."

"There was nothing happy in that moment, but in this one, you can see Athena's genius."

"Her genius? All I see is defeat. Enki need only order me away and all my friends and allies arrested or worse, and I'll be bound to obey his edicts."

He placed his hands on my shoulders. "Don't you see now why I was hidden from Olympus thus far? --

Athena's genius."

"Are you going to take them on alone?"

"No, Aiden, it was for this moment I was hidden. The Cabal thinks they set aside all their potential challengers only for me to be her able replacement. Her last instructions were to move the portal to my new dwelling here and for me to coordinate our countering of the Cabal."

"What do you mean, 'our countering?' I am bound to Olympian law."

"I was hidden and now I will hide you, dragon."

"What good will I be to anyone hiding?"

He wagged a finger. "We'll make it work. That will be a small matter. For you to trust me like you did Athena—that will perhaps be your greatest challenge."

I nodded. "You're a chaos god."

"And there's the rub, but for now, let's assess our situation. All of Athena's people are with us. They will be our most reliable assets."

"Your wife included amongst them."

"Uh, yes."

"The Empusa of course."

He tapped his cheek. "Not as much as you'd think. I need still to keep them in the dark as to who I am, for a time. Elektra and her Oceanids, on the other hand, are solidly with us, even the one who escaped your wrath, I'm told."

"Okay, so a bookstore owner, an archaeologist, a psychoanalyst, and a fraction of the remnants are with us. So far, I'm not encouraged."

"Gabe tells me the Children of Galinthius are trying to avoid being available for orders from the throne. They are trying their best to hide themselves in their duties. It's not a new tactic for them. They use it often whenever the goings-on in Olympus become unorthodox."

"That helps."

"Now as for the Titans, they are best not trusted. They're opportunists."

"Epimetheus?"

"He's a recluse for good reason."

"Okay, so none of the Titans. What of Oliver?"

"He's with us, of course, but he doesn't know about me yet. I could spoil the picture for him."

"Do you think maybe I could try to find Apollo? That would double our god-count."

Thumper appeared at Siet's side. *"Hunter and his pretend witches and wizards are back in San Jose."*

I went flush. I pulled out my torch amulet for Siet to see. "I may have made a huge mistake. I forgot I had this on me."

Siet laughed. "That would have been a big mistake if Filius and I had not met while you were away."

"Filius?"

"Thumper is what I ask to be called."

"Yes, Thumper. Forgive me."

"But the Children of Galinthius aren't exactly with us."

"They're not and it's best they yet not know about me, but this one found me out while helping you and has agreed to try to keep the secret."

Thumper closed his eyes. *"For the cause."*

"Thumper being with us is the best news I've heard so far."

Siet walked to the window. I worried I upset him. "Sorry, Siet. I know you're powerful and skilled in deception like no one else I could imagine, but I can't see how I as a dragon of order can work effectively with you. We're like discordant."

Siet tapped the glass. "Speaking of discordant, Thumper, you told me about a destructive raven you no longer saw nor heard from while Aiden was away?"

"Yes. Have you figured out what it might be?"

He tapped louder. "Two blocks that way."

20

We joined him at the window. The streets below distracted. I forced my eyes to the level Siet pointed. Once I saw it, I knew the raven. It hovered in a way that defied physics. Magic of some kind had to hold it. I worried more about the magic it had brought in past encounters. "Thousands of people may die if that thing starts arcing."

"I can teleport you to within about fifteen feet of it," said Thumper.

"Why don't you just teleport it away from here?"

"I can't teleport that close to it. There's some kind of magic field around it."

"Odd," said Siet.

"No arcs yet," said Keith.

"Take me as close as you can, Thumper."

"Boss, are you sure we should provoke it?"

"Good point. Thumper, wait and see if it's going to attack."

"I won't give it but a fraction of a second if it does."

I sprouted my wings. "I'm ready."

Siet pressed his hand against the window. "I'll cover you with a storm when needed."

"Boss, your shirt doesn't rip when you bring out those wings?"

"Keith, of course not."

"He's a dragon of order," said Siet.

Keith moved to the window. "I sure wish we knew what the hell that bird is."

A blue arc radiated from the raven and I appeared fifteen feet above it. Arcs spread across a skyscraper's windows. Thumper delivered me sideways which made a direct dive impossible. I could either swoop around to level or pull in my wings and plummet. The plummet, though not graceful, would get me to the raven faster.

A floor of windows blew in and out in a wave pattern. Shards scratched my side. A woman's scream pierced my eardrums. The woman, in business attire, fell past me and I needed a snap decision. I could try to fly faster than gravity's acceleration of the falling woman or, if I acted immediately, I could do something I knew would be faster. I grew into a large enough dragon form to reach my tail beneath her.

Like a drowning victim, she grabbed it without discrimination. Siet's fog hid most of me from her. That is until I lifted her into my front legs in the midst of becoming my arms again. She hugged me as I glided to a blown-out opening. *Where was the raven?*

She touched a wing and asked her own question. "What are you?"

I found the raven across the street and two floors up. It hovered and radiated more blue arcs. I pushed the woman's hand off and moved to leap. White lightning arcs met the blue arcs head-on and both vanished along with the raven. Thunder shook the buildings. Again, the woman hugged me. "Please don't leave me up here."

I thought about what to say. Before I had words, Thumper put some of his in my head. *"Siet seems confident the raven's gone. Are you ready for me to get you back?"*

"Not just yet."

"What," said the woman.

I gave her back a pat. "It's over now. Just move away from the broken windows. I need to go back to where I came from."

She let go and allowed some space between us. "Where did you come from?"

"Take me now, Thumper."I made it a point not to look up or down or anywhere she might mistake for an answer to her question. In an instant, I was back in Siet's penthouse.

"How are you so certain the raven is gone?"

Siet turned. "I countered its magic convincingly enough that it won't want to come near me again."

"Do you think it knows who you are now?"

"It has no reason to make that assumption. As chaos magic users go, that raven's far from the most powerful. Powerful enough to be a menace, but nowhere near the most."

"You think it may leave Earth altogether?"

"No. You know it's got to be seeking you out for a reason. It will continue its stalking until we stop it. But as long as you're here with me, it will have to hold off."

"How can we stop something that vanishes at will?"

"It's teleporting. If I ever get close to it, I can stop that?"

"So, if I leave here and you follow me without being seen, we could catch it?"

"Yes, something like that, but I don't want that thing slowing us down any more than necessary."

"Okay. Then we deal with the raven as soon as possible. Do you have a plan or do you want me to devise one."

He walked over to a desk and pulled something out of a drawer. "Athena seems to anticipate everything."

"You mean to tell me she made a plan for this already?"

"Not exactly, but she told me she wanted me to give this to you until this war in Olympus business is over."

He let a white-translucent ball the size of a golf-ball roll out of his hand and swing on the end of a chain. "It used to be my soul-stone."

"What's a soul-stone?"

"One of the first means by which mortals obtained virtual immortality; before dragon contracts, before golden apples, before transformation curses."

"Are they something like a kitsune's star ball?"

He pointed and smiled. "The core essence of the ball's owner is protected in the ball and as long as the ball and the rest of them remain together, they can regenerate from any damage."

"And you say this one used to be yours?"

"A long story about how I nearly died for Alexandra's sake and was brought back using a golden apple. The ball is no longer the source of my permanence."

He held it out to me.

"What use will it be for me? I too don't need it."

"Take it and look at it carefully. You may recognize what you see in its center."

The ball had a void in its midst, shaped like the pendant his wife wore.

"Alexandra's pendant is gold."

"A magic alloy in fact. It coats the piece that came out of this. The point of you having this is that while it no longer serves me as it did, it still allows its holder to share some level of consciousness with me."

"Shouldn't this be Alexandra's then?"

"Take it for now, so when that raven finds you again, I'll be able to help you."

"You think that's what Athena wants us to do?"

"I have no doubt. Like so many things with Athena, what seems to work against us may be unwittingly working for us in some ultimate way. I get that sense here. Take this."

I took it from him. I felt the torch amulet and looked to the sky. "I should be running out of room in my head, but here it goes."

21

I hung the soul-stone around my neck. It touched my chest with a static shock.

"What exactly is the nature of this link?"

"That question is like asking a bird how it flies. Everyone, follow me to my library. There's one more thing I need to show you before we disperse."

The room's floor space could have barely allowed the four of us to stand and look over Siet's shoulder. Harold saw the point of this first. "A second soul-stone? What do you intend to do with that?"

"It's not mine to use. You'll notice it glows."

"And that means?" I asked.

"This one is still in use by someone; someone I sent on a mission for me."

"Aren't the owners of such things in a bit of distress if they're separated from them?"

"If they're separated long enough, their bodies die, and their minds are trapped in the stone. They're condemned to eternal solitude."

"You need me to return this to its owner?"

"We're too late for that. This one's body was completely destroyed."

Keith stuttered. "Why, why would you show us this?"

"A very unfortunate kitsune," said Thumper.

Siet lifted the stone. "This is all that's left of my friend and ally, Hana."

"I'm so sorry for your loss," I said.

"Don't be. Not yet. The Gray Wolf may be convinced to help her."

"That's going to be a challenge for Oliver, considering his grandfather's state of mind, but he's with us."

"Okay, so what are we here to see and why?"

"My redemption left me with a powerful sympathy for those trapped in soul-stones without bodies to reunite with, so much so that I became interested in that of the evilest of kitsune, one named Koseina. I asked Hana to find it for me."

Keith cleared his throat. "How do you know that one is Hana's and not this evil one's?"

"Good question, wanderer. The one who did this to Hana tried to trick us into thinking it was Koseina's, but he underestimated Thumper and me."

"And Hana," added Thumper.

Siet placed the soul-stone onto a scale, only with a metal box attached where the counterweights would go. "When Thumper went to extract Hana from her mission, he returned with not only the soul-stone but this machine."

"A machine?" said Harold.

"A magical device if you prefer. Thumper came upon a scene with a soul-stone and a note in Hana's writing, telling us this was Koseina's star ball, but fortunately, Thumper saw this device on his way in."

"A seeming stray mark in her note resembled the strange machine, so I brought it back as well."

"This Hana left a clue?"

"In the note, she was forced to write. It said that since her task was done, she would leave us. If we had not retrieved this device, we might have thought we had Koseina's star ball when instead it was Hana's."

"What does the device do?" asked Harold.

"It allows one to communicate with the mind inside the stone. I speak with Hana every day now, and intend to continue until the day she is no longer trapped."

"So, you want me to help you with this as well as all the other things we need to do?"

"No. As I said before, Oliver is working on that."

"Then what are we to do about this?"

"Hana told me what happened before she was overwhelmed and forced to write that note. It's not what you must do so much as what you should know."

"What then?"

"When Hana found Koseina's star ball, someone else had beaten her to it. That someone else was Enki."

"Enki? Don't kitsune tend to chaos? What would Enki want with Koseina's star ball?"

Keith tapped my shoulder. "And what would he want with Dakk's library?"

"That's right," said Harold.

The hair on my back rose. "What would the slayer of the mother of dragons and chaos want with a chaotic evil mind and the research of a monstrously chaotic wizard?"

"Harold? You worked for Dakk. You know what was in his library. Do you have any idea what Enki would want with such things?"

"Perhaps he fears their use against him."

Siet tapped the device. "But why, wizard, would he go through the trouble of talking with Koseina?"

"He needed her input on some of Dakk's notes?"

Siet shook his head. "I don't know of any reason why she'd have insight into wizardry, or at least why Enki would know if she did. Dakk never mentioned her, did he?"

"No. He had nothing to do with Earth."

"Then, wizard, that's the mystery I share with all of you today; an ominous one."

"You want us to ponder it on our travels then?" asked Keith.

"More than that, wanderer. We need to figure it out—on our travels."

"Like a homework assignment without instructions, neither in the lecture nor the text," I said.

"Yes, dragon. Like that. My wife would never give such a thing to any of her students, even the best of them, but I'm afraid we're going to have to take it on, all of us."

"I could end up doing a lot of teleporting because of that," said Thumper.

"I realize I may be asking much more of you in this, Child of Galinthius, but we all must do what we can in it. For us to ultimately know how to stop Enki's plans, we must know what they are."

Thumper left us immediately. Siet provided bedrooms for the wizard, the wanderer, and me, the dragon. We had tasks and tasks ahead of us.

22

I opened my eyes to the morning sun in a New York City sky.

Keith shook my shoulder. "They're already planning things and we're not up yet."

"Thumper's back?"

"No, Siet's talking to Harold about something to do with Dakk's library."

I slept in my clothes, so I moved straight to Harold sitting at breakfast with the former god of storms and destruction. My old teacher raised his voice. "But I don't think you understand. I can't go back there. Suunt will have told them who I am by now."

Siet answered with a sickening sweet calm. "Things will be different now."

"I'm responsible for the deaths of hundreds of innocents there. How can things be different?"

I interrupted. "I went through a lot of trouble to get Harold out of that place. I can't have him go back there to die now."

Siet stood. "Oh good, your up, dragon. I need you and the wanderer to go speak with Earth's greatest expert on lore of all kinds, my wife."

"We want her input on all we've discovered thus far?"

"Yes, and I also need you to try and convince her to not put herself in harm's way."

"And why are you having me do this instead of you?"

"She and I still can't be seen together, and also, if I can persuade the wizard here to work with me on this library task, he will be needing my help."

"You want him to go back to a place where almost everyone wants him dead? I don't want that. Can't you send Keith? He's got some experience with ancient tomes and such. If you give him a list of the things you're looking for—"

"That's just it, dragon. What we hope to find is not what's there but what's missing. Harold knows what's supposed to be in that library. Only he'll know what's missing."

Harold scooted his chair. "Yes, my boy, and what's missing will tell us what Enki took, and in turn, perhaps, what he's up to."

"But the problem is that you'd be in immense danger if you went back there."

Harold rubbed his hands. "As in not just one but three gold dragons and a dozen or so spell-casters from the remnants of Toth's court. It wouldn't be a battle; just an execution."

"Maybe I could escort Harold there and back?"

"Not you, my boy. Those gold dragons all know your father and wouldn't miss the connection if they even so much as caught scent of you."

"What about Thumper? Surely they couldn't keep him from pulling you out of trouble."

Siet glared. "I need Thumper and you doing other things. Besides, do you all forget who you're speaking to?"

"A former god," I said.

"I'm still a master of deception."

"I remember that part and it frightens me."

"Like I said yesterday. Trusting me, like you have Athena, may be your toughest task in all this, but dragon, know this, I can place an illusion upon your wizard that no one over there will be able to see through."

Harold threw up his arms. “Well, of course. Why, Siet, didn’t you mention this at the start? If you can make me unrecognizable, I will go without hesitation—Just as long as it’s not permanent.”

“Yeah, a transformation curse left him wary of permanent changes,” I said.

Siet waved his hand across the room. “Then are we agreed?”

“You’re in charge Siet as long as your instructions continue to make sense. Athena had the excuse of being as much more intelligent than everyone as we are to cats and dogs. Sometimes things were beyond our comprehension. I’m not granting you that same excuse.”

He nodded. “Understood. This won’t be easy for either of us, dragon, it seems.”

I RENTED a car and drove to Lexington. It was six of one, half dozen of the other as to if we could drive it or deal with airports and fly in less time. I chose the option that would give the raven the least potential mayhem.

She didn’t answer any of six attempts to call Alexandra. I called Marcus. He answered. “I’m so glad you’re back. Did the one immune to sunshine make it back too?”

“Keith, Marcus asked about you?”

“Oh, please. I am happy he’s okay too, but I don’t want to sit in a hot basement with him ever again.”

“Marcus, we’re trying to call Alexandra and she’s not answering us. Maybe it’s because we’re using burners. Can you try for us?”

He hung up and called me back after a minute. “She’s not answering my call either. You don’t think something could be wrong, do you?”

“We’re an hour from the university. Hopefully, she’s there or at least someone there can tell us where she may be.”

We ran from guest parking to her office. We called her as we reached her door. We heard her phone ring. Keith tried the door. I knocked. A twenty-something woman came from a neighboring office. "Are you looking for Doctor Saint-George?"

"Yes," I answered.

"Did you two miss class yesterday?"

Keith quickly gave the answer I couldn't. "Yes. What did we miss?"

"She had to leave in a rush because of something found in Ireland."

I felt sick to my stomach and wanted to confess not being a student. Instead, I swallowed hard and asked a question. "Ancient writing?"

"Of course. That's what she's known for."

"Her usual sponsor?"

I knew she did almost all her research at the behest of Athena's front-people.

"I think so."

I sensed her doubts came just as she thought about it. "Was there something unusual about this assignment besides it interrupting her semester?"

"Yes. She said it had something to do with some Babylonian myth."

"In Ireland?"

"I know. It doesn't make sense."

"The god of cities?"

"Yeah, something like that."

I tapped Keith's elbow. "Enki."

"Yes. Enki, that's it," she said.

Keith and I ran. He reached for my shoulder. "What's going on?"

I didn't want to speak my guess out loud. I didn't want to frighten Keith any more than he already was.

23

The SUV rocked when we tumbled in. Its electric engine hummed and we drove as quickly as my legalism allowed us.

"Boss, maybe I should drive and, you know, ask you not to look at the speedometer?"

I tapped the phone on his belt. "You'll speed us up more by getting us a flight to Ireland. The airport's not far. A wait there is almost certain."

We pulled into the parking lot by the time he hung up with arrangements. "We've got a small jet to Dublin with a stopover in Greenland."

"Sounds optimal considering our stalker."

"I would have expected it to show by now."

"Me too. It showed at the graveyard, the storage place, the book collector's mansion, and Siet's penthouse. All my destinations. Why not the university?"

We left the SUV and walked. We watched our surroundings on the way.

"No ravens or birds of any kind," said Keith.

A car passed us. The woman inside flirted with me. No imagination on my part. I knew she flirted with me. I recognized her face, her wavy brown hair, her nereid charm. It was Ylera, Apollo's lover the last I knew. She flirted with an innate magic with any man she pleased to, like my innate ability to detect a lack of sincerity. I detected a lack of hers.

Keith must have noticed my head turn. "See something, boss?"

"Yeah. Apollo's girlfriend or at least the last I knew he had."

"Here?"

"That is odd. For a nereid, she has an unusual fondness for urban places, but Lexington, Kentucky?"

"Do nereid's commonly drive cars?"

"No. I'd like to know the reason for her being here, driving a car and all, but we have more pressing needs."

"Yeah, we do. Still no sign of that bird."

"Count our blessings, I guess."

"Hey, boss. Do you have any idea why that Egyptian guy calls me wanderer?"

I laughed, though I couldn't blame him for not wanting to use Siet's name in public. "I wondered about that too. My best guess is that it's a reference to your immortality. Because of it, you must wander through time, almost without a destination."

"Almost?"

A bird's cah came where an answer might have been. The raven hovered over the building. I gripped the stone hanging from my neck. "Siet, it's here."

The blue arcs came. They dangled like a cat's cradle between the sky and the roof.

"Oh no you don't," I shouted and ran at it.

A golf cart raced across the pavement toward us. The man inside wore an airport worker's uniform and had a shotgun slung over his shoulder. He yelled, "holy shit. People get away from the doors."

Blast my nature. His words compelled me to change course. The man slid the cart to a stop and readied his gun. Keith approached him. "Sir, that's not a good idea."

"It's my job, son. No birds allowed near the runways. Now cover your ears."

The crack of his gun brought a ring to my ears. The man's aim impressed me and, no doubt, the raven. The slug knocked the raven up to a point where I could barely see it.

"What the Hell? That slug should have blown him apart, not like a damned billiard ball."

I took advantage of the distraction to jump onto the roof and move out of sight. The raven came back. The blue arcs resembled a spearhead as he flew. I yelled and hoped Keith could hear me. "Get that man to cover."

A thick blue arc jumped from the raven to the area I last saw Keith and the man. The thunder, though loud, defied normalcy, as if a giant sock softened it. The corresponding hum made my head wish it could split.

I felt Siet's stone. "You got something to stop this thing?"

My own thoughts said, *"Jump."*

Siet didn't speak inside my head. He caused me to do it for him. I jumped. The air became a thick mist. My wings and claws appeared at my behest, though I didn't remember willing it. I enveloped the raven before it could blink away. My claws became a vice around it. I squeezed it, no give.

The bird seemed like the hardest of rock against my efforts. A white flash blinded me for a moment and my clawed hands held nothing but my own blood from where my claws closed on themselves.

My thoughts, like before said, *"It's gone for now."*

"What the Hell?"

I remembered Keith and the airport employee. I landed under the cover of the mist and found Keith. He dropped something. It clanged the pavement. He saw me and pushed me back. "We need to get away from this, boss."

He held back tears. What he dropped consisted of golf cart parts and part of a human torso. Some of it bled. Other parts smoldered. I could tell by the Airport's emblem on the torso's uniform remnants who it used to be.

"Was he the only one?"

"I think so, boss. I hope so."

Back to normal human form, I gripped Keith by his shoulders. "Before the mist clears, let me clean you off."

We moved well away from the unfortunate man's remains and passed into the building without further trouble. I called Siet from a secluded area of the airport lounge. "You know about the raven, but I think you really want to know about Alexandra."

"Yes. Why are you at an airport?"

"Through her usual connections, she got called away to Ireland to investigate some recently unearthed tablet."

"Her usual connections work at Athena's behest and she's not close enough to communicate. How can this be?"

"She seems to have wondered the same thing and left enough clues, like leaving her phone behind, for anyone checking up on her to assume something's wrong."

"That's why you're at the airport?"

"Yes. Following her seemed like the only thing we could do. Especially considering she told her colleagues at the university that this tablet in Ireland has something to do with Enki."

"Flying would be a horrible idea for you with that raven harassing you."

"Yeah. About that. Too bad you and I came up empty-handed this time."

"Give me your plane's itinerary and I'll try and get Elektra's remnants to monitor your travel."

"So, if we plummet out of the sky, they can pick up the pieces? Nice."

"You and the wanderer are tougher than that, and a good thing. You may end up needing to be."

24

We landed in Greenland. Kieth and I stretched our legs near the tarmac while the plane refueled. Our clothes didn't suit the cold. That meant nothing to me but to Keith, it gave him reason to shiver. "Don't worry about me, boss. I actually like the cold as long as I know I can get out of it when I want."

"Good. Stay near the plane for me. I see stars."

He knew what I meant. "By all means."

Keith's understanding of the hierarchy between us followed randomly. I didn't mind this. I needed to be reminded of both sides of things. I was his boss; the dragon. He was my employee; my hoard manager and whatnot. Yet he' was also someone who could easily live without me. As a matter of fact, if enough force hit to pulverize us; I'd be truly dead. He'd probably reassemble. I didn't envy him.

"Aiden, my pretty boy," Vedi spoke through the stars and into my head.

"Vedi. I have so much to do to get you back."

"I'm disappointed."

She lied. She still spoke in code to keep things from Nix.

"I discovered ..."

"Your lost cat. You liked that cat and I didn't. I wish you hadn't found him."

All lies, yet I knew what she inferred by my lost cat. Harold had been cursed to be a housecat until I lifted it after the wedding.

"He and I have come to be at peace with each other."

"Sickening. He is of no use to you whatsoever."

"Why?"

My question applied to the opposite of what she said. I hoped she'd tell me why it was so vital that I fetched my teacher. She answered in her code of lies. *"I hoped you wouldn't forgive him. Your current friends and allies are so reliable that he certainly will not be of any use to you."*

"So reliable, you say? Who do you think is the most reliable of them?"

"Siet and then Thumper second."

Her sincerity moved from none to low across those words.

"It seems I have to trust Siet."

"Billions of dead over countless time means nothing now that he says he's repented of his ways."

I paid extra-careful attention to that sentence. Billions of dead meant the opposite of nothing to her. I didn't marry an antihuman. As for the value of his repentance, her certainty wavered. I couldn't hang much hope on that.

"Vedi, what do you think I should do."

"Athena keeps information from people until the time is right."

She returned to honesty with that.

"Even some of our most important allies?"

"Yes, though she would never hide things from Nix or Siet."

A yes and then a couple lies corroborated a couple of theories. Vedi was trying to keep Harold's return to Earth a secret from Nix. Likely only Athena knew the wisdom behind that. The other theory was Athena somehow accounted for Siet's character or lack thereof and used him despite himself; even now in her absence. It could work out despite my understanding.

For my heart's sake, I wanted to hear Vedi speak the truth to me. "Vedi. Never forget I love you."

"I so hate causing you pain."

"I know that's true."

"Of course, you of all people do. I miss being with you. I only bear our separation through the hope that the day of my return grows closer through all of these things we endure."

"Blessed truth."

"Try not to cry, my pretty boy. Your tears may freeze on your face. Leave the crying to me this time."

Keith shouted from the plane. "Boss, they say we've got five minutes before departure."

"I need to go now, Vedi."

She didn't answer.

Halfway to the plane, another woman's voice came from the night air. "Imagine us on the same side."

I knew her too well; Ayla, the Oceanid who got away.

"So, you finally dare show your face to me?"

"I went out of my way to ask Elektra for the task of seeing you to and from Greenland."

I kept walking to the plane. "Yeah. I was told you're with us. Not being drawn by the accumulation of power like you, I can't imagine your reasons."

"Someone who lusts for power as I do has good reason to resent others who seek it to my disadvantage."

"What have you to lose in this?"

"Dragon, you don't understand Nereids. A nymph named Ylera is playing the same game I once played, only I think on a bigger scale."

"Ylera? I've encountered her. She was Apollo's love, last I knew."

"She may still be. I don't know who, but whoever it is, they're on his level of connections at least. I saw her with a transformation wand."

"Those are bad news and near impossible to get."

"Unless you're an Olympian of high status, and that uppity

nymph wouldn't be involved if it wasn't part of a play for major power."

She believed what she said.

"And you went out of your way to be here so you could warn me about this? Why?"

"Don't flatter yourself, lizard."

"But you did go out of your way to tell me? Why?"

"Because you killed the Titan who killed my sister and Kern. I owe you something."

She owed me more for all the time I spent in self-destruct mode because of her trickery. Oceanids make for both formidable and spiteful enemies.

"So, I'm off your shit-list?"

She sighed. "Yes. Am I off yours?"

"As long as Elektra remains my friend and she grants you to live."

You'd think thousands of years would teach an Oceanid to understand how a dragon of order thinks. Her face didn't show it. Her jaw dropped. I shrugged. "I am what I am. That's why your trick caused me such suffering. How can you now expect any different of me?"

I boarded the plane. Keith had been watching through the window. "Someone you know boss?"

"Someone helping me see how that nymph at the airport and the raven may be related."

"Things become clearer?"

"Apollo is probably behind the raven. That could be clearer, but what the raven is just became a lot less clear."

25

My phone rang upon us reaching Dublin. A good friend and Athena's psychoanalyst, Gabriel Schalken called.

"Hey, Gabe. Have you heard about Alexandra?"

"Yes. That's why I'm calling you. She thinks this assignment stinks. I understand you're heading to Ireland?"

"Yeah. Keith and I just landed in Dublin."

"Good that you're already in Ireland. I'm sending you a file with the directions to the dig. She left from the Dublin airport about an hour ago."

"I'll hurry after her."

"Good thinking. No time to talk between friends. Just get to her."

I LET KEITH DRIVE. I'd understand Gabe's wording better. At least that's what I told myself.

Kieth enjoyed driving. "Don't look at the speedometer, boss."

Luminescent orange ribbons clung to trees along the dirt road to the dig. Keith slammed the breaks to avoid cows.

"I thought you said cows don't commonly run, boss."

"They don't. I suspect there's something very uncommon going on up ahead."

We drove across a makeshift bridge over a ditch and stopped. A mix of screams and laughter assaulted our ears. Normal screams, male and female interrupted laughter like from men failing an attempt to imitate women. We jumped out of the car.

The air tingled of unfamiliar magic. I walked further in. Keith stayed behind his door. "What the Hell?"

His words were closer to the truth than I wanted them to be. A woman's head and shoulders stuck out of the ground. What looked like two naked people with red skin and no genitals stepped on her. She screamed for a second. That was all the time it took before her head disappeared into the soil. The two red things let out perverse laughs.

The only thing worse than being buried alive and unable to escape is all of that and being immortal. I thought of my assistant. "Keith, get back in the car and get out of here."

"Boss?"

"I don't know what these things are, but there's nothing to protect you from them. Now go. I'll call you when I need the car back."

He followed my directions. *Good boy.*

I ran to where the woman went under. The red things showed yellow fangs and pounced. My claws came out in time to draw blood. They flew back and landed on their backs on opposite sides of me. Streams of white trailed from their faces. I dug at the ground where the woman dissapeared. Twelve inches down and I knew she had gone somewhere else.

The things growled at me with perverse sounds. I called out, "Alexandra?"

A man ran in my direction. Three of the red things followed him and laughed. I ran his way. Before I could reach him, one of the three dived and grabbed his ankles. In an instant, only the red thing's upper torso remained above the ground and it pulled the man's feet under.

I slashed and knocked back the two above ground. With a free arm, I grabbed the man and yanked. He screamed. Joints cracked as I pulled him out. I placed him away from the thing in the ground and grabbed it by the head. Its mouth fell open and I heard it scream. Its high pitch reverberated in my gut until I pulled it up; half of it. White fluid splattered. Purple bits fell out of his torso. I tossed the limp remains. The two things I knocked back ran into a tunnel entrance.

"Alexandra?"

The laughter stopped. I yelled again.

"Alexandra?"

Footsteps, a lot, came from inside the tunnel. I hoped to find her before I discovered their source. "Alexandra?"

No Alexandra, just the reason for the sounds exited the tunnel. The red things, dozens of them, spread out before me. They bore their yellow teeth and hissed like a human might hiss when out of his mind. I sprouted my wings and let my eyes glow. I hoped to send them off without a fight.

"What are you?" I said.

They dashed my hope and charged me en mass. I suspected their magic had something to do with the ground. I hovered before they got to me. They leaped higher than I expected. I couldn't carry all the ones about to land on me, so I took a house-sized dragon form.

Their angry screams filled the air and made my insides turn. I flailed with all four limbs and tail. More of their screams along with white blood radiated from me. They frightened me. Not with any threat to my health, but with their dedication to forcing me to kill them; all of them. After minutes of gore without apparent meaning, I landed and took human form again. The last of their white blood rained about me. I remembered Keith's words. "What the Hell is right."

Silence followed. I broke it. "Alexandra?"

I suspected my ears rung in the aftermath and they probably did. Yet some of that ringing became words.

"Aiden, down here."

Did my ears deceive me?

"Alexandra, you're alive?"

She stepped out from the tunnel clasping her pendant. "I guess it's not a day for logic, is it?"

I laughed my relief. "They confused me too."

"Come on in. You deserve an explanation, as best I can give."

I accepted her invitation and pointed at her pendant. "He protected you?"

"Yes, but it's a good thing you came. He was running out of tricks he could pull at a distance."

"What were those red things?"

"The last of the Galla."

"The last of the what?"

"They were Enki's enforcers back when his pantheon mattered."

"So, Enki sent them?"

"Perhaps but that question will require some thinking through."

"You said they were his enforcers. Did they stop being that at some point?"

"When the Olympians left Earth, Enki left too and left his Galla behind as remnants. He supposedly relinquished them to the administrators. Between Iapetus and Elektra, you can be certain they didn't order this attack."

"Have you translated the tablet yet?"

"No. The Galla attacked the moment I got to this chamber."

"Like they didn't want you to read it."

"Yes. It seems that way, doesn't it?"

"And here I was thinking Athena couldn't have gotten your sponsors to send you after this. Maybe she left them a delayed message?"

"Maybe."

"So many maybes."

26

Alexandra leaned over the pieces of a tablet. She seemed to listen to the silent stone. She reached out as if to offer comfort. "So, the Galla were willing to die to keep you from telling me something? What? Are you going to be stubborn or are you eager to tell me your tale?"

She framed some of the etchings with her hands and thumbs, paused, and stepped back.

"What does it say?" I asked.

She picked up a camera. "We're short on time. The legal authorities are coming."

"Your husband knows that?"

"The CoG and the locals shortly to follow."

She snapped a few shots and swapped the camera's memory with one in her pocket. "We need to move outside quickly."

"I don't feel unwelcomed here. Why must we leave?"

"I need to count the bodies before they're gone."

I followed her out and called Keith. "Time to bring the car back. The battle's over."

Alexandra walked through the variously sundered bodies and penciled chicken scratch into a notepad. She crossed the area when my spatial awareness detected split-second comings and goings. "The CoG."

"I counted them just in time, it seems."

Bodies and body parts vanished here and there until all vanished. I caught glimpses of a couple of different felines as they found their hauls and left. She double-checked her count. "Fifty and three. Yep, Aiden, you got all of them."

"You knew how many came?"

"I wouldn't put it that way. Rather, I'd say I knew how many Galla were left in existence. Congratulations, Aiden. They made a fight with you their final act as a species, or whatever one might classify them as."

I didn't want to believe. "You've encountered them before?"

"No, but my late predecessor did, and he was quite the one to catalog his findings."

A rustle in brambles distracted me from my sense of guilt. The man I saved wrestled his way out. "You're, you're alive, Doctor Saint-George, and you, you're the one who saved my life."

"Rick Jones, right?" asked Alexandra.

I helped steady his stagger. "Are you hurt in any way?"

His face contorted like a tragic mask. He tried to speak but no words escaped before the sobs came. I held him and placed a hand on the back of his head. "You remember what attacked us here?"

Alexandra caught my eyes. "I am not new to this sort of thing, Aiden. Trust me to take care of him."

"How?"

"He should be okay. My husband is good with minds."

I knew I didn't want to know more details of what had to be a deception of some kind. "I would guess he is. I can settle his fears."

"Don't. What you do makes people face their memories and that's not what's needed here."

Keith drove up and noticed one of the few Galla corpses not yet taken away. The pile of red and purple flesh in puddles of white got to him. He bent over and wretched. Alexandra grabbed his long hair and held it out of the way. "Rick, you should go sit down in your car until the police arrive."

The man did as she told him. Keith, for his part, headed back to our car.

"So, did you manage to translate anything from the tablet before we rushed away?"

"It looks like a unique telling of the battle between Enki and Tiamat, but I'll need some time to translate it. The stylus marks are unusual and leave me uncertain as to if it's as different an account as it first seems."

"Why would such a tablet be in a recently discovered Druidic gravesite?"

"It makes no sense and that's the currency I deal in."

"Well, you're talking to a dragon right now and you're married to a former god. Only now has any of this started to not make sense?"

"Neither you nor my husband should flatter yourselves. You're not outside the rules of reason. This tablet and its context are trying to get there, but I won't let it."

"I'll stay with you as long as you need me too."

"I'm only staying here long enough to unintentionally baffle the local police about how ten archaeology grad students have disappeared. After that, I intend to go back to Lexington and look at the pictures I took. Which reminds me, with the police coming, you and Keith need to get going. You don't lie well at all."

I EXPECTED the raven for a couple of days and so far, it hadn't come. Rather than risk mayhem for others we spent the night in the car off a remote road. Clear skies blessed me yet again.

"Aiden? Aiden?"

"Yes, Vedi, I'm here."

"I am very worried."

I'd never known her to say those words. "After all we've been through, what could worry you?"

"I don't know what it is, but something is heading my brother's way."

"I thought you had a special view of things where you are?"

"I do, of things involving chaos and magic, but there's something out there I can't see. I just know it's coming for Hunter."

"Add him to the list."

"What's that, Aiden?"

"We're flying back to the states in the morning. I guess we can pop back to Milpitas and check on Hunter."

"I need you to do more than guess. I need you to get to him as soon as possible. I really sense danger approaching him."

"Okay, Vedi, I will."

"I know you two don't like each other, but he's my brother and I believe there's hope for him."

"I love you and you love him and that's enough for me."

"I love you too—I need to go. Nix is asking for my attention."

I wanted to complain about women's hunches and how they've got me running around. I couldn't though. So far I've needed to be where they've sent me. I returned to the car and found a place on the ground.

"Have a good talk with her, boss?"

"I don't believe you've ever met her brother. I'll apologize for the experience in advance."

27

The local authorities in Ireland, like most Earth authorities, had a bias against supernatural explanations. Alexandra caught up with us at the tarmac. "They'd rather not know how ten people disappeared than consider any supernatural explanation that fits the evidence."

Keith took her bags. "And all of the natural explanations didn't involve you needing to stay, Doctor Saint-George?"

"There was no natural evidence, no evidence they could see, touch, or hear. They're for all purposes done with their investigation even as they started. They made me promise to help them if anything came up for them. Considering their standards of evidence, that will be a very easy promise to keep."

We dropped her off in Lexington. The CoG promised to keep an eye on her. Unlike the locals back in Ireland, they had an open investigation.

We chased the sun to Milpitas to see what danger may approach my brother-in-law. A call found us on the way to my car.

"Hey, son, are you back from Ireland yet?"

It was the only human who worked for the CoG.

"Zeke. Good to hear from you. So, it's okay for you to call me now?"

"No time for small talk. Where are you?"

"San Jose."

"Good, you're back. Oliver called me and asked you to get Hunter into a safe-house right away."

"Why didn't he call me?"

"Damnit, kid, why do you have to be so suspicious? You'd know if I was lying. He called me first and I can't do it, but he tells me he knows you can."

"Well, if anyone can talk Hunter into hiding. That's going to be a task."

"Best of luck to you, son."

"Hey, can you tell me what he needs to hide from? That might help me."

"Yeah. The Feds have classified his coven as a suspected terrorist group. If not for Oliver's efforts, they'd be more than suspected. The Feds got things in motion to bring Hunter in for questioning."

"They have an arrest warrant?"

"No. Again thanks to Oliver, but he says he can't bat this away indefinitely. Someone's pulling big strings and you and I know where that's likely coming from."

"So, I've got some time?"

"Think, kid. You know Hunter better than I do. What are the odds he'll cooperate with them when they ask him to come with them to an interrogation room?"

"Yeah, Zeke. I got it. Keith and I will be driving straight to him."

When we pulled into Hunter's apartment complex, we noticed a car with government plates. Two men with badges on their belts got out. I walked fast to beat them to Hunter. They took their time. They seemed oblivious to our rush ahead. I spoke discretely to Keith. "I may need to knock him out and climb out the back with him. If I do, I'll need you to get the car and drive around."

Keith's face didn't assure me he understood.

"You got that, Keith."

"Yeah, boss."

I couldn't fault his disbelief at my plan. I found it hard to believe circumstances could leave me with just that option. Hunter, however, was never easy to persuade, and I had no time.

I knocked on his door. "Hunter, it's me, Aiden. It's important I come in."

He opened the door. "It's always important, isn't it?"

His gesture gave me passage, just before he placed his hands over his ears. The raven's hum attacked my skull. *Why now of all times?*

A muffled crack paired with blue flash left a hole in the parking lot. I saw the raven just in time for it to vanish. It moved somewhere else, not far. The hum persisted.

Hunter slammed the door behind us. "Shit! What's that?"

"It's some sort of chaotic creature. It seems to follow me around as of late."

"And you brought it here, stupid lizard?"

"I came here to save you from being in trouble with the law. I didn't expect it to follow me here of all places."

Out the window I saw the Feds run back to their car. I relocated the raven in time to see it launch another thick bolt at the ground, vanish and reappear somewhere else. I clasped the soul-stone around my neck. "Its new tactics are making it next to impossible for me to respond."

It launched a new bolt from a new location once every couple of seconds. Thumper appeared in the apartment as if he just landed from a leap. *"Get out of this structure before we have to dig you out."*

"Can you teleport us to the refuge where Mr. Asta is?"

"Will do."

He moved next to Hunter's leg. He paused and both he and Hunter were still there. Black saucers appeared in his eyes.

"What's wrong?"

"I can't teleport."

Hunter grinned. I remembered the depths of his stupidity. *"When you hunted down those terrorists you collected more than just their gold teeth, didn't you?"*

The building rocked amidst continued humming. Hunter steadied himself to answer me. "They had these anti-teleportation glyphs. I'm under constant threat to be teleported to a rock in space. You bet I grabbed some."

"Some? How many? Where are they?"

"Nine, I think, and I'm not entirely sure. I spread them around."

I wished he lied, but he didn't. Another crack and the windows shattered. "We're going to have to run out of here. We don't have time to find the glyphs."

The door jammed in the distorted doorway. I rammed it open. Thumper ran out first. *"Catch up to me between the cars. I can teleport us from there."*

My thoughts spoke for Siet. *"Just go."*

Keith grabbed Hunter's shoulder but Hunter pushed him into a wall. "I'm getting out of here but I'm not going to that hole in the ground."

He finally said words I welcomed. I shouldn't have wanted them. I found only a short moment of pleasure in delivering a haymaker to his chin. I caught him before he hit the floor and threw him over my shoulder. I had to thank those magically perverted genes his great grandfather passed to him that I hadn't just killed my wife's brother with that punch. Instead, I saved him.

Siet's words proved the best advice I could get. Once Thumper had us out of there, I'm told the raven stopped its latest batch of mayhem.

28

Hidden in the mountains of the Pacific Northwest, the Empusa, not to be mistaken for vampires, operated an underground complex. Colorless plastic walls and carpet still emitted formaldehyde. More importantly, they provided refuge for those needing to hide from the Cabal. Keith hid there just weeks ago. Vedi's father still hid there and we hoped her brother would too.

The Empusa worked for Siet. They didn't know this. They knew him as Iapetus; a fake Titan identity arranged by Athena. The Empusa, I was told, weren't ready to trust the former god of storms, destruction, and deceit. We had that in common.

Gabe, Athena's psychoanalyst, arrived with us and used a sedative to prolong Hunter's "placid state." Those were his words. It kept him unconscious. Those were my words.

"You're not going to keep him like that the whole time it may take us to sort out the Cabal, are you?"

"No, Aiden. Of course not, but I think the rest of you need time to discuss that thing that made a Milpitas apartment complex look like a warzone. I don't think him being awake will help that."

"He didn't push me that hard," said Keith.

Gabe looked bemused. "This isn't something to be frivolous about. Whatver that is must be dealt with."

I tapped Gabe's shoulder. "I've been told it's something that will help our cause in the long run. You know, an Athena thing?"

"I'd think I of all people would know if that was the case."

Words in my head formed for Siet. "*Don't say I said.*"

Gabe grimaced. I suspected he mirrored my own expression. I needed a way out of this. "In any event, whatever that creature is will likely be a mystery to us until it does something to reveal more about itself."

Thumper writhed his tail. *"If Dakk had used this bird's current tactic, I'm not sure our fathers could have stopped him."*

Gabe's eyes moved between us. "You both aren't sounding like your usual, how might I put it, gung ho selves."

"We're the ones in the trenches."

Gabe gaze came to rest on the stone hanging around my neck. His eyebrows rose and he took a long breath. "I think that's most unwise."

"For a later moment, Gabe."

Keith raised his hand. I nodded to him. "Keith, you have something you think should be said?"

"Just a note about this raven's behavior. For all the destructive force it has, it has yet to actually directly attack you, boss."

"That is interesting," said Thumper.

Siet's use of my own thoughts planted the words, *"Already noted."*

"Good observation, Keith."

Gabe glowered at the stone. With the hand I held it, I pointed at him. "Gabe, might you think you have an insight as to this thing's motivations."

"If it's sentient, and—well, it is that, isn't it? Its tactical adjustment, as I've been told of them, are more than simple trial and error."

He rubbed his chin.

"Is there any rhyme or reason behind its choices as to when to attack and not to?"

"So, far only in the United States," said Keith.

"Probable fluke," came my own thoughts at Siet's behest.

I squeezed the stone. "Alexandra's analysis?"

"No, my own," said Keith.

"Yes," was my answer.

"Sorry, Keith. I'm getting input from a New York penthouse. Alexandra has applied some of her logic to the significance of the raven not attacking us in Ireland, and she suspects it's not."

Gabe shook his head.

"You have another thought on that, Gabe?"

"No. Just ignore me for now, and I wish you'd ignore the man on the other side of that stone too."

I didn't blame Gabe at all for having a severe issue with Siet. Unlike him, however, I didn't have the luxury of isgnoring him. "Okay, then, we have what we have about why the raven does what it does, as little as that is. Now for the more urgent question. What should we do the next time it shows up? Any ideas?"

Thumper placed himself beside me. *"We should get you away from this place."*

"I agree, of course, but I should talk to Hunter before I leave."

"I can pass on a message," said Gabe.

"What he needs to hear, he won't believe from anyone on Earth but me and in person."

"Okay, dragon, then quickly. Let us decide our future tactics. Perhaps we can modify and correct them later?"

"Yes, later," came from the stone and through my thoughts.

One of the Empusa entered the room; my friend, Praxis. "Noble dragon, your brother-in-law has awoken."

Gabe stepped to the door. "What? I expected him to stay out longer than this. Just how much of his great grandfather's genes did he inherit."

I led him out. "All the thick-headed and mean for no reason ones."

Praxis followed us to Hunter's room. Two Empusa, in their usual dark well-tailored suits, stood by the door.

"I pulled everyone out and locked him in," said Praxis.

"You couldn't handle him?"

Praxis peered up. "Not without hurting him."

I knocked. "Hunter, it's Aiden. Your sister would want me to tell you something."

I had to choose my words carefully. The Empusa weren't to know Vedi still lived; like other things, not yet.

"She would, lizard?"

He didn't catch my subtlety. I feared he might blow it. "Hunter, between you and me and the stars, we need to talk. Can I come in?"

"The stars? What the hell are you talking about? Have you lost your mind, death lizard?"

I checked the door. I could open it without pain to my gut. I closed it behind me once I entered. I whispered. "They're not to know she's alive."

"Well, I'm going to tell them."

"Not if you want her to return. They must not know."

He paused. His eyes read empty air. I gave up after a few seconds of waiting for him to reach the end of his material. "Hunter, I know you hate me, but your sister loves both of us, and she sent me to get you out of danger's way."

"I don't run from my enemies."

"Vedi tells me she will be able to return just as soon as the Cabal is defeated, but they and the rest of Olympus can't discover she's alive before then."

"I won't squeal."

"But you'll tempt your sister to risk revealing herself to protect you."

"Why should she need to?"

"Hunter, your tough, but the schemes of connivers tend to find you tied to altars."

"But I'm tough."

"Toughness doesn't protect you from trickery."

He bowed his head. "True."

"For some tricky reason, the Cabal wants you in a fight with the law. If not for your sake, then for your sister's, you need to hide from them until we no longer need to hide the fact she didn't die."

"So, I can beat their trickery by staying hidden until then?"

"Yes."

"Then I'll do it."

His sincerity and his words meant one thing right then. I grabbed the torch pendant. "Thumper, now, I'm best away from here."

"Right away."

29

We stopped in a remote field to transition between altitudes. The woman who believes herself to be my birth mother, Nikki, called me. She was my mother in every way but birth and I treated her like my only mother. "Hey, Mom."

"Aiden, I took in your mail. I wasn't looking through it or anything like that, but I noticed an important-looking envelope. It's from Egypt."

"I'm traveling on business. Just put it on my kitchen table with the rest of the mail and I'll check it when I get back."

"I don't know. It has a very official-looking seal on it and it says it's from the estate of Ari Bishara."

Thumper was impatient. *"Can we move on now?"*

"Take Keith first and come back. I need just a little more time."

"What?" said my mom.

"I was talking to someone else. Just leave the mail on my table and be sure not to open any of it. If it's from someone's estate, it probably needs to be opened by me."

"Okay, but I don't think you should take too long."

"I won't. You know me."

"Okay. I love you, Son."

"I love you too."

Thumper returned. *"Ready?"*

"There's a piece of mail at my house in Milpitas that I should pick up if we can."

"How important can a piece of mail be?"

"There's an official letter to me from the estate of a former Egyptian ambassador."

"Estate? Doesn't that mean he's dead?"

"Could be. Whatever the case, Ari Bishara, is an old former ally of mine. I'm indebted to him. If he or his estate wishes to contact me, I should respond as quickly as I reasonably can."

"But with the Cabal to deal with, we are not in any position to be answering the requests of terrestrial governments."

"I'm not a fool. I did say 'as I reasonably can.' I just owe it to him to see what it says, in case there is something I can do sooner as opposed to later. It's a matter of honor."

"Hmph. Oh, very well, dragon. It won't add but a couple of minutes to our trip, but I'm not at your service to help you do the bidding of an Egyptian ambassador."

I ARRIVED at Siet's penthouse; letter in hand.

"Why did you delay, dragon, Child of Galinthius?"

I held out the envelope and tore it open. "A former Egyptian ambassador's estate sent this to me."

A lot of formal language couldn't make its news kind. An old allie of mine, Ari Bishara, was dead. Authorities suspected murder but had yet to catch anyone. One set of lines meant the most to me. I read them aloud for my company to hear. "It was his dying wish that you, Aiden Ferris, be informed of his death. He said he has faith in your commitment to justice."

"No. We don't have time for this matter," said Thumper.

I refolded the letter and placed it back in the envelope. "You're right for now. His killer probably can wait for me to catch up later."

Siet faced the window. "It seems to be part of an interesting pattern, nonetheless."

"You mean, Alexandra, Hunter, and now Ari Bishara?"

"Yes, dragon. All allies of yours."

"What about me?"

"I suspect, Enki this and he doesn't know you're not still in captivity to Lord Suunt."

"He doesn't?"

Thumper closed his eyes. *"With Zeus away, the Children of Galinthius have been avoiding making any reports to the throne. Enki believes you've been dealt with."*

"Then it's important that I not let him know I'm back until it's necessary."

"Agreed, dragon."

Keith raised his hand. "Getting the kids off the street."

"What's that Keith?"

"I've played a lot of bridge for someone my age. Enki has sent Zeus and Athena on a long journey. He thinks he's dealt with you and doesn't know about Siet. He thinks he has a very strong winning hand. What a wise Bridge player does with that situation is to get the kids off the street, as in get what few strong cards remain in others hands out of play and do it straight away; no fooling around; no taking chances."

"So, if this pattern is real, he's going after the allies, no matter how weak, of myself and Athena."

"How long of a list is that?" asked Keith.

"Gabe, Marcus, Epimetheus, Praxis, Harold, maybe Dogan, perhaps Ezekiel Roe, definitely Thumper, and you."

Siet turned around. "This, 'getting the kids off the street' idea of the wanderer's makes sense for Enki's way of thinking. Now he also thinks the wanderer and the wizard are in captivity and the Children of Galinthius should take good care of their own. That shortens the list."

"Gabe, Epimetheus, Praxis, and maybe Dogan. Siet, can you look after Athena's allies? If so, I can concentrate on Epimetheus and

Praxis."

Siet rubbed his chin. Yes. I can take care of Doctor Schalken myself and thanks to a large body of water near Chicago, Elektra can look out for the librarian. We'll have to work together on Praxis, though. As long as he can stay safely in the refuge, we'll let him be, but after that, I'll send him out and let you take care of him from there."

"And what about Dogan?" asked Keith.

I wanted to leave that one on his own. My honor required otherwise. "Yes. If we can find him without unreasonable effort, we'll check on him too."

Siet grinned. "That one has even managed to drag my name through the dirt. He's fortunate to have happened to help a dragon such as you."

"Yeah, yeah. Siet, before we set out, what are we planning to do about the raven?"

"Until I say otherwise, dragon, whenever it shows up, leave as quickly as you can."

"That doesn't sound like progress."

"We'll see that when Athena's wisdom in this becomes clearer to us. For now, we tread water."

"Is that what we're treading?"

He pointed. "Dragon, go save your Titan friend."

"Thumper, take Keith and me to the Yukon."

Keith spoke words laden with sarcasm. "Woohoo. Of course, the Yukon. Where else?"

30

Thumper left Keith and me near a Yukon store where Kieth could buy a coat. He bought one a bit large and left to meet Thumper. I noted how the sleeves covered his hands. "You know you're not growing into it, right?"

"I'll make it work."

Thumper appeared at my side. *"You could hide in that."*

"Did you find our Titan already?" I asked.

"Yes. I got lucky and came across Iris. I think she's with us, or at least she was more than happy to tell me where to find Epimetheus once I explained he was in danger."

"Someone sent him a message?"

"No, he was trying to send one to Zeus."

"He has near perfect deduction. How could he not know Zeus is away?"

"He's secluded himself."

"Yes, that's right. Did Iris tell him she's unlikely to get the message to him for a while and why?"

"No. She respects his wishes to be told as little as possible."

"Okay, Keith, let me do the talking. He's going to hate learning the bare minimum of what he must. Let any mistakes in that area be mine."

"Are we ready, dragon?"

"Yes, Thumper. Let's go see my tortured friend."

The oranges and golds of fall danced off the tundra below. We arrived in the snow of the mountains. Planks peaked from under a plateau's snow cover. A casual climber could easily have mistaken it for just a pile and not a structure. Thumper hopped toward it. *"He was inside, just minutes ago."*

"Is he alone?"

Thumper vanished and reappeared. *"Yes. Like how I last observed him."*

I knocked. "Epimetheus, it's me, Aiden. We need to—"

The Titan in his human form threw open the door. His bushy silver eyebrows furrowed. "Son of Order. Hurry in."

We all entered, and he slammed the door behind us. He offered us stools and sat in a recliner in front of a shelf of books. "The forces of chaos are gathering like a storm; one that could bring a cataclysm. My curse may just save Olympus if Zeus will just heed my warning."

"I'm aware of some of those forces."

He shook his finger. "Siet? Yes, dragon, he's alive."

I considered my words carefully. "The immediate threat to Olympus and Earth is Enki."

He cringed. "No. I don't want to know. Stop Siet and you should be able to deal with Enki, whatever he's doing, please don't tell me."

I paused to think. Keith opened his mouth and I put my hand over it. "What you don't know about Siet and Enki is why you can't see the wisdom of my priorities. I am here because I believe you're in danger."

He looked at Thumper. "I don't have glyphs to protect me from the Children of Galinthius because I choose not to. Do you know why?"

Thumper stared.

Epimetheus pointed at his head. "It's because I know too much.

My deduction is a curse and it's compounded by my hyperactive immortality."

Keith raised a finger. I pushed it down. "You actually would welcome being separated from Earth. Perhaps you could die then? You wouldn't mind the Children of Galinthius teleporting you away."

"Yes."

"I could do that for you," said Thumper.

"No," I said.

Epimetheus offered a rare smile. "I'm afraid the Son of Order is right. As much as I may welcome death, it has no interest in me. It would be rude of me to impose, especially if it means breaking Zeus's agreement with us Titans to remain on Earth."

"Then you'll accept our protection?"

"How can you protect me from what I don't know without me discovering what that is?"

"I'm afraid, Epimetheus, you may have to learn a little more."

"I may? You're not sure that I do? If you're not sure, I insist you not tell me."

I listened to wind outside. He scowled his earnestness. I noted our circumstance. "All seems quiet for now. Grant us stay here the night. My fellow travelers and I will asses our reasoning during that time. Only if we become certain of your danger, only then will we tell you. If we can't become certain by sunrise, we'll leave you alone for the time."

"I accept your proposal. Please feel free to eat whatever food you wish from my kitchen and help yourself to my reading materials."

Keith gave himself permission to speak. "The books on your shelf are all science fiction novels. Why is that?"

"I tried mystery novels. They have little to teach me that I don't already know. That I welcome but they annoy me in that I either solve the mystery well before the end or I find their solution implausible. I didn't read but a couple of fantasy novels before I realized I took a great risk of learning new things about reality from them. Now, science fiction, on the other hand, is full of predictions and speculations based on empiricism. That may spawn questions, but the scientific method allows me to safely insulate myself from answers."

Keith's eyes shot open. "You're Epimetheus, right?"

"Yes, bother of Prometheus and former advisor to Zeus."

"Isn't your thing perfect hindsight?"

"That's the myth. The reality the myth is based on is that I have perfect deduction."

I slapped Keith's shoulder. "Save your critical thinking for Thumper and me as we discuss Epimetheus' safety."

The three of us stepped outside and talked it through. Thumper and Keith agreed and Siet chimed in with input from Alexandra. The odds that Epimetheus was in danger was high enough for statistical certainty.

"Alright then. It's still quiet around here. Allow me to sleep on my choice of words and I'll tell him in the morning."

He offered his bed but we all chose the floor and fell asleep. Well before the sunrise, a rumble woke me. A roar accompanied it.

"What's that?" said Keith.

Thumper had left. He spoke in our thoughts. *"Dragon, step outside and look downslope."*

I stepped out. I saw men wielding cleavers. They rode horses up a cliff that would have given a climber a challenge. The horses moved as across level ground. A gale roared behind them and shot towers of snow into the sky. I shouted as loud as I could. "Epimetheus, we are certain now."

31

My largest dragon form could have covered the mountainside. It also would have made it obvious the son of Ferus walked the Earth. I settled for the largest form I could hide behind the plateau's crest. My tail pushed banks of snow along the width of the slope. The avalanche's roar drowned out the sound of horses' hooves.

I returned to the edge in human form and watched. The moonlight bounced white off the falling snow and ice. The mass swallowed the horses and their riders. The rumble grew distant. I shouted. "Epimetheus. This is likely only the first attempt."

He joined me. "This one's not over, Son of Order."

As the avalanche's rumble grew more distant, horse's hooves pounding returned louder than before. They cut through the cloud. Their riders clung close to their necks. Some of them lost their cleavers as their only trouble from my efforts.

"All that did next to nothing. What am I up against?"

"Hyperboreans. When they get up here, you'll see that they and their horses are giants."

"Thumper, get Epimetheus away from here."

"On it."

I watched for the Titan's disappearance. Thumper appeared and leaned into his knee. Instead of them vanishing, Thumper's tail reeled. *"What is as of late and ways to stop me from teleporting?"*

He vanished and left Epimetheus with me.

"You just did, just without Epimetheus. What's up?"

"I don't know. Let me try this."

He reappeared at the Titan's side and they both vanished.

"False alarm?"

"No. I moved him back to the cabin. Something is limiting me."

Blue reflected off my skin. The rising flumes ahead of the horses also reflected blue. My hairs stood. I worried about the raven for a moment until I noticed what wasn't there, no hum, no arcs. The blue came from another source. A blue cloud moved across the moon. I called to the cabin.

"Keith. Shine a flashlight straight up."

The riders neared. My spatial awareness told me Keith hadn't located his flashlight yet. His report on my suspicion could wait. I had an idea to try.

I flew into the rider's view. The one's nearest I noticed. I pointed at one of them and yelled. I used no discernible words. I hoped he'd see it as a universal challenge.

He compelled his horse with his heals and growled. He accepted and pulled ahead of the others. He pulled back his cleaver and closed. Just as he reached me, I pulled in my wings and dropped. I pushed off the ground into his horse's legs. At that point, I realized the scale of things. The rider had twice my height and his horse almost triple. The legs I collided with were like iron tree trunks.

Just my pure thick-headed determination allowed me to knock the horse off its feet. My back punished me when I caught the beast's chest. I screamed in pain as I launched the mass into the next horse over. I fell to my knees and huffed.

The thrown horse knocked the other down and my effort ended there. My visions of knocking several down like bowling pins died in the reality of physics. My regeneration worked just fast enough that I could get up and avoid a trample. I launched into the air and back toward the cabin.

"Got it, boss."

I saw Kieth's flashlight beam. It reflected off something translucent and blue. I moved closer to the cabin. "Thumper. Whatever's limiting you looks like a dome of some sort."

"Noted."

He vanished. I returned my attention to the giant cavalry charge. I landed on a horse and wrestled its rider off. My claws ripped the giant's flesh wherever convenient. I jumped to another and repeated. Unfortunately, the other couple dozen or so horsemen reached the cabin.

Logs flew and the wood cracked. Only a hole in the snow remained of Epimetheus's home. Keith and the Titan ducked among the ruins. The giants gathered on the other side and turned as a group; ready for another run at their objective. Their next try had fewer obstacles. I grasped my torch amulet. "Thumper, I'm running out of options before I need to use my scream."

Where many dragons breath fire or poisonous gas, my specialty is a sonic blast. Besides breaking bones and cracking structures, on this mountain it would probably cause numerous avalanches and perhaps worst of all; people would hear it for miles around. Of all the restrictions on me, not using my scream ranked near the top. I hoped Thumper might have a less desperate alternative.

"I think I can hold them off for you, dragon, but you need to find the source of that dome while I do. I won't be able to keep it up for long."

Giants and their horses vanished one horse and rider at a time. Thumper relocated them to different places within the dome. He did this quickly enough that only six of them reached Epimetheus and Keith. The Titan had taken his full size and swung a large blade. Three of them veered around him. One ran over Keith; nothing the wanderer couldn't get up from. Two got Epimetheus with their cleavers. One grazed him. The other took a chunk out of his shoulder. Thumper caught up with them shortly after.

"That many teleports so fast is exhausting. Hurry up and find the source."

I flew to the edge. "Thumper, I think I see it, or rather I should say him."

"A him? Take him out."

Amidst the flying snow, a flame burned. The flame shot down from the feet of a shirtless man with waist-length silver hair. I knew this man; insane enough to go shirtless in the snow; once my most hated ally and at one point a most annoying enemy, Dogan.

I flew apprehending everything because a brilliant talent for spellcasting is a terrible thing to find in a mad man. I knew I could take him, but how much of the Yukon might burn in the process?

32

Snow rested on Dogan's shoulders. Goosebumps rose from his pale skin. His body abhored the cold. His stare, however looked beyond it. Steam poured from his mouth. "Young dragon? --- No matter."

He started an incantation. He liked near-instant ones. This one, unusually, had some verbiage to it. That worried me and it also gave me time to do something. I could interrupt it by attacking and start a fight between us for sure, or I could try to talk him out of it.

"Dogan, why after our last meeting would you go back to the same employers?"

He kept mumbling and moving his hands in circles.

Giant horsemen charged past us. I gestured to one. "A Child of Galinthius is going to keep teleporting them back to the bottom. How about we talk?"

He spread his hands and shouted, "Ita."

His cast completed. A glowing circle appeared ten yards off. A horseman with a bloody cleaver rode to it. He flung the piece of the Titan's shoulder into it. The flesh vanished. Dogan waved his hand and the portal also vanished. He cocked his head. "We can't kill Epimetheus, just scatter his pieces around the world so it takes a long time for him to reassemble. That's all we're doing, Aiden, so please just let me finish."

"Epimetheus is my friend. I won't let you torture him."

"So, now you object to torture? Those words are rich coming from you."

It eluded me as to how he knew enough to say those words sincerely. I determined not to let it be a distraction. "Rich or not, Dogan, you should know better than to think you can shame me over such a thing. I won't let you torture Epimetheus. He's my friend."

"I'm getting tired. How much longer?" said Thumper.

Dogan brushed snow off a shoulder and smiled. "And what of us, Aiden? You've been inside my thoughts. My hand has been inside your guts in order that everything healed in the right place. Remember that? Am I not your friend?"

I cringed. "Sharing in your thoughts was as disturbing as it was helpful. As for the rest, you got what I owed you in that you still live."

He began another incantation. I gripped the torch pendant. "Have any of them gotten to him since he lost a piece of his shoulder?"

"No, but I can't keep it that way much longer. I'm slowing down and the Titan says those horses are literally tireless."

Dogan finished creating a second portal and grinned. "Problems, young dragon?"

"I don't want to hurt you, Dogan, if I can. You having helped me in the past and all, but I can't let you finish what you're doing here. Perhaps a price?"

He laughed. "If you had any idea what my reward will be, you'd know you couldn't match it."

"The last time we met, you asked if you could speak with Harold. I might be able to arrange that."

"Harold? You might? Oh, dragon, even if you did, it wouldn't compare."

"I might be able to do even better than that."

I could say that honestly because I suspected Siet to be a wizard of sorts. I took care not to touch the soul-stone lest the former god corrected me.

Dogan turned up his nose. "How can you do better than to appoint me to the court of Hecate."

"Enki promised to get you into Hecate's court?"

"No, silly. Poseidon. He's the one with the in."

"Wouldn't that be Hades?"

"Actually, that would be no one," said Thumper.

Dogan put his hands in motion for another incantation. "They both do."

I made sure I had Dogan's attention and held out the torch pendant. "Thumper, why do you say no one has an in with Hecate?"

"Because she's dead. Siet and Athena had something to do with it. I don't know what. All I know for sure is that she's dead."

"It's because she's dead, Dogan."

Dogan wagged his head. "Not true. Not true."

I held up a finger. "The Child of Galinthius tells me the truth. Hecate is dead."

"He lies. Poseidon doesn't."

"Dogan, remember who and what I am."

"You're not a god."

"That's right. I'm not. I'm the Son of Order. I know when someone lies to me, and he isn't."

"Poseidon wouldn't lie to me. Why would he?"

"He needs your services and knows you won't accept riches as payment?"

"No. It can't be true that he lied to me. I'm about to be with Hecate. You can't stop me with your lies."

Purple reflected off his skin. I knew the source and I calmed myself to make it stop. "Don't die a fool, Dogan. You know the Son of Order cannot lie to you."

His flames extinguished. He fell to the ground and squatted. He ran his fingers down his chest and mumbled. A cloak appeared. He pulled it tight around him. He stood and shook the snow out of his hair. "Hecate is dead? That god lied to me?"

"Athena would tell he isn't a god."

He pouted. "She's such a killjoy."

"She anticipated Enki and Poseidon's takeover and has plans in motion to stop them. Their offer of payment to you is a lie. The closest things you have to friends are with Athena."

He waved away his latest portal and shrugged his shoulders. "I'm afraid the Hyperboreans do welcome riches as payment and your hoard is no match for that of Poseidon."

"They won't matter if you remove that anti-teleportation dome."

He held out his hands. "You said something about me meeting Harold again?"

"Yes. Allow my Child of Galinthius friend to teleport freely and I'll ask Harold to see you."

"You are the Son of Order and you cannot lie."

He raised his hands high and snapped his fingers. The snow and all other reflective surfaces turned white.

"Okay, Thumper, get us all, including Dogan, out of here."

"Are we that desperate?"

"I call it two birds with one stone."

"You should have used a heavier stone."

33

Thumper moved Epimetheus and Keith first, then me to a meadow. He'd used that meadow the last three times he's transitioned me. He brushed me with his tail. *"Now for that wizard. If I'm not back in a few minutes, you'll know you've blown it."*

His faith in me needed some work.

"Keith, did you hear that?"

Keith finished up a makeshift bandage on Epimetheus' shoulder. "Did the big cat say something to you, boss?"

"Nothing worth sharing."

I could tell from Epimetheus face the wound pre-occupied his concentration. In his case, he might prefer the distracting pain over arriving at new insights. I left him to his discomfort.

The clouds in the night sky teased me with the possibility of clearing. One large cloud left an opening in its wake only for wispy cirrus clouds to fill it. Stars blinked between their strands; close and only so.

Thumper appeared with Dogan. *"We'll be moving on in about a minute's time."*

"Got that," said Keith.

Epimetheus grimaced.

I asked, "can we get Epimetheus' missing shoulder piece before we move on?"

"How long will that take?"

"Dogan?"

He grabbed his head. "That thing's talking in my brain."

"Dogan, so you've never met a Child of Galinthius before. I think right now would be a good time to get Epimetheus missing piece for him."

"Those portals require hard to obtain reagents and a great deal of skill and talent to create."

"You were prepared for several of them."

"His missing piece will come back to him on its own. Why should I waste the reagents?"

Keith yelled, "because he's in pain."

He shrugged. "He's a Titan. They practically live for pain. You know, like giant voodoo dolls, only you skip the make a copy step."

"We can kill him here," said Thumper.

I knew Dogan well enough to have a clue as to his angle. "Dogan, your teleportation skills have dramatically improved since we last met. Really quite amazing over such a short time."

A smile crossed his pale face. "Yes, it is."

"Harold may just be impressed."

"You think?"

His sincerity dipped telling me he had little doubt.

"How quickly can you use this new mastery to retrieve the missing piece of Epimetheus' shoulder?"

"Less than a minute."

"Are we to take your word for it?"

"You'll know if I'm telling the truth."

I raised a finger. "I can tell that you honestly believe you can do it in under a minute, but I can't tell if you actually can."

He pointed his chin. "Watch me, Son of Order."

He did his incantation and waved his hands around. Fifteen seconds and he created a portal, three feet across. He leaned in as if through a window, then fell the rest of the way through. Twenty-five seconds and his hand came through holding a lump of flesh. Keith had it at thirty-three and Dogan rolled through at thirty-six and bowed.

If I had been capable of insincerity, I would have clapped. None of those capable of it did either.

"He's like a child," said Thumper.

Dogan held out his hands. "What, no applause? Nothing?"

A clap came, that of muffled lightning. The headache-inducing hum followed. The raven hovered over the meadow's edge.

I watched Dogan's face. His hands flew over his ears. The nature of his wince read to me as sincere horror.

Keith ran to Epimetheus and pulled off his bandage. The chunk of flesh jumped to the Titan. His face expressed a new pain, though I could not be certain which one of two causes brought it; the hum or the deductions he had to draw from what he saw.

The raven shot a bolt at the Titan who seemed to channel his brother and dodge it a split second before it launched.

"Thumper, get us out of here."

"Everyone, come together over me and touch me."

Even Dogan hopped to as three hands touched white fur. Wood floor replaced dirt and weeds, and the piercing hum ceased. My ears rang for a moment. As they cleared, Siet spoke in an apologetic tone. "For different reasons but to the same inevitable result, Titan, as with the Son of Order, I cannot hide who I am from you. I'll show you the respect of not trying."

Epimetheus glared at us. "Please don't tell me how the Son of Order aligns himself with this god of chaos."

He hated finding the answers to the questions his situation compelled him to ask. I gestured Keith to stop before he spoke. I offered what I hoped to be the best answer for the moment. "If it brings you any comfort, I can't completely answer that question myself. It is only what is. The why still eludes me."

Siet took a seat and gestured for Epimetheus to do the same. "It's noble of Aiden to try and comfort you, but I'm afraid Olympus and Earth are in peril and may need your help. You may need to learn a little more and share it with those of us who wish to preserve civilization."

The old Titan took up a place on a couch and studied the New York skyline. "I have seen more in the last few minutes than I have in the last few years. I need to rest before I make any promises."

Siet gestured to Dogan. "Of course, Titan. Now as for you, wizard, we should plan to talk as soon as the Titan has found a bed. Wanderer, there's an empty room next to yours. Help him find it."

Keith put his hand on Epimetheus' shoulder. "When you're ready."

Epimetheus kept staring out the window. "I've been avoiding seeing that."

"New York?" asked Keith.

"No. What's gone."

He winced and left with Keith.

"You avoided that?" asked Keith.

"Especially things like that."

Dogan's eyebrows seemed stuck to his hairline. "Who is this?"

Siet waved a hand in front of Dogan's face. A sort of magic came from it that made me cringe. "You and everyone else are better off with you still believing that I'm dead. You merely see me as someone who looks like Siet."

Dogan looked at me. "Why is this guy dressed up to look like Siet?"

I chased away a sick feeling in my stomach. "I only know when people lie. I don't always know why."

34

Three of us sat with New York's skyline lit behind us; order, chaos, and insanity. I wanted away from the moment Siet touched Dogan's perception to deceive him. "So, the matter that hangs ominously over us, what do we think Enki's up to?"

Something lay under a cloth on the table. Siet pulled away the cloth. He revealed the device he used to communicate with souls trapped in stones. "I want Hana to be in on this."

"She can see and hear us now?" I asked.

Siet's hand trembled as he placed it on the device. "Hana, do you see our two guests?"

He whispered, "when you're trapped inside a soul-stone, watching the world beyond it is uncomfortable, to say the least."

"She has my sympathy."

He looked up. "Son of Order, she's especially pleased to see you. She says, thank you."

"Thank you? For what? My sympathy?"

"You saved the Gray Wolf and thus her hope to get her body back."

"Do you know if Oliver's talked him into that yet?"

"As soon as he gets him to lift the stone curse from Astraeus, he will move his attention to Hana."

"And how goes that?"

Siet rubbed his forehead and then a tear. "The trap you saved the Gray Wolf from traumatized his already fragile mind. It's a struggle but Oliver tells me to not give up hope."

"If I touch that device, could I talk to her?"

"You mean and hear her? Yes, but that's best left to me for now. It's an effort for her to keep her attention with us and not pull back. Let's not waste her effort. Wizard, you've recently come into command of chaos tainted magic. From whom or from where did you obtain it?"

Dogan leaned back. "How do you know I didn't derive it on my own?"

Siet leaned forward. "Because you didn't, wizard."

"I have talent, a lot of talent."

"You're a quick learner."

"That's talent."

"Who or what did you learn from?"

Only a mad man could stare down the glint in Siet's eye. Dogan started and then with a second thought, looked away. "Dakk's library."

"When?" I asked.

"Enki has access to it and needed my help."

"Enki, the slayer of Tiamat? What did he need to do in Dakk's library? Enki is anti-chaos."

"He had other spell-casters there working to derive new counter-spells against chaos magic. He needed me to show them how to cast some of Dakk's spells so they could test their counter-spells against them."

I knew about some of Dakk's chaos magic my wife experimented with and what they were related to. "Teleportation spells?"

"No. Teleportation was my own personal research. The spells he wanted to counter were destruction spells."

"Destruction spells, wizard?" said Siet.

"Yes."

"Don't you mean, wizard, disruption spells?"

"Yes, or as Dakk's notes occasionally called them, purification."

Siet bowed his head. "My words, my lie; my lie to myself."

"What?" said Dogan.

At that moment, Siet almost convinced me of his redemption beyond just his wife's perception. A life of lies by a master of deception, unfortunately, creates an army of doubts. I remembered Hana's struggle. "Whatever they're called, Dogan, did Enki get the counter-spells he wanted?"

"Yes."

"Hana has a question, wizard," said Siet.

"I was wondering when this Hana would," said Dogan.

"She wants to know if Enki gathered any of the chaos magic from the library for himself?"

Dogan shot a finger toward the device. "As a matter of fact, he might have tried to."

"Really?" I said.

"Yes, Son of Order. He asked me if there were any notes on how Dakk transformed himself into the creature that four dragons and Toth saw a need to kill."

"And you just pointed them out to him? Have you no wisdom at all?"

"I didn't see the harm. Dakk's tome with those notes is sealed inside a vault with magic traps. I showed him where it is, and he dismissed me. Even if he gets at the tome, without me, his spell-casters are unlikely to figure it out."

"Enki is the Sumerian god of intelligence and crafts, Dogan. Did he watch you work while you were there?"

"Well, yes, but he's not a wizard."

Siet cleared his throat. "By definition, but not necessarily by function."

"I don't think he could get through the traps to the tome."

Dogan's sincerity waned with those words.

I couldn't look at him. "You mean, Dogan, you hope he couldn't."

"Wizard, Son of Order, Hana tells me that when her stone was placed where the Child of Galinthius would find it, instead of Koseina's, Koseina spoke to her; taunted her."

"What might we learn from that?" I asked.

"Koseina said to her that it was such sweet irony that Enki of all gods was about to complete the task that Dakk had failed to complete. Even sweeter that he would do it with both Koseina's and Hana's help."

"What does she mean by with Hana's help?"

Siet gently removed his hand from the device. "She's paid attention as long as she could bear for now."

"Siet, do you know what Koseina meant with those words?"

"No, I don't. Koseina and Hana are kitsune. As magically powerful as they can be, they're no more wizards than you are, Son of Order. Now Enki on the other hand ..."

Dogan perked up. "Enki's a powerful wizard?"

I caught Siet's eye and then gestured to Dogan. Siet picked up on it. "No, wizard, just a capable emulator. His learning only goes one way, to him."

"Most important here, Dogan, if he's gone through the trouble of getting Koseina's star ball, he's probably trying to use Dakk's tome."

"How can he use Dakk's tome to achieve the ends of a god of creation. Shouldn't he be on your side, Son of Order?"

I remembered Apollo's rhetoric before I persuaded him out of the Cabal. "Reset."

"Yes, of course," added Siet.

Dogan shot out of his chair. "I don't want to start over. I've worked too long and hard to become a wizard."

I grabbed his arm. "And those are the words of someone on our side of the war."

Siet grinned wryly. "Welcome mad wizard."

35

Despite a looming cataclysm, I got what rest I could without messing up my sleep cycle. Of all my weaknesses, the most dangerous I found to be the lack of rest.

I woke to Beethoven's Moonlight Sonata. I found Siet in the same chair I left him. He listened to the slow yet persistent cadence and watched the waking city. I think I understood his choice in music. It seemed an anthem to a civilization not yet ready to pass away.

I dared interject. "We're all that stands in the way, aren't we?"

"Irony on irony."

"How so?"

"It used to be I was all that was needed to end a civilization, an in the greater power of my past I destroyed many. Your ancestor, Tiamat, once filled that role too. Our excuse was the corruption of humanity. Now here we are, on the other side opposing Enki, Poseidon, and the throne of Olympus. Civilization is finally working as it should, stumbling but getting back up, and a destroyer and a dragon lead its champions."

"I'm a dragon of order."

"A contradiction."

"Like a master of deception who I must trust?"

"Yes."

He turned off the music. Thumper appeared. *"Should I take Epimetheus to the refuge."*

"That's a good question," I said.

Siet dismissed it with his hand. "I'm already holding up a request from Olympus to meet with Praxis. That and Dakk's great-grandson being there means we dare not hide any more of Enki's targets all in the same place."

"So, our theory holds. Enki is trying to get all of my allies out of the way."

"And we've frustrated him in all cases but one."

"At this point, he's got to know there's more out there against him than he previously believed."

"Yes. He must. More clever strategists might have let him get more of his targets so as not to reveal what we know. Perhaps we should have left Epimetheus unprotected."

"And let them chop him to pieces and scatter them across the Earth?"

"He would have reassembled eventually."

"I couldn't allow that."

Siet winked. "And I suppose Athena knew what she was doing when she left so much to us; your nature and all."

Keith walked in and leaned on a chair. "Epimetheus doesn't want to leave his room. He's afraid he'll learn something."

"He's going to need to, wanderer."

"It pains him so that even considering it makes his face take on a look that makes me hurt."

I patted Keith. "Siet, Epimetheus is safely hidden here, right? Why not let him hide in the room until the war passes?"

Siet walked to the window. "Up until now, we've been self-serving; protecting ones we love and feel obligations to. We've done well at that, but now Enki knows there's a significant resistance, and on top of that, Epimetheus is in that resistance's hands."

I scoffed. "That's his fault. If he had left him alone, so would have we."

"Yes, dragon, that is true. If he had left the Titan alone, he would have stayed out of this. Like a Greek tragedy, Enki's efforts to make sure Epimetheus stayed out of things has brought him in, and here's the crux of the matter, he knows he's made this error and understands the magnitude of it. Epimehteus knows more than anyone in power or seeking it would want anyone to know."

"And so he must wonder what destructive secrets he Epimehteus will tell us."

"Yes."

"Well, let Enki suffer in anticipation. The worry alone should hinder his cause. We can leave Epimetheus alone."

Siet tapped the glass. "Enki's going to act because of this. Our actions have used up what time we had to operate from shadows. He's going to come for us now, even if he doesn't yet know who we are."

"And we can deal with that without torturing Epimetheus any further."

"I say, dragon, Child of Galinthius, wanderer, if we're going to pay the price, we would be fools not to get what we're paying for. We should ask the Titan to hear what we know and give us his deductions."

"My ears burn," said the old Titan. We missed noticing his approach.

Keith turned. "Are you sure you want to be out here, sir?"

Epimetheus glared at Siet. "I wouldn't trust that lord of chaos and deception with the contents of a chamber pot, but the words he speaks belong to reason, not him."

"But the pain," said Keith.

The old Titan sat where he could see the city and gripped his chair. "I first banished myself to avoid sharing with Zeus things about one of his brothers that would have caused a war in Olympus. Well, now I know enough to know that horse has escaped. Now, I can suffer toward the ends of ending a war already begun."

He forced a smile through his face, contorted in discomfort. "Besides, Son of Order, it can't be worse than the fate you saved me from."

I assessed his sincerity or rather, in this case, his determination versus his dread of more pain. I couldn't comprehend the amount of pain that required the determination I sensed.

"Siet, Thumper, let's tell him what we know about Enki and the Cabal, but please try to avoid telling him anymore. Epimetheus, my friend, we'll start when you're ready."

The old Titan's eyes widened. "There is no 'when I'm ready'. I must be ready now for I have already deduced from the incidental that our time is short."

36

We took turns telling him every relevant thing we could; first me, then Thumper, and finally Siet. The old Titan turned pale and sweat beaded on his brow through the whole process. Even pleasant things like the undoing of Lord Suunt struck him like grief.

He asked follow-up questions; few to me; more to Thumper; many to Siet. He found Siet's recollection of his redemption most relevant for reasons he didn't explain. Finally, he stood. "I've heard enough."

"You have valuable deductions to share with us then?" I asked.

"I have arrived upon multiple deductions and I'm afraid your ears will have to wait a little longer. I need to ponder out yet more deductions to be drawn from the combinations of them."

"Is this complicated even for you?"

"Forgive me, Son of Order, for I am exhausted and need time to rest."

"But you said yourself, we don't have much time."

He looked blankly at Siet. "You all told me what I need to know; all we need to know. You'll get your answers after I rest."

He returned to his room while the rest of us sat and exchanged glances between ourselves, his bedroom door, and the cityscape. Dogan broke the silence by throwing a handful of nuts into his mouth. Keith finally spoke. “We’re expecting an imminent attack?”

Siet moved to the window. “Yes.”

“Are we planning to just wait for it?”

“Wanderere? It’s going to be near impossible for Enki to find us here. He will attack in some way, but it will have to be indirect; something to draw us out.”

I said, “I was hoping Epimetheus might help us foresee that.”

“Son of Order, you have the wrong brother for foresight.”

“True, but is it your plan to just wait and react?”

“It’s all we can do for the moment. We must wait for an opportunity to take the initiative from him. Until now, we must react.”

“I can scout about,” said Thumper.

“Yes, of course, Child of Galinthius, do what you do so well.”

Thumper vanished. Keith stretched himself across a couch. “And I’ll do what I’ve done so well as of late, wait and do nothing.”

Kieth had the order of the rest of daylight. I noted clouds as they filled the night sky. “Siet, do you think we need those?”

He smiled. “They’re not my doing and as much as I’d like to blow out a clear spot for Aiden, it’s best not under our current circumstances.”

I continued to study the sky. Siet left me alone. I thought about what I might say to Vedi if I could. A small thought leaped in my heart. For all the dread of Enki’s unknown next move, one thing, she assured me would be true, it would be one move closer to her return.

A light peeked around a cloud. At first, I suspected a bright star but the colors, red, orange, yellow, green, blue dispelled that. Kaleidoscope wings carried a Titan. Iris approached.

“Siet, Iris is flying our way. Should we open a window or something?”

Siet returned to the window. “She’ll find her way in fine. I need to make sure she’s not being followed.”

His eyes glowed red. Iris flew up to and through the glass as if it weren’t there. She greeted me, “Son of Order.”

"Do you have a message for us?"

She held up a scroll with a crooked and off-center seal. "I have a message for Epimetheus."

Siet glanced back with his eyes still glowing red. "Deal with her. My attention is needed here."

I gestured and walked her to Epimetheus' room. "He's asked us to give him time for what he believes to be much-needed rest."

"Perhaps we shouldn't disturb him?" she asked.

"I don't know. Do you know what the nature of the message is?"

A groan came from the old Titan's room. She brought her voice to a whisper. "You're the Son of Order. I know this much. You can be trusted to open it and determine things from there."

She handed me the scroll. When she did, I recognized the seal on it. I walked her away from the bedroom door. "This is Athena's seal. How can this be?"

"The message is from Melia, the child in Athena's care. She has sent the message on behalf of Prometheus, Epimetheus' brother."

"The little girl? Is she alone? Why is he having her send it?"

"Athena left Melia in his care until she returns from her journey. He's been taken against his will by Ares. She was instructed to inform his brother."

Siet met us with his normal eyes. "Hermes followed you, Iris."

"Oh no. I didn't know."

"We're discovered?" I asked.

"No, Son of Order. I confused his mind on this matter, but you, Titaness, need to take my portal here to Archai."

He handed her another scroll. "Take this to the dragons at the court of Toth. It's a message from Doctor Schalken about scheduling counseling."

She stared at Siet. "Peculiar timing and method. Why didn't Doctor Scahalken call me to take it directly from him?"

"He'll forgive me for sending messages on his behalf in this circumstance, I'm sure. Eventually."

I recalled Gabe's reaction to Siet's name. "I wouldn't be If I were you."

He looked askance at me. "Athena trusted me to do what I'd do, and this is what's needed to protect both us and Iris. Titaness, once you deliver this message return directly to Olympus. Hermes will be under the belief that you flew to the outskirts of this city and then to the court of Toth and that he lost you on the way."

"I'm a messenger. I can't lie."

"You won't need to. The only person who might want more details than that you went to Toth's court after reaching these city outskirts believes you did just that. Now, go."

I broke the seal and with Dogan's help, read Melia's message. It read, "Prometheus refused to help Enki find his brother. Enki said he admired his loyalty too much to punish him and let him go. But when we got back to the dwelling, Ares took Prometheus away to re-punish him. He wanted me to be sure I wrote that down, re-punish."

Siet slapped a chair. "He's trying to draw out whoever helped Epimetheus."

"Re-punish?" said Keith.

"Gabe told me Ares has psychological issues he couldn't help with. He could be working on his own and for reasons of madness."

Epimehteus stepped out. "No."

"Are you ready to share your deductions with us?"

"Not yet, Son of Order. Only this one as it pertains to my brother. Ares made a point of using the term 're-punish' because he wanted me to know where he took him."

"He wants to draw us out."

He raised a finger. "More than that. Enki intentionally let my brother off so that Ares' re-punishment would not be with the legal authority of the throne of Olympus. Why would he do that if not to give someone like you the freedom to try and rescue my brother?"

"Enki knows I'm free."

"Not yet. He only suspects for the time, but if you go, he will know and that will be when the rest of his plan will happen. He will use your nature against you as only someone with the authority of the throne of Olympus can."

"It's like a mousetrap."
"One you can't subvert."
"Yet, one I must enter."

37

Epimetheus stumbled to a chair. Keith caught him. "You should go back and rest more, sir."

"Ares has taken my brother to a place in the Caucasus mountains. I know the place. I will go and deal with it like I should have the last time."

Siet pointed at the bedrooms. "We need you to rest up and arrive at your deductions. I can go."

"No, it must be me," I said.

Siet placed his hand on my shoulder. "As you say, I'm a master of deception. I can go and leave any observers totally confused as to who performed the rescue."

"But, Siet, of all our secrets, that you're alive is the greatest by far."

I clasped the torch pendant. "Thumper, I need you to take me somewhere as soon as possible."

"But, boss, why can't Thumper do it without you?"

"Ares is an Olympian and he could easily be anticipating teleporters. If Thumper goes there and can't teleport away, and he's alone, he's not a dragon."

Thumper appeared behind us. *"Here now. --- Why does Epimetheus look ill?"*

I walked to the old Titan. I placed my hand on his head. "I can tell you're tired by your words. Your body though seems fine. It draws no healing from me."

"Then I can go with you."

"No. Just tell Thumper where your brother is so he knows where to go."

He waved at Thumper. "It's the place in the Caucasus where they chained him before. I can show you on a map."

Thumper closed his eyes. *"No need. I know the place."*

Dogan studied a bowl he'd recently emptied. "Son of Order, I don't understand why you feel it necessary to rescue Prometheus at all."

"Because, Dogan, of something called honor. I'm not sure you're familiar with it."

"No need to insult me. I know what honor is. I just think it's a foolish thing, but more of a mystery to me is why it's so important to you? Your thing is order. That's all you're magically bound to. How do you justify letting this thing called honor get in its way."

"My magic contract makes me a dragon and I have no choice in it. Caring for honor, for the individual dignity of those who make sacrifices in our cause, that allows me to be more than just a dragon."

"It gets you into so much trouble. It's almost like you're a glutton for punishment."

"You don't understand, Dogan, and I pity you that you don't. Epimetheus has accepted great pain in order to help us stop the Cabal. I cannot then let his brother be tortured as well."

Dogan threw a hand into the air. "Just so long as I get to speak with Harold, what do I care."

"Thumper, transition us there now."

"Gladly."

We landed in a new meadow. Thumper whipped his tail about. *"I have to say, I don't understand myself why you choose to walk into a trap."*

"I don't see any other choice. Besides, with Siet, the cause may not even need me."

"Well, at least you don't have a messiah complex."

"I recommend you drop me off about a mile out. That way you shouldn't get caught up in it."

"From the first mention of the word trap, that was my plan."

"I know you're brave, Thumper. You just don't want to repeat your father's mistake."

"It wasn't his mistake."

"Sorry. Poor choice of words."

He leaned against my knee and we teleported into the mountains. *"If Epimetheus is right, you should find his brother on this mountain's peak. You're just below the tree line, so your approach will be wide open."*

"Thanks. Hopefully, there won't be any climbers to see me."

"Worry about more than that, friend."

I used my strength to bound up the mountain. As I neared the peak, light glistened off metal. I heard a calm voice in a conversation. I decided to get out my wings and survey things.

I saw what had to be Prometheus; a nine-foot-tall man bound with chains embedded in rock. I flew around to make sure nothing might surprise me on the other side. I tried to make sure. I couldn't.

A giant eagle nested on that other side. It caught sight of me in no time and took flight. I dived. It followed. Its feathers created more drag than my scales and I lost it. I came back to where Thumper dropped me off and started back up, foot and hand.

My plan was to sneak up and release Prometheus and then, in dragon-form, carry him down and away from the eagle. I didn't want a fight if I could help it.

I reached the Titan and so far, so good. I found a boulder to break his chains with. I had him loose in four hits; one too many it seemed. The Eagle rose over the peak. Prometheus spoke. "You don't have a bow? That's not good."

"I'm a dragon. Get on my back when I take form and we'll fly away from it."

"No, dragon. No matter what size you take on, either I or your greater size or my presence on your back will allow it to catch you."

"Then I'll have to fight it."

"Ares had the poor bird's beak and talons replaced with dark metal. You know what that means?"

"Yes. Stay out of the way."

"Have you ever fought a giant eagle with dark metal talons before?"

"Yes. I almost died."

38

The mere sight of those black talons stung my flesh with memories. My inner thigh cried the loudest. My nerves could not forget the fight against similar talons in a pre-historic vault.

From the peak's crest, the bird swooped. I dodged. Adrenalin served me more than any magic. My hand slapped my thigh to make sure. The absence of warm liquid meant I hadn't started bleeding.

Prometheus called out. "He turns already, dragon,"

This bird maneuvered more quickly than my last talon-bearing attacker. I remembered in the last such fight I benefitted some from misdirection tactics, though it was always a dangerous gambit.

My heart thumped between my ears as I flew out, ready to try what worked before. I flew about and waited for another swoop. He came. I pulled into a ball and fell beneath him. I swung over my head, hoping to rip flesh. I got claws full of feathers and blood sprayed. The spray followed me and not the bird; my blood.

My forearms both gushed. I pressed the wounds together and turned my fall into a dive. I asked my memory for more lessons from the last fight. I noted the last one failed. This bird's natural quickness exceeded the automatons.

Unlike the vault, I had no place to hide. On the positive side, I could out dive this one and I had room. I flew beneath the treetops and zig zagged between their trunks. My regeneration caught up with the bleeding before the eagle caught me flying level. I couldn't count on that every time I needed to dive. I couldn't afford to try and replay my last such fight. Where the automaton eagle left me almost bled out and dead, this natural giant eagle would complete the job.

After healing I flew for another minute. I needed an idea other than just another attempt at misdirection and counterstrike.

A thought struck me with enough plausibility to return me to the peak. The outdoors allowed me to outsize the eagle. Perhaps I allowed unpleasant memories too much power over my reasoning. I could outsize him if I to took care not to be visible more than a mile away. I flew above the trees and looked for the eagle. He flew away from me and I flew close to the mountain and back to Prometheus.

My spatial awareness told me if the eagle changed course to chase me I wouldn't reach Prometheus before he caught me. I turned and hovered. I transformed quickly in hopes I could end the fight with intimidation. I became as large as a typical barn. My tail and wings could have dominated a football field.

The eagle turned, not to flee, instead to gain altitude for a dive. So much for intimidation. I went for a cautious counter. I met the eagle's dive with a tail sweep. He evaded the predominance of my sweep. He fell off course for a moment before returning to soaring. Deep slashes and an opportune bite stung my tail.

Before I could gauge the merit of my new tactic, he swooped in. My spatial awareness couldn't spare me from the surprise. His quickness left me only able to repeat my last maneuver. More slashes and this time the eagle hung on and dug and gnawed. I flew about and whipped to no effect. He hung on and moved from gnawing to ripping.

"The rocks," yelled Prometheus.

The Titan knew the future. The rocks had to have a use. I swooped toward the peak and bashed my tail against it. The Eagle cried out and released my tail.

I remembered I beat the automaton by knocking out the lights. It lacked night vision. A sun in ascension dashed that thought. The Eagle picked himself off the rocks and flew at me again. Again, I swept and hoped the eagle learned not to hang on. He learned. He settled for adding more gashes to the mass of bloody flesh I called a tail. It lacked any major arteries. It only bled profusely instead of fatally.

I looked to Prometheus for an insight. He only watched. I wondered what that could mean. *Had he seen the future and given up on me?*

Again the eagle swooped and again I swept my tail to keep him away from more vulnerable areas. The eagle seemed content to slice at my tail and watch me bleed. I bled faster than my regeneration. Thanks to faintness the mountain threatened to spin around me. Time worked against me.

Another swoop of slicing open flesh to bleed yet faster. My flesh proved no match for his dark metal talons and his quickness gave me few options. He rose up for a more forceful dive. He, no doubt, expected to deal something close to the final blows. He expected.

My mind made as much use of its oxygen as it could. I unwitingly got the eagle used to my sweeps. Why would he expect any other response this time? He dove. I waggled as a fake to reinforce his expectations. When he neared I flipped and met his head with my claws. I tore at his eyes. That time the blood came from him.

He caught my forearms. This time, however, not as well. My surprise threw off his deft aim. My hind legs pushed him off. His flight wobbled. I roared at him; not my sonic attack; just an "over-hear." He turned at me and I dodged. He struck the mountainside and tumbled down.

He came to rest on a precipice and struggled to rise. Before he could, if he could, the ground beneath him shook and a cliffside tumbled and buried him.

"Oh my. You're a bloody mess, dragon."

I returned to human form, almost. I wanted to heal my tail before finding out where its injuries might be in total human form. I couldn't locate Thumper. "Where are you?"

"Down here. Where else would I be? I delivered the coup de grace for you. Saved you a little extra trouble."

"How do you know I'm a bloody mess?"

"You've been bleeding all over the forest down here. Take care of yourself, get that Titan down here and we can go. We need to hurry."

39

Prometheus paused at the pile of rocks. I noticed a tear run down his face. "You were talking to the eagle before I came, weren't you?"

He wiped the tear. "A tragic life for a noble beast."

"You may wish to take on human dimensions, Titan. Where we're going has eight-foot ceilings."

"Your brother is probably eager to see that you're okay."

He shrank to the frame of an average man. "Yes. Take me away from this place."

We kept quiet at the transition meadow. Prometheus stared at me. A second tear welled in his eye just before Thumper took us to Siet's penthouse.

Epimetheus stood when we arrived. "Brother, it's good to see you're well."

They embraced and kissed each other's cheeks. Siet's gaze remained locked on the window. "Congratulations on a successful rescue mission."

"What's wrong, brother?" said Epimetheus.

Prometheus spoke to me. "Like that noble bird, noble dragon, I see tragedy in your future."

"I warned him it was a trap," said Epimetheus.

"Chaining me to that mountain again? Yes, that was a trap, but I'm not speaking of the springing of that trap when I say I see tragedy in the dragon's future."

Keith's voice trembled. "Prometheus, what do you see?"

"I'm not an oracle. I see where things are going but not the details. I told Ares that posting that noble bird to guard me would only get it killed. I wasn't certain as to how. He wouldn't listen and now the poor thing's dead."

Keith pressed the point. "But what of Aiden Ferris?"

Prometheus' face stiffened. "Like the noble bird, he will serve his masters as best he can, and he will die doing it."

Siet turned. "Titan, you see possible futures."

"Yes, destroyer."

"So like Ares with his bird, he could have avoided the tragedy if he had headed your warning."

"Yes.

"So, what warning have you for the Son of Order that he may avoid this tragedy?"

Prometheus shook his head. "He is the Son of Order. He cannot act against his nature and it leads him to this tragedy. I don't see a way to avoid it. I am sorry."

Keith shot to his feet. "Then why tell him?"

He stomped toward his room. Prometheus bowed. "So, you can prepare yourself, noble dragon. I hope you can meet your demise with honor and purpose."

Siet patted Epimetheus. "Your brother must be tired. I should have a spare bed for him."

The two Titans left for the bedrooms and Siet took me to the window. "Don't fret, Son of Order. You and I have both met tragic ends before and we're both still here."

The only person in the universe that can get away with lying to me told me not to worry. Such words from him lacked the reassurance I wanted. I ran my hand along the glass. "At least he says the springing of the trap won't be so tragic."

"Yes, but that's what I'm worried most about at the moment."

"Well then, Enki, bring it on. I don't want to wait too long."

Siet glanced at me. "That's the spirit."

THE SUN PASSED its zenith when Iris and her rainbow wings passed through the window glass like light. She handed me a scroll, this one neatly sealed. "Aiden Ferris, the throne of Olympus summons you. You are to go to Milpitas and wait for Hermes to transport you."

"You weren't followed this time," said Siet.

She spoke with false humility. "Only Hermes or the best of the Children of Galinthius can do that, and Hermes is probably waiting in Milpitas."

I lifted the torch pendant off my chest. "Thumper, I need to go to Milpitas."

"I'm not far, dragon. I'll be with you soon."

I felt him lean into me and we appeared in his favorite American meadow. His tail brushed my arm. *"Enki springing his trap?"*

"Most likely. I'm to meet Hermes in Milpitas so he can take me to the throne of Olympus."

"Most assuredly then. Note that he needs to use Hermes. The Children of Galinthius continue to avoid Enki."

"You know if they took sides, they'd probably end this?"

"That's why it's a good thing we avoid him. Like you, we can't defy edicts from the throne. The best we can do is to just not be available to receive them."

"That must be tough to do."

"Our leaders have decided it's a good time to round up all the criminals we previously considered too minor to waste time on. Thus, we have no free time and none of us are in Olympus."

"And you, Thumper?"

"What does it look like I'm doing? I'm following old leads. You know, like why exactly Apollo tried to capture the Gray Wolf?"

"Yeah. I know the game."

"Play it as much as you're allowed, friend."

Thumper took me to a bus station in San Jose. *"I can't have Hermes seeing me or I may be ordered to do something we don't want me to do."*

"Understood."

The idea that Hermes would be kept waiting by a couple of city bus exchanges amused me. Something had to. I needed something to distract me from the plate of gloom before me. The city passed my bus window like an old friend saying goodbye.

At the next bus stop, I made a point of sniffing the smog for old time's sake. Seagulls flew overhead and bombed the shelter. I risked a little to walk around the edges and allow my aura to clean things up. I even brushed off an unfortunate woman's sweater. I thought, why not. If Prometheus is right, I could afford one more incident of the supernatural to perform some good.

A raven followed the seagulls; the raven. At first, a blue aura became a web of arcs and that awful hum. My skin crawled. I began to wonder if I'd make my meeting with Hermes after all.

The arcs reached out in fingers of chaos to buildings on both sides of the street. Some panes of glass blew out and others in. I could make out no pattern to it. My fellow would-be bus-riders dropped to the ground.

"Put your heads under the benches," a man yelled.

He followed his own example. If only we dealt with an earthquake his idea would be more useful. I knew the best way to maximize their safety was for me to get away from them. I ran.

A man in running sweats appeared in front of me. "There you are, Aiden Ferris. I was told to look for you near any chaos storm that happened to brew."

I figured it had to be Ares. "How did the Son of Order get into using chaos magic?"

"What?"

"Ah but we don't have time for questions, do we? We have an appointment to make."

He grabbed me under the arm, and we left San Jose in an instant.

40

The throne of Olympus surprised me, I should say, in that it didn't. A purple cushion rested on the white stone in the shape of a grand chair. Marble pillars flanked it with no purpose except to thrust into the sky. Enki paced before it and brushed his woven beard.

Hermes, now in a toga, waived a gold stick at him. "Lord Enki, I have brought Aiden Ferris to you."

Enki's gaze moved from the ground to me and then to Hermes. "Good. Thank you, Hermes."

He paused. "Is there something else, Hermes?"

"I was waiting at Aiden Ferris's house when I noticed a chaos storm a few miles away. On a hunch, I went there and found him there."

"In the storm?"

Hermes squared his shoulders. "Yes. The pattern we were told about holds. You know what that means?"

Enki tapped his beard. "No, no. I don't want to consider nonsense. The Son of Order cannot command chaos magic."

I sensed fear in his last sentence. He didn't so much know I couldn't as he dreaded the thought I could. Hermes squeezed his gold stick. "The pattern is completely unbroken, Lord Enki. You weren't appointed Zeus' proxy to ignore reality. Every one of these storms has happened in the presence of Aiden Ferris."

"Did you see him cause the storm?"

"No, but that doesn't—"

Enki raised his voice. "Enough."

He turned to me. "Aiden Ferris, have you stopped being a dragon of order?"

"No," I answered.

Enki studied the ground. "A contradiction of evidence."

"You can't ignore it," said Hermes.

"Very well, Hermes, you are right. Aiden Ferris, you are to stay in Athena's dwelling while I consider this evidence. You are commanded to stay there by the authority of the throne that Zeus has given me. Do you understand?"

"Yes, "I said.

Hermes took me to Athena's dwelling and left me there with the child under Athena's care, Melia. She brought me a blanket and a pillow. "I remembered, sir, from your last visit, that you prefer the hard floor."

I nodded my thanks and set the bedding aside. "You may wish to know that Prometheus is okay. I freed him from the mountain."

"Did you hurt Ares Eagle?"

"I'm afraid I had to. Prometheus was sad about it."

"Were you?"

"I never met the eagle before I had to fight him. I was happy not to have bled to death."

She left and came back with food. Her eyes watered. "Birds are pretty."

"They are pretty."

She walked to a bench. "Is it okay if I sit here for a while? With Athena and Prometheus gone, I get lonely."

"Of course, it is. This is your home."

"Thank you, sir."

"I wish I could get someone here to take care of you until either of them returns, but my near future is very uncertain. They think I may have turned into some kind of chaos monster."

"That's nonsense, what they think."

"Nonsense or not, they think it and because of that and some other things, I can't even help myself. I'm so sorry Melia."

"Well, sir, don't worry about me. I've taken care of myself these last few days."

I had to look away from her. She just lied for some reason.

"You've had no help from anyone?"

"No one, sir."

She lied again. I wondered why she'd lie about something like that.

"Melia, do you know what I am?"

"Athena told me that you're a dragon."

"Yes, and I am one of those kinds of dragons that can tell if someone's lying."

Her skin turned pale. Her movements slowed.

"Who has been here to help you since Prometheus left?"

"If I tell you, you have to promise not to tell anyone in Olympus."

"I don't make promises easily. Breaking them can kill me."

"Alright, then it would be alright for you to tell Apollo."

With the mention of his name, I changed from unwilling to commit my dragon nature over a little girl's secret to considering it a worthy gamble.

"Why is it alright to tell Apollo?"

"Because he already knows."

"Then in that case, if it's important to Apollo, it's probably important to me too. Very well, Melia. I promise not to tell anyone in Olympus except Apollo."

"He loves her very much. You must keep the secret."

"Alright. I will. That's no small thing for me to say about a promise. I make it, Melia and I will keep it."

She walked over and whispered in my ear. "Ylera."

"Apollo's ..."

She shushed me.

"But how can she be away from Earth?"

"You must not tell, dragon sir. Apollo and her would get into very bad trouble, like my mom and dad."

The pieces of a puzzle necessary to make a picture of Apollo and his wood nymph lover together in Olympus fell together in my head. More important than how is what it means. Remnants depend on Earth magic for their long life and other abilities. That means she either became mortal to live a few decades with him before dying or he found a new way to make her immortal, like a golden apple. The throne of Olympus rarely allows their use and strictly forbids their use on remnants.

"And to think he gave me a lecture on preserving order," I said.

"He loves her."

"Olympians and their weakness for such things."

"I don't understand, sir."

"I'm sorry. I meant no offense."

"So, you'll keep your promise?"

"Yes. I must and besides, I see no reason not to."

She returned to her bench. Lines formed on her forehead.

"Thinking about something?" I asked.

Her eyes fixed on me. "If you see her bird, try not to hurt it."

"As long as it doesn't attack me or someone I care about, I won't."

"Good."

"You must find it pretty. What does it look like?"

"It's very pretty. It's black and has blue squiggly lights around it."

"A raven?"

"Yes."

This all confirmed my expectations. I still wondered what Apollo meant to do with it. "You've seen it once?"

"I've seen it a lot. Just before you came here, I did. I think you'd like it."

I knew it worked into Athena's plans, just not how.

41

The next morning I woke to Hermes standing over me. "Enki calls you before the throne, dragon."

I began to fold my blanket. Melia stopped me. "I'll do that, sir. Grab some cheese and bread."

I stepped toward the table and Hermes grabbed me. I didn't reach the table before he moved us before the throne and Enki.

"You think I answer questions better on an empty stomach?"

Enki, still not seated, leaned on the throne. "You, Son of Order, answer questions from the throne of Olympus equally as well, hungry, sated, and all points in between. Isn't that true?"

His eyes drilled into me.

"Yes."

"Very well, then, now that we've gotten your first attempt at evasion out of the way, let's get to the more important questions. Do you know what the source of the chaos storms is?"

Thanks to philosophy, I could honestly answer, "no." Who really knows anything for sure?

Enki looked askance. "You say, 'no,' do you? I see your second attempt at evasion. I will reword my question. Do you know anything that may be a clue as to the source of these chaos storms?"

"I know the storms are brought by something that looks like a raven."

"A raven, you say?"

"Yes."

"A giant one?"

"No, a normal-sized one."

"Is there something else that brings these storms?"

"Not that I've seen."

He paced twice and stopped in front of the throne. "So, every time you've seen these storms, this raven has brought them?"

"Yes."

He smirked. "You like it when I let you answer with a simple yes or no. You like it especially when the answers lead me away from where you don't want me to go."

With no question asked, I kept silent. He wagged his head. "Yet, what you've told me is that this raven has brought these chaos storms every time, and when I asked you if you knew the source, you told me you didn't know."

"Yes."

"How is this not a lie, Son of Order?"

How dare he suggest I could lie.

I took a deep breath. "Would you credit a raven with causing chaos storms, Enki? Like Ares' eagle, someone directs this bird."

"I find it strange, Son of Order, that you could not know the source of the storms, though probably the raven, yet now you seem somewhat confident that this raven operates on someone else's behalf. You actually know this?"

"Yes."

Enki began to pace again and thought aloud. "I could ask you why and you could give me any reasonable answer that just happens to not be the one you want me to hear, thus moving me away from where you don't want me to go. And, oh do I ever want to go there. Let me think about how to word this."

If not for my oath of allegiance to the throne of Olympus, I would have interrupted his train of thought. Like a chess-master against a novice, he moved me closer and closer to a place where I couldn't go, that is and live.

Enki stopped. "Son of Order, by the authority granted me by Zeus, I command you to list for me everyone who you suspect may command this raven."

"Everyone?"

I hoped he'd not want a long list, though I had a short one; too short to avoid breaking my promise to Melia.

"Yes, Son of Order, everyone."

Checkmate. I kept silent for as long as Enki allowed. He enjoyed the first few seconds. Then his tone turned stern. "Answer my question, dragon."

He had me caught between two promises; one to Zeus and one to Melia. If I broke either, my nature would destroy me. He cornered me and I tried the only path that may not involve me dying.

"Lord Enki, my nature which I cannot deny, tears at me in two directions at once. I cannot answer your question without violating it, but if I can ask for your mercy, I suspect Apollo could answer your question better than I can."

I thought of myself a coward at that moment. A grin crossed Enki's face. It told my dragon senses that he took pleasure in hearing Apollo's name. "Aha, now we're getting somewhere, dragon."

He pointed. "Hermes, bring Apollo before the throne. Tell him it needs answers to questions he's best able to answer."

Hermes disappeared. I asked Enki a question. "It? You refer to the throne as if it has its own will. The throne is Zeus's authority."

He snickered. "You think you can just chit chat with me now, dragon?

"I meant no offense."

"While we wait for Apollo, let me make some things clear. When I slew Tiamat, I hunted down all of her spawn I could find. That I missed some, is the greatest regret of my life."

"A dragon of order is not Tiamat. She would have hated me. You and I, on the other hand, are of similar natures."

He shouted, "you're an abomination. Dragons have no more business protecting civilization than foxes do chicken coops. It doesn't matter what sorcery tries to make it seem as though you're not. You are still what every dragon is, you are a dragon."

"I am my father's son."

He took a long breath. "You're the one before the throne of Olympus, and I want you to know, I would happily make you answer that question or do anything else to cause your death and I fully intend to. The only reason I'm keeping you alive for now is that you can serve me as a lie-detector."

"You want me to keep Apollo from lying to you?"

"Yes, and perhaps a few others, but I want you to remember this. I'm holding your leash as long as it's useful to me. After that, I will kill you."

His words reminded me of what Prometheus told me. Like Ares' eagle, I will serve my masters as best I can, and I will die doing it. Perhaps, I hoped, that meant I'd die fighting—something; a better death than self-destruction.

42

Hermes delivered Apollo next to a flanking pillar. "Lord Enki, I have brought the son of Zeus, Apollo, as you requested.

Enki put a hand on my chest and nudged me. "By Zeus' authority, I command you to listen."

Apollo spoke with the volume of an orator. "What help does the throne of Olympus need of me, Lord Enki."

"It has come to be my understanding that a raven has brought all of the recent chaos storms to Earth, and that you would be able to tell me who this raven belongs to."

"I see you have the Son of Order with you."

"Yes, now back to the throne's question?"

Apollo stared at me. "I don't know."

He spoke the truth. Could he not know what Ylera's up to? My gut didn't twist. Enki seemed to share my confusion. "Does he tell the truth, Son of Order?"

I reviewed Enki's question to Apollo and his answer. He didn't know who the raven belongs to. I saw the hole he stood in.

"The raven may belong to no one, Lord Enki, but still be at someone's direction," I said.

Enki laughed. "Of course, dragon, you have experience at this game. Very good observation. Apollo, do you know at whose direction the raven had brought these storms to Earth?"

Apollo glared at me. "I don't know of any raven that has brought chaos storms to Earth."

Again, he told the truth. He had a slight drop in sincerity around the word 'raven.' Not enough for a lie, though. Why not a simple 'no'? He needed the word 'raven' in his answer for it to be true. The rod of transformation made his answere possible.

"Well, Son of Order? What of this answer? Do I need to return the questioning to you?"

I bowed my head. "Apollo, I must ask you, do you know at whose direction, whatever brought the recent chaos storms to Earth, did so?"

I saw fear in Apollo at that moment. His eyes darted from me to Enki and after a pause, to Hermes. His shoulders raised. "I do. I commanded the creature to bring the storms."

He told a half-truth and I knew why; Ylera.

"Does he tell the truth now, Son of Order?"

I considered my answer. If I helped Enki draw out Ylera's involvement from Apollo, would I have broken my promise to Melia?

"Well, Son of Order?" Enki said.

Apollo's face tightened as did my insides.

Enki shoved me. "Dragon, serve me and tell me if he told the truth."

"Don't answer him," said Apollo.

Enki laughed. "No need, dragon. Apollo has just now admitted to the lie himself. So it wasn't Apollo, but someone else who commands the creature."

"I do now, though," said Apollo.

The static fuzz, the aching hum, the blue arcs emanated from a black dot in the Olympian sky. Enki grabbed his ears. "How can Apollo, a god of civilization, command a chaos monster?"

Apollo yelled, "how can a non-Olympian rule Olympus?"

"Zeus made me his proxy. I have the authority of the throne."

"You don't understand Olympus, Enki."

Apollo pointed and a blue bolt struck the throne. Shards flew out and pillars fell in. The throne reduced to a mix of rubble and glowing black regions of the air. A gauntlet encompassed Enki's forearm; Imhullu. He pointed it at the raven. The roar of wind drowned out the hum. The raven darted and vanished.

Enki scowled. "You dare attack the throne of Olympus, Apollo?"

"The throne of Olympus that you had has been destroyed. All that remains of its authority now, in Zeus' absence, resides in Zeus' chosen, and with Athena away, that leaves only me."

Enki raised Imhulu. "Zeus appointed me his proxy. You have gone mad, Apollo."

Apollo turned to me. "I understand you are what you are, Son of Order. You are now free to go."

Enki pointed Imhullu at Apollo. "I will destroy you and the dragon in turn."

I leaped at Apollo and moved him behind a pillar just as wind carved a trench in the ground where he had been. I grasped my torch pendant. "Thumper, get me and Apollo out of here."

"Let me stay and die," said Apollo.

"And leave her vulnerable?"

"You know, don't you?"

"Melia told me. We'll fetch her too."

Apollo nodded. Another gust from Imhulu broke a pillar from its base. It struck us and threw us backward. Thumper appeared standing on my chest. We fell on our backs atop a plateau, well away from the destruction. Apollo grabbed Thumper's shoulder. "You need to get Ylera from my dwelling before Enki finds her."

"And Melia from Athena's, while you're at it."

"Thanking me will come later, I assume."

He vanished.

I addressed Apollo. "I'm not sure your reasoning about Enki's authority holds water, "

Apollo got to his feet. "Well, do you feel compelled not to go back?"

"No."

"Blasted Athena! She knew my feeble efforts to frame you would end up leading to this."

"What exactly?"

"I wanted to stop you and instead I've put the authority of Olympus into dispute, leaving you free from it."

"When do you finally just accept that she knows best?"

"When do you?"

He had a point. That still left a few things to make clear. "Okay, now, Apollo, why did you have that thing follow me around causing chaos storms?"

"I hoped to convince Enki that the forces of chaos were too strong to risk resetting human civilization."

"Why have it follow me?"

"Because you married a chaos witch and we all know it gave you new power. You removed a transformation curse from your old teacher, Harold the Dread."

"But, why would I also have the power to cause chaos storms?"

"The power you gained from your marriage is chaos magic. Many in Olympus worried greatly because of your marriage. I hoped the storms would be all they needed to be terrified."

"Well, it didn't work."

"Now that they know I was behind them, yes."

"No, even before that, I suspect."

"Why?"

"Enki has been studying chaos magic for his own uses. He dug through Dakk's library and obtained the soul-stone of Koseina."

"What would Enki want with chaos magic and a trapped evil kitsune?"

"What did you want with whatever that raven is?"

"You mean we haven't even begun to see what he has planned."

"We're still reacting and not responding. Maybe with you, we can make that change."

"A few weeks ago, dragon, I couldn't imagine coming to your side, but in this messed-up universe, you're clearly the lesser of evils."

"You think I am? You haven't seen anything yet. Wait until you meet who your sister left in charge of the resistance."

43

Apollo and I observed the lowlands.

"Do you know this place, dragon?"

"I think it's about an hour's drive north of Sacramento. If I were Thumper, I'd try mixing up his transition spots a bit more. I mean I could probably find this place, camp out and wait for him if I didn't have an easier way to contact him."

"So, you're saying he's too predictable like we are to my sister."

"Yes, but who isn't predictable to her?"

"She used that to bring us here."

"Yeah. She brought us here with one simple move. She arranged for Prometheus to take care of Melia in her absence, knowing he'd be taken away. I wondered about that, but now I know why."

"Yes, dragon, she knew something very few do; that my Ylera has a very soft spot for children. It was a certainty that she would visit the child."

"And she knew of Melia's great fondness for birds. Combine that with her anticipating your scheme, and everything set up for this moment."

"How could she know I'd destroy the throne?"

I laughed. "Apollo, you're her brother. She gets extra bonuses predicting you. She knew you'd do enough to create a crisis of authority, thus freeing me."

I touched the soul-stone hanging next to the torch pendant. "Are you ready to meet with Apollo?"

Apollo's eyebrow cocked. "What?"

My thoughts spoke for Siet. *"Not yet."*

"Sorry, Apollo. I'm being telepathed to. "Where should we go?"

"Send Thumper."

"I assume that question wasn't for me?" asked Apollo.

"Correct. When Thumper returns with Ylera and Melia, we are to send Thumper ahead for some reason."

"Who is this you're telepathing with? Who are we arranging a meeting with?"

"I think it's best he introduces himself."

"Who in the universe could this be that you feel it necessary to preserve the mystery until I meet him?"

"I think you'll understand when you do. Remember two things. Your sister, Athena, in all of her wisdom and intellect, believes in this individual to do what's best."

"Yes, yes, she always believes she's doing what's best, but you know I don't always trust her. What's the second thing you want me to remember?"

"She knew I'd save you. She wants you alive. She loves you."

"That's a second and third, Son of Order. She loves her brother so much that she wants me to owe you a favor."

Thumper returned with Ylera and Melia in one arrival. *"And now everyone can thank me."*

Ylera grabbed Apollo's side. "Is it true? Have you claimed the throne?"

He brushed her hair. "You know I'm no fool. I did the only thing I could to protect you."

I placed my hand on Thumper's head. "Thank you, son of Rumbler. You do your father's legacy justice."

The big cat closed his eyes. *"Nice to be appreciated now and then."*

"Thumper, you need to go ahead without us at first."

"Why?"

I pointed at the soul-stone. "He wants to speak with you before bringing Apollo, I think."

"Understandable. I for one am not sure if we should be ready to trust him."

He vanished. The irony didn't miss me. Thumper and I weren't ready to trust Apollo and yet followed the orders of Siet, a master of deception. I fought off a chill from the thought.

Melia's little voice broke the moment. "Is this our new home?"

"No, not here."

"Then where will I stay. The pretty kitty told me I couldn't stay where I was."

Ylera placed her hands on her shoulders. "You'll come and stay with me."

"In Apollo's dwelling?"

I knelt down to her level. "We're going to find out, but it will be with Ylera until Athena comes back."

Thumper re-appeared and sent his voice into everyone's heads. *"Prepare to leave. Everyone touch my back."*

We did as he asked. Melia did more than just touch. She couldn't resist petting. I knew Thumper disliked that. I had to give him credit for patience. He only said, *"keep your little hand on me, Melia."*

A bright sun assaulted our eyes from near the horizon. Sand scratched our faces. We weren't in New York City. Siet called to us. "Come inside the temple. We can't talk very well out there."

"Temple?" said Apollo.

We moved toward his voice. Ylera helped Melia with confusion and we all left the sandstorm outside. The storm's roar transformed from menacing to soothing. Siet wore only a serape and sandals. I thought only an Egyptian god could use their smooth skin to affect awe.

Apollo lacked the same appreciation. "Siet, the destroyer of worlds, a chaos god, this was my sister's choice? Surely not."

Siet answered him. "Apollo, the god of arts, a god of civilization, my friend Athena's beloved brother, she knew you'd be on her side if just given enough time."

"I was told you and Hecate killed each other and I mourned her death. What evil sorcery is this that you're alive?"

"Hecate brought me close enough to death to be seen as such. Then one of your sister's allies killed Hecate. Your sister saw it wise to use a golden apple to save me. She has faith in my redemption, and I have neither reason nor intention to disappoint that faith."

"You say my sister helped kill Hecate and saved you? How am I to believe that?"

Apollo turned to me. "Son of Order, do you believe what he says to be true?"

"Someone besides him told me Siet's personal character has been redeemed."

"Someone besides him told you? Why do you answer me that way?"

"I can only tell you that person believes what she told me and that Athena acts as if she trusts Siet. As for Siet's own words, he is the only person in the universe my sense of truth doesn't work on."

Thumper's tail tapped me. *"Dragon, can't you at least embellish a little."*

Apollo put his arm around Ylera. "Siet, you are a master of deception like no one else I know of in the universe. You simply don't deserve my trust."

Siet raised a hand. "Fair enough, but perhaps we can still find ways to cooperate by working toward the same goals, just without getting in each other's way?"

Apollo turned his back. "Child of Galinthius, take Ylera, myself, and the child to Astraeus' portal. We will find our way to a refuge from there."

"Can we work with you at all, Apollo?" I asked.

"Not as long as you work with that monster, Siet. Child of Galinthius, take us now."

Thumper took them away. Siet stared at me. "What have we gained?"

My honest nature prevented a hopeful answer.

44

The desert wind sang through the stone walls. Siet gave up on an answer to his last question and asked another. "What do you think of this place, Son of Order?"

"I hope the Egyptian government doesn't catch us amid their antiquities. Last I checked, they don't approve of interlopers."

"How can I be an interloper in a temple dedicated to me? Besides, I've kept this place hidden for the last several centuries."

"Hidden? Even from your wife?"

"I'm debating if I should let her discover it. Do you think it would be doing her too much of a favor? I mean the archaeological community would be green with envy."

"Good point. I'd advise you to wait for Athena to return so you can get her input."

Thumper appeared. *"I'm back."*

The sun cast a shadow through the temple. Siet shaded his eyes. "Time to return to New York."

We needed no transition for air pressure and soon cool air and electric lights surrounded us. Before the New York City skyline, Dogan's skinny paleness stretched across a couch.

He kept reading a science journal rather than look up. Keith closed his laptop. "Boss, so good to see you've come back."

I pointed at Dogan, a wizard reading a science journal.

"He made me fetch him those," said Keith.

I noticed stacks lining the floor beside him. "What does he want with science journals?"

"He says science and magic may as well be the same thing. I didn't talk to him much about it." Keith whispered, "I didn't want to."

"Where are the brothers?"

"Epimetheus is in his room. He's used to being alone and seems to like it that way."

"And Prometheus?"

"You mean Killjoy? He's out exploring the city again."

I looked at Siet. "Is it okay for him to wander?"

"He's Prometheus. He knows when he can go out and back without causing any unwanted consequences, so I let him."

"Is that how you got those journals, Keith?"

"Yes, but that's the only time I went out. I'd rather avoid that guy. He's the voice of doom."

Siet walked into the kitchen. "The wanderer seems very picky about who he associates with; Epimetheus and me. At least he knows an interesting person when he meets one."

"Keith, what have you been doing to pass the time?"

"Reviewing John's inventory of your hoard. You know he's got your ancestor's corpse listed in it?"

"Yeah. That's because his bones turned into a gold alloy for some reason."

Siet carried out a plate of cold cuts. "You must be hungry, dragon."

I nodded my thanks and dug in. The moon moved through clouds. I couldn't speak with Vedi that night. I found my bed and tried to rest despite the time-lag. Just five hours from waking in Olympus and I had six hours till sunrise in New York City.

~

SLEEP surprised me just before my thoughts woke me. *"Dragon, Harold."*

I lifted my hand from the soul-stone. "What? Harold?"

Sunlight played between skyscrapers. I realized I just spoke to someone who couldn't hear me, and I threw myself to my feet. My feet remembered the idea of walking by the end of the hall. Siet stood beside the portal. "Good, dragon, you're up."

Prometheus moaned from his room.

"Who's all up?" I asked.

"You, I, and that."

Siet pointed at Dogan who still read science journals.

"Just the three of us?"

"I assume Epimetheus and Keith are sleeping still. Keith stayed up late. Prometheus is recovering from a night of drinking."

"He doesn't see liver disease in his future?"

Siet raised his eyes at my stupid question. Titans are immune to such things.

"Dragon, the wizard Harold told me to expect him any minute now."

As if to emphasize his point, a hand reached out of the portal and waved before pulling back. Out of curiosity, I looked at Dogan. He had put down his journal and studied the ceiling instead.

After a long minute, Harold stepped through. Dogan sat. Harold shook a sleeve of the thick robe he wore in Dogan's direction. "What is he doing here?"

"Long story, Harold, but the short of it is that he hired out to Enki to help spread Epimetheus around the world. I talked him out of it and took him home with us since he was on my list of Enki's potential targets."

"Seriously, Aiden? If you wanted to make my life as miserable as possible, you couldn't have done much better than to bring him here."

Dogan stood. "Harold, my old master, it's like old times. You and I and Aiden; like when we fought goblins together."

Harold scowled. "You were on the goblins' side, Dogan."

"I was and I wasn't. I put Aiden's insides back together, and when it was all said and done, I betrayed the one I was working for to help you."

"Dogan, ever since Dakk's death you've made it a habit to switch sides, all while chasing the next mentor-to-be. Can't you see how that makes people not want your help, let alone to mentor you?"

Dogan opened his mouth and I raised a hand. "Dogan, save it for later. We've been waiting days for Harold to get back from Dakk's library to report on what he found there."

Dogan still spoke. "He and I have been there many many times. What can be so important?"

Harold closed on him. "Sit down and shut up, you long-haired ghast of a man. If you must know, what's important is what isn't there anymore."

Dogan fell into the couch and ogled like a brat.

Siet gestured Harold to a chair. "Tell us, wizard."

Harold negotiated the chair like a man much older in body. "All of Dakk's notes on his transformation are gone."

"But, I was certain Enki couldn't get to them," said Dogan.

Harold shook a finger. "Well, of course, that's what you do, Dogan, isn't it? You help all sides, no matter the potential consequences."

"I'm helping you now, Harold."

"Too little too late, I'm afraid, not to mention you're probably still helping him unwittingly, but that's not the worst of my findings, anyway."

"Not the worst? What could be worse than Dakk's dragon form that took three gold dragons, my father, and the wizard Toth to defeat?"

Harold gripped the chair's arms. "Aiden, my boy, you and Siet should probably sit down too. You really should be sitting down for this."

45

An easily frightened man doesn't get 'the dread' attached to his name. He doesn't fight giant automatons while trapped in a housecat body. He doesn't risk me killing him just to restore our friendship. The fear I sensed in him as he asked me to sit demanded my attention.

"As you know, Dakk's transformation drove him mad. That madness gave him a vulnerability your father and his allies were able to use against him. Enki knows this too."

"And?"

"Enki doesn't wish to adopt Dakk's transformation. He wishes to adapt it."

"You mean to improve it?"

"That could be true except for one thing," said Siet.

"And that would be?" I asked.

"Enki is, to use Harold's language, a great adopter but has no significant talents as an adapter. He's all about learning, but his intellect stops there. Always the top student but never the discoverer. He's derivative."

Harold fingered his gray beard. "Far be it for me to contradict a god, but allow me to share more of my findings. Based on recent notes taken by spell casters Enki took with him to Dakk's library, Enki took particular interest in Dakk's research on magic-driven automatons."

Siet's finger quivered at Harold. "Dakk did research on automatons? That's not something I've heard before."

"Yes, he did. He abandoned it because he couldn't—"

Siet finished for him. "Get chaos magic to work with automatons, correct?"

Harold batted his eyes. "To my point, the chaos magic destroyed the automatons it was supposed to animate."

"As I said."

"Not exactly, sir."

Siet pointed his chin. "Semantics, Harold?"

"No, significantly more than semantics, Siet."

I raised a hand. "How so, Harold?"

"The chaos magic would, for a time after the automaton fell apart, continue the task the automaton had been given. Then the magic would dissipate because its container had been destroyed."

Siet held out his hands. "Organized chaos bombs. Perverse, but hardly more frightening than a dragon the size of a couple of mountains."

Dogan grumbled and shook his hand at Siet. "You may be a god, the destroyer of worlds and all, but you've got no right to talk down to Harold, my former master like that."

Harold gave Dogan a knock. "Sit down and shut up. I'll not have you die in the mistaken notion that you were defending me."

I placed my hand between them. "This is not a time for losing tempers."

Harold moved back. "I found scraps of notes they failed to completely burn. There wasn't enough there to tell exactly what they did, but this non-adapter of a god had his casters find a way to triple the time the disembodied chaos magic would continue working on its task."

"So, wizard, you're saying Enki may, if given enough time, be able to adapt Dakk's work to his ends?"

Dogan peered from the slouch Harold had knocked him into. “More than may.”

Harold huffed. “Dogan, of all people, I certainly don’t need your help.”

“I’m not helping, Harold. I’m saying.”

“What, Dogan, have you known something all this time and just not bothered to tell us?”

Dogan held up a science journal and smiled. “I’ve been doing my own research, master Harold. I only fully arrived at this insight just yesterday. Enki’s spell-casters are not all that talented as potential wizards go, but they were all trained in Toth’s court in this sub-discipline of magic called science. Following its methods, they could easily adapt Dakk’s work to whatever ends Enki wishes.”

I shivered. “I wish he just lied to us but he hasn’t. He speaks what he believes to be true, and with confidence.”

Harold picked up a journal from the pile and handed it to Siet. “Have you ever given much time to this subject? I have.”

Siet perused it. “I haven’t. Why would I?”

“I suppose the destroyer of worlds would have little use for the machinations of science which only approach your power, but applied to the work of a chaos wizard like Dakk and under the directions of the god of learning, I believe even you’d be wise to beware the result.”

“Wizards with science?”

“Toth, in his last days, had many in his court studying things like science and medicine.”

Siet rubbed his head. “Toth, I thought his death meant I was done being tormented by him. But now I see I should never underestimate the malevolent reach of one who seeks power to advance their good intentions.”

Keith entered the room in time to hear what Siet said and seemed to share my confusion. “What?”

Instead of answering, Siet walked to the window. “We can no longer afford to wait for Enki’s next move.”

“What, what happened while I was sleeping in?”

"Wanderer, I hope you're well-rested."

"I am, Siet. Should I load up a backpack?"

I squeezed Keith's shoulder. "If I understand our circumstances and the intent of Siet's words, we are about to launch some sort of attack."

Keith pointed at his back. "Backpack?"

"Wait for our plan. Then we'll know."

"Right, boss."

"I recommend we launch some sort of a probing attack, "I said.

Siet nodded. "Yes, one powerful enough to potentially draw out some of what Enki has in store for us."

Harold took on his teacher voice. "It needs to be subtle enough that we can pull out of it with minimal losses."

Another voice chortled from behind. "Am I actually forgotten. Oh, how wonderful a day that would be."

Epimetheus took a seat at the table. I waved fingers his way. "If your deductions are ready for us, Titan, we would be foolish not to hear them as we plan our attack."

He cocked his head. "They are, Son of Order. Perhaps you should call in your Child of Galinthius ally before I share them?"

Siet knocked on the window. "Do call the Child of Galinthius, dragon, but Titan, hold your words for the time being."

"What? Why?" I asked.

"I fear Enki may still have the initiative."

"Of course, he does, until we take it from him."

Siet knocked again on the window. Wings rose up from behind a row of skyscrapers; black dragon wings. It came right at us.

46

I gave my torch amulet a pull. “Thumper, I need you to get me out of this building in the next few seconds.”

Siet swung a hand my way. “I can cloud enough minds to cover for you, dragon.”

Keith touched my arm. “Whoa Boss, we’re about to have a real kaiju battle in New York City?”

“As nice as it is to know I can use my full size around here, Siet, I really don’t believe this dragon is Enki’s doing.”

Thumper appeared at my side. Keith’s grasp on my arm tightened. “Clouded minds or not, the collateral damage is going to be huge.”

Siet peered. “Why do you say this isn’t Enki’s doing, dragon?”

“Because Enki hates dragons. Thumper, take Keith and me to the closest possible building top to that dragon.”

“Me too, boss? You plan to use me as a decoy?”

“No. As what you are, my assistant. Be sure you’ve got your phone.”

“Dragon?”

“Thanks to Harold’s teaching, I know my dragons and that’s a chaos dragon.”

“I knew that too.”

"And, your point, dragon?" prompted Siet.

"Its chaos attack can't harm me."

Harold's teacher voice erupted behind me. "True, but its teeth and claws can, my boy."

"Thumper, take us, now."

The last words heard in the penthouse before we teleported came from Keith. "I'm ready."

I appreciated his spirit if not his weak sincerity. I asked a lot of him in that moment. Thumper brought us within a block. *"This is as close as that thing's chaos aura will let me teleport. I'll stay as close to you as I can."*

I brought out my wings and flapped them. "Dragon, over here."

"Taunting?" asked Keith.

"I hope not. I want the people on the top floors of this building to make it home tonight."

At half a block's distance, the black dragon filled the sky. Kieth's voice quivered. "Oh shit."

The black made details impossible to see, except for the eyes. They almost seemed to hover in dark air like floating blue boulders of fire. I had to remind myself that what seemed like black air was armored flesh. I tried to recall if Harold told me what sort of sight a blue glow indicated.

The dragon's eyes closed in to see us. I gave my wings one more wide flap. "Let's talk this out."

The sky emptied of the blackness. Instead, a winged human form hovered. Her black hair clung and twisted as air rushed into the void her transformation left. "If I only talk to you, you won't harm me?"

"You knew something the rest of us didn't, boss?"

I nudged Keith back and answered her. "If we can avoid fighting and causing harm to this place, yes. Let's talk."

She vanished and reappeared in my face. "Is this too close for you?"

I stepped back. She winked. "Very well, as you wish." Her eyes explored me. "It wasn't too close for me, if you know what I mean."

Kieth stuttered. "Uh, uh, he's married."

She sneered. "To you?"

"No, not to me, of course."

She laughed. "Don't worry. As interesting as the offspring of chaos and order dragons might be, it's not possible. Now you on the other hand—I don't know. You are cute but I'm not sure you're —"

I stopped her. "We should talk."

"Oh yes. Forgive me. The auras here are rich in contrast and questions, but I must not forget why I came."

"Yes."

"I was told by Apollo that I owe you for my freedom from his transformation curse."

"Well, of course. You were the raven. It all makes sense. He controlled you through the use of that transformation wand."

"Yes. I was told I could only free myself by harassing you. He hoped to convince his fellow Olympians that you are both order and chaos."

"You didn't but it stopped mattering."

"Yes, what you did before the throne played Apollo's plan out and he no longer needed my services. Now, I'm free because of you. I came to thank you."

Two questions bothered me.

"How did you know where to find me?"

"I am especially sensitive to the aura of chaos magic and I was told you're with Siet. For me, his location is like a shining beacon."

"Do you know if you were followed?"

"I teleport. It's hard to follow that."

Her sincerity caused the second question. "Besides thanking me, what else did you come to me for?"

She dropped to a knee. "Dragon of order, I know we are natural enemies, but our common enemy, Enki wants us both dead. I beg your help in escaping Earth before he finds me."

Kieth tapped me. "After all she did?"

She bowed her head. "I helped you escape your commitment to the throne of Olympus."

I understood the meaning of her exposing her neck to me. "I owe you some help at least. Keith, call Alexandra and explain the situation to her."

She kept her head down. "Thank you. I owe you more than you do me."

"Transformation curses are truly horrible things, worse than legal commitments. Yes, I agree that you may owe me more. Why not join Siet and me in our fight against the Cabal?"

She got off her knee. "I don't understand how you and Siet can work together, or for that matter that you and that one can. Chaos is strong with both of them, and you --- I'm confused. Somehow there is subtle chaos in your aura. That's not possible."

That her sincerity maxed out in her last sentence gave me a chill. She not only believed what she said; she had strong reasons to.

"I married a chaos witch."

Her eyebrows jumped. "A powerful one. A most powerful one. Why haven't I seen her aura around? It would be hard for me to miss it."

Keith leaned in. "Boss, she says we can't hide a chaos dragon. She suggests Siet let her use his portal to leave."

"Dragon of order, it's almost assuredly best I find distance from you and your efforts, but someday I would love to meet your wife."

"Yes, a distance would be best and it's probably best for both of us that we not know each other's names. In fact the less we know about each other the more help we can be to each other. You can consider your debt to me paid if you never tell anyone what you've discovered about my wife today."

"Really? It's a secret of great import? Very well, I promise you, but will Siet help me leave?"

Kieth nodded. I extended my hand to her. "Yes."

She grasped it and shook it. "Umbra. My name's Umbra."

"But ..."

She smirked. "Just for good measure."

47

Storm clouds gathered. They grumbled as if miffed at Siet for summoning them. Keith, Thumper, and I waited atop the skyscraper for Umbra and Siet to finish their meeting.

"We're like lightning rods up here," said Keith.

"Only if Siet means us harm."

"How long do they need to talk?"

"Maybe Umbra's sharing what she knows with Epimetheus."

"He'll hate that."

"Yes, Keith, he will, but he's committed himself to help us figure out what Enki's up to. So, there's no good reason not to get a little more information."

"I'm just happy she's leaving Earth voluntarily. What was Apollo thinking bringing a chaos dragon here?"

"Come back," came my thoughts at Siet's behest.

"She must have left now. Siet wants us back."

Thumper vanished for a second and reappeared. *"Confirmed. Come with me."*

We touched his fur. Dry air and indoor light engulfed us. Epimetheus straddled a footrest and held up a hand. He studied the new arrivals. Harold, Dogan, and Siet were already seated. We did the same and the Titan held up a hand. "Here are my deductions about Enki and what he's up to."

"In your hand?" said Dogan.

The Titan looked daggers. Harold leaned in. "Dogan, just keep quiet until he's done, please."

"Besides from the people in this current conversation, I have gathered information from Hana, the unfortunate kitsune, Doctor Alexandra Saint-George, and the chaos dragon, Umbra. It all came together to tell me three things; what motivates Enki; what Enki believes and has discovered; and what he's almost assuredly doing because of it."

He scanned the room. "I don't want to have to repeat myself any more than necessary. Are there any questions at this point?"

"Almost assuredly? You know almost assuredly what he's doing?" said Keith.

"Yes. The thing about contemporary information is that there's often not enough to draw a clear deduction from. I am, after all, not my brother."

"Then could he tell us what you can't?"

Epimetheus took a breath. "Not in the way you're thinking. His gift is intuition. He can't give you or me the missing pieces involved in a line of deduction."

"Hmph," said Keith.

Epimetheus laughed. "What people think about him and me and what's true, we are well misunderstood. Now, if there are no further questions, I will continue. Two things motivate Enki more than any else, polity and hatred for dragons. He believes current human polity has failed because despite technology there is still suffering. He believes, like the dragons, who he failed to eliminate, certain human faults have been allowed to infest the very structure of things."

Keith spoke again before I could stop him. "He sees dragons as an infestation? There's only one on Earth."

Epimehteus waved me off. "Don't stop his questions, Son of Order. He's asked good ones so far. This is one of Enki's greatest weaknesses if one wants to call it that. He's consumed by a belief that the very existence of dragons corrupts the universe and everything in it. Your presence on Earth only compounds it as he sees it."

"Might he stop his plans if I left Earth and promised to never return?"

"Putting aside the fact that you would never do that? No. You having ever been here, since the death of Tiamat, has done the damage. Human civilization, in its current form, is hopelessly corrupt for him."

"So, I was right that he wants a reset."

"Yes, and that brings us to what he's bothered himself to discover since his conclusions. He's studied the libraries of both Dakk and Toth and taken from them things having to do with how to instantiate large amounts of chaos magic and how to counter it. This I've been told by Harold and Dogan. Where my curse of complete deduction comes in is to reveal what he's almost assuredly up to with this. Hana's accounting of her last days before her body was destroyed completed the insidious puzzle."

"Insidious?" said Keith.

"Yes, again you seem to see the key question. How can a god of civilization be up to something insidious? --- Because of his unbridled commitment to civilization working to certain ends that he imposes upon it and his irrational hatred of dragons, his zeal to make civilization work drives him to destroy it so he can rebuild it."

Keith started, "But ..."

Epimetheus smilled. "With the destroyer redeemed of heart and purpose and now on civilization's side, its champion even, Enki has made himself the destroyer."

I missed the gravity of that at first. "Okay, so we have a role reversal. How does he intend to achieve this reset?"

"He either has or is about to create a powerful chaos entity, probably non-corporeal since that's where he found Dakk's progress has gotten and it would be very effective to leave that aspect."

"How?" asked Keith.

"That he obtained Koseina's soul-stone suggests he will somehow put her soul into the entity to control and maintain it."

Siet shook his head. “No. Koseina would never work for anyone, let alone Enki.”

The Titan bowed. “Siet, he only needs her to do what she wants. He wants her to push human civilization to the brink of destruction, so he can introduce his solution; almost assuredly one that involves a restructuring of society to achieve it.”

“You don’t know what his solution is?” I asked.

“Only that he has one,” said Keith.

The Titan stood. “I’m doubly afraid. I’m afraid the probability though high is far from certain. I’m afraid also that Enki’s state of mind makes it quite possible his plan is incomplete, and he doesn’t yet realize it. That could be more dangerous than it working as he planned.”

“What of Koseina?” said Siet.

“That part, I’m afraid it is almost certain and it's likely she’s already free. It’s just a matter of where she strikes first and what that will look like.”

I saw my eyes glowing purple off the window. “We can’t just wait and see. We have to somehow stop just reacting.”

Siet’s hand landed on my shoulder. “This, dragon, is when we stop just reacting.”

48

Clouds brought night to day across the city. A forest of lightning bolts blinked in and out of existence. A chorus of thunder defied rhythm. The glass muffled. Siet's animal head appeared in his hand. "Child of Galinthius, bring my wife here."

"But what of Athena's instruction?"

"The end of the time for secrets nears. I will soon be revealed to our enemies."

Thumper vanished. I brought out my wings. "We're about to act?"

"Just as soon as Koseina reveals herself, dragon."

Thumper reappeared with Alexandra beside him. She held a laptop which she flung around Siet with her arms. Except for Dogan, we averted our eyes out of respect. My sensitive ears told me more about their preferred kissing styles than I wanted to know. After long seconds, Alexandra tore herself away. "We need to think of Earth right now."

She threw open her laptop. Her fingers flew over the keys and landed on enter. "Good, it still works."

"What still works?" said Keith.

"What Athena's techs set up for me a few years ago. It monitors mounted cameras in most of the world's major cities. They were able to set it up to identify anomalous imagery and alert me."

"What if the first attack isn't against a major city?" I asked.

Alexandra's eyes lit up. "It's probability plus eventuality, young man. Koseina's coming for people and considering her cultural affinity, she's likely to start with Japanese or Anglo, and most of those people live in cities. Even if by chance she starts more rural or culturally remote, her thinking should soon enough come for a major city."

"How do you know it's Koseina? You've barely just got here?"

"Epimetheus asked me over the phone to help him organize his conclusions before he presented them."

"Okay, so we're okay with some rural areas being destroyed before we try to stop her?"

"Let's hope statistics work for us and them."

Kieth peered over her shoulder. "So, we just wait now?"

Siet admired his storm through the glass. "I should be able to easily defeat a god created of automaton magic. Thanks to Athena's super-genius planning, Enki's plan makes no account for me, an actual chaos god. This could be over fast."

A thought struck me. "Perhaps we should consider not revealing you just yet? Shouldn't I be immune to the chaos magic Koseina will be throwing around? Why not just send me?"

"Caution, my boy," said Harold. "This isn't just chaos magic you'd be dealing with, but a noncorporeal automaton that just happens to be powered by chaos magic. Chaos spells may not hurt you but matter and energy propelled by it won't care what that source is and nor would your flesh."

"Wouldn't the fact that it is non-corporeal mean that it's all magic?"

"I wouldn't want to wager your life on it."

Siet tapped the window. "No, dragon. This is my moment. I feel it. I will fight her. I will give you a task you're better equipped for than I am."

Alexandra waved an arm. "I think I've found her."

She punched, clicked, and pointed at her screen. "Look, here.

Miami. I think we may be able to save even more lives than we hoped."

I studied the display. "The sun is blue. Everything is in blue light."

Siet placed his finger on the horizon. "Koseina's out at sea, hovering over the ocean. She hasn't come ashore yet."

"She must be huge to fill the sky like that," said Keith.

Siet put the black fox headpiece on. "Child of Galinthius, take the dragon, my wife, and me as close to there as you can."

We appeared in a swamp. Distant skyscrapers peered over brush, backlit by a blue glow. Siet grasped my forearm. "Dragon, I need you to carry my wife to within sight of Koseina but also to keep her safe. That is your only task. I'll need her insight."

"But how?" she said.

He yanked the soul-stone off me and handed it to her. Between this and what you're already wearing, the communication should be clear enough."

He moved my arm over her shoulder. "Pardon the spray."

"You're confident you can defeat Koseina?"

"It must be Athena's plan, right? This must be the reason she kept me a secret till now; a decisive blow. And once I deliver it, Enki's schemes will unravel."

He shrugged. "Again, dragon, the spray."

A whirlwind lifted water around him. My aura abbreviated the duration of the drenching for both of us to a second. The whirlwind moved toward the city and grew as it traveled into a tornado.

I took dragon form large enough to carry her on my back. We followed Siet and his storm. Blocks of varied rooftops passed beneath us and then lines of foam on the water. One line thicker than the others rushed the shore. The ocean jumped across a city block and quickly enveloped others further in.

"Oh my God!" cried Alexandra.

The water receded and I grunted inaudibly. The rooftops and the walls beneath them left with the water; blocks and blocks of buildings; businesses and dwellings gone in seconds.

"A million people washed out to see."

I hoped for less. My mind couldn't fathom even the smallest likelihood. A sound of voices filled distant air. I used my dragon sight to look for people on the water. None could be seen. The sound, I realized, came from the air; from the direction of a dark region of the glowing air.

The sound sickened. The same female voice duplicated a multitude of times. It laughed with glee.

Siet floated before the darkness. "Koseina, I've come to end your misery."

The voices all answered. "Misery? I am happier than I've ever been, Master Siet. It's been so long."

49

The ocean danced. It swirled and chopped beneath Siet. Beneath Koseina it rose like fountains and fell into pits. White lightning bolts and blue arcs formed opposing armies on a field of surf. Alexandra squeezed my neck so hard I grew larger to keep from choking. Her first attempt at words stopped short to hold back other stuff from within her. I moved to put us behind Siet's waterspout and wrestled with my constitution.

A chorus of the same woman's voice mocked. "Shall we have a contest to see who can cause more damage to the mortals, Master Siet?"

Alexandra found a path for words. "Why does she keep calling him 'Master Siet?'"

In a sea of chaos, that stood out to Athena's researcher. I wished I could have discussed it with her. I needed my dragon form to protect her, so I trusted Siet to listen through the stone.

Siet swung his position between the darkness and the shore. I kept us behind him; always behind him; our only cover over the ocean.

An island jumped to the ocean surface beneath the darkness. My knowledge of Earth science told me another and a possibly bigger wave was about to strike the city.

Siet gestured behind him as if calling forth a hidden ally. A deafening roar surrounded us. An army of waterspouts sprang and pulled the ocean to the sky.

Alexandra cheered. "I've never seen him when he wasn't just toying with his foes before."

The other female voice haunted the sky in multitude. "You're suddenly no fun. Oh well. Let's see if you can hold all that water up and still fight me."

Blue arcs birthed from all sides and unified about Siet. I had to turn away. The intensity hurt my eyes even passing through the side of my dragon skull. I raised my tail to shield Alexandra.

Siet cried out. The crack of thunder and white light replaced the blue. I could look again and Siet hung in the sky with wings of white lightning. His voice thundered like his storm. "Koseina, why do you fight me? You know my power. Did you think you had more with this?"

"It seems I was mistaken, master, but you must know that now that you've betrayed all you stand for, I must fight you with all my being to the bitter end."

"If you persist, I will have to kill you."

"Then you shall have to, Master Siet."

"Then you know you're about to die?"

"You and I must do what we do. Yes, I know, so do it. I tire of your words."

She lied about knowing she was about to die. I shouted a warning to Siet that came out as a growl and not words. I flew away from the dual. I both hoped Siet might read a warning in my actions and I also sought to maximize Alexandra's safety.

"Get both of you away from here," he shouted to us.

Alexandra shouted over the wind. "He must be about to use his destruction power. The most powerful chaos spell at his disposal."

I flew between the waterspouts and beneath the ocean they suspended. The spouts faded and the ocean returned to its place. I took comfort in that. We stopped and hovered over the flattened city shoreline.

A bright white flash like a second sunrise burnt the eastern horizon. Then a blue one.

Alexandra's voice quivered. "I don't think that should have happened."

The blue darkness vanished. I flew us back out. The ocean's calm belied my worry. On the new island, a body lay. Blue arcs crawled about it.

"Is that Koseina? Where's my husband?"

My eyes could answer her question before my voice could. The best I could do on the approached was moan.

She cried. "Oh no. Oh no. Get me there right now."

I landed and became human. "Koseina lied when she said she knew she was about to die."

Alexandra tore off her necklace and ran to Siet's body. He lacked hands and feet. Blue arcs danced about the rest of him. Bits of him faded into nothing. She pressed the soul-stone against his chest. "You can't die again."

His words struggled between here and someplace else. "She absorbed my power. How could Athena have been wrong?"

Alexandra pushed the stone down with all the weight she could. "Save yourself in the stone like you used to. This isn't over."

The stone shimmered.

"Yes, that's it. We can save you later."

The stone dulled again. Siet raised a stump to her cheek. "She took too much from me, sweet Alexandra."

"No, you can't give up."

His stump fell to his side. "I'm so sorry."

His eyes closed and the rest of his body vanished. Alexandra screamed. "No."

"Where did Koseina go? Why did she leave?" I asked.

Alexandra spoke as if to the ground. "She's got to go and relish her stolen power, now that she's the new god of chaos."

She pounded the sand. I couldn't give her the time to grief; not with Koseina able to kill millions more at her whim. "I have to say, I share Siet's confusion. How could Athena have been wrong?"

"She's never been wrong before."

Alexandra lied.

"She has been, just not in my experience," I said.

Alexandra rose against pain and turned. She projected a false confidence. "I don't how she can be right this time, but she must be."

Her facade collapsed and I caught her before her body followed.

"I see why you were able to redeem that guy of yours, Alexandra. You're an amazingly strong woman, but none of us are too strong to grieve."

She cried a few sobs before clearing her throat. "Whatever Athena's plans were, I better not discover she planned for my husband to die. Not after all she put us through. Or you'll have to protect her from me."

"Athena has honor and honor wouldn't let her do that to you."

She gestured to the sand. "Then what is this? Right?"

She hung the soul-stone around my neck.

"What is this?" I asked.

"What little may be left of my Siet. Wear it as you avenge him."

The island seemed empty despite the two of us. Indeed the world seemed empty.

50

Koseina disappeared for a time. With a new chaos god set on destruction, the Children of Galinthius stopped hiding in other tasks and tracked her down. Due to her chaos magic, they couldn't get near her. They found her by finding a place on Earth they couldn't go, an area of the eastern Atlantic Ocean; the place where most hurricanes are born.

Dogan took Siet's old place at the window. "All that glorious power and she just sits in the ocean doing nothing? It's maddening."

Keith guffawed. "You find something maddening, Dogan?"

"Yes. Why doesn't she just light into things?"

"She can use her powers to maximize hurricanes and shepherd them to strike in the worst possible of places," I said.

Dogan threw his arms out. "But why? She could use her power directly and do far more harm more quickly."

"She may want humanity to blame weather at first. Perhaps this will give her some desired advantage later."

"Good thinking, my boy," said Harold.

"How does she know what's been in the news for the last twenty years?" said Keith.

"Thirty or forty, I've been told. People have exaggerated the immediate implications of human activity on the environment to include monster storms and earthquakes. Well-meaning I guess, but fear is a tool chaos and evil won't hesitate to exploit."

Dogan squatted. "But all that glorious power."

"Take a cold shower, Dogan," said Harold. "The Son of Order's thoughts are not only sound but dare I say probable. We know Enki intends to use Koseina to unite Earth against her. She's no fool. She knows better than to think Enki actually wants her to destroy the world. She must suspect his intentions and is trying to do as much damage as she can without revealing herself."

"Why start in the Atlantic, Harold?"

"Because, my boy, those storms can strike over half the people in the most powerful nation on Earth. Devastate that and she will be well on her way to pre-empting any response the people of Earth may make to her."

"How does he know so much about Earth?" asked Keith.

"He spent the first sixteen years of my life with little to do but be my family's housecat. He read a lot during that time."

"And there's something else I've read, as it were, young dragon. Now that Siet is dead, you're our cause's leader. It's time you hold a meeting to determine what we should do next."

Dogan ended his couch-nap. "Him? Leader? You should be the new leader, Harold. You have by far the most knowledge and experience with strategy and tactics."

"Dogan, you can never let me forget that you're a fool, now can you. No one's going to rally around me, Harold the Dread, unless they're either insane like you or looking to commit atrocities."

"But the dragon is stuck in a rut of rules."

Harold raised a finger. "Dogan, your nap?"

He closed his eyes. Harold placed his hand on my shoulder. "So, now the weight of the world may truly be on your shoulders."

"I'm afraid he's right, dragon," said Thumper.

"Okay. Athena must have expected this, right?"

I wanted someone to show me more confidence than I had. Only a mix of cold expressions and insincere nods answered me.

"We have to be honest with ourselves. Koseina is now more powerful than Siet and we don't have enough power in this penthouse combined to challenge her."

"So, my boy, what then?"

"We have to look beyond this penthouse."

"We have allies out there, "said Keith.

"Elektra and her remnants, even all remnants combined would be nothing against her."

"The CoG, boss."

"They can't get near her. They can shuttle whatever allies we may find, but we'll need more than us and Titans and remnants."

"There must be someone powerful who doesn't want to see civilization wiped out."

"Yeah, exactly, Keith. I should have thought of that sooner."

"No need for sarcasm, boss."

"I'm not being sarcastic. If there is one thing we may gain now that Siet is dead, it's that Apollo may join us now."

Thumper lashed his tail. *"He's hiding in a dryad refuge."*

"The Children of Galinthius can find him there, right?"

"Yes, but as you know he's got the Olympian sickness that saps their judgment."

"I need him found and invited here. You can take him here when he accepts the offer."

"How do you know he'll accept?"

"I'm not sure I can afford for him not to."

"This is not good, dragon."

"Yeah. That's the summary of our circumstances. Now, please, Thumper, my friend, just go and get him here."

DRYADS MUST HIDE WELL. I'm told it took dozens of Children of Galinthius to find Apollo. It took the better part of two days. We waited in the New York penthouse. Koseina waited in the cradle of hurricanes.

Thumper appeared with Apollo and Ylera. *"He comes with a message."*

I extended my hand and we grasped arms.

"Son of Order, I should let you know I've exchanged messages with Enki."

"Do my allies here need to leave before he attacks?"

Apollo smiled. "No. He doesn't know where you are. I wouldn't tell him. Like you, I despise him, but things have changed a great deal since the three of us last spoke."

"You mean, fought."

"And that, yes, but Enki's plans did not account for Siet and especially not for what happened in Miami."

"What, he didn't think she'd attack? Was he expecting something else?"

"You play the games to avoid telling what you know too well, dragon. The distance the Children of Galinthius need to keep from her is much greater than Enki admits his teleporters had to keep before she defeated Siet. He told me his planned way to stop her is now inadequate to stop her."

"And?"

"Instead of waiting for Koseina to kill us before stopping her, he now needs us to work alongside his solution."

"What if we don't like his solution?"

"And we don't work with him? He loses, we lose, civilization loses, Earth loses."

"What choice do we have?"

"Exactly."

51

Two long years had passed since I last stepped foot at the corner of First Avenue and East 42nd Street in New York. Other than the removal of hazardous materials and other loose debris, little had changed. Back then I left through a cloud of smoke and didn't look back.

When the UN headquarters building still stood there, leaders of the world met in it. I ended that. I grew inside it until it surrendered to the rules of relativity; two objects can't occupy the same space at the same time. Back then I had an automaton to stop from plunging the world into chaos, and a building I could collapse on it to hold it still. Zeus understood though withheld approval. I doubt Enki understood.

This new threat dwarfed that one and this was the place Enki wanted to meet. I wondered if he meant to rub my nose in the broken concrete and rebar and hit me with a rolled-up newspaper. "This place brings back memories. Why here of all places?"

Apollo stopped by a remnant of a wall. "It's a fitting place to plot how we might save the world?"

"A place I tore down?"

"I don't want you to waste energy on that past. That this place is in ruins, makes it a place we can gather without interruption. How it became this way doesn't really matter in the here and now."

He meant that sincerely. I guess I should have expected such pragmatism from Athena's closest rival of intellect in her family. Harold peeked around the wall. "I see someone has set some things about before our meeting."

I joined him to see. The center of the ruins had been cleared in a wide circle of eight alternating knee-height stones; four cubes and four pyramids. In the circle's center stood a ten-foot statue; a crude depiction of a child; so crude I couldn't tell the gender or the ethnicity. The child sat on a throne.

Keith let out with, "what the Hell?"

"Yeah, Keith, you may be onto something. Harold, any idea as to what that's supposed to be?"

He walked to the circle's edge. "The black and white stone these are made of is combined like no natural rock I've seen. I'm guessing magic, my boy. Nobody touch."

Apollo walked along the circle's edge. "Enki did say he was going to show us what he intends to use against Koseina. Wizard, would you say this could be the setup for a powerful incantation?"

"It could well be."

I stepped further away from the circle. "If Enki wants us to participate in an incantation involving an idle, I don't think I can do that."

"Nor I, " added Keith.

"Not even to save the world?" said Apollo.

"I was raised a Christian so no idles for this dragon."

"Or this wanderer."

Harold smiled. "Your adopted mother Nikki is a saint, isn't she? Aiden, I wouldn't worry. I doubt Enki needs us to participate in whatever incantation he has prepared here. He probably just needs us to help the results defeat Koseina."

Apollo shook a finger. "Well, for the world's sake I hope the wizard's right. My sister practices the same silliness."

Keith glared. I patted him on the back. "Okay, let's wait for Enki to see that he has to say."

"Besides, lads, I really don't think that statue's an idle so much as it's a really big spell component."

We let Harold's words end that conversation. In a short time, Hermes appeared inside the circle with Enki behind him. "Zeus' proxy, Lord Enki," he announced.

Hermes wore running sweats. Enki made no attempt to blend into 21st century New York. A breeze kicked up dust. His thick robe and braided beard defied it.

"At a time like this, Hermes, we should leave lesser disputes behind us. We can dispense with titles laying claim to this or that authority."

Hermes's quiet acquiescence lacked sincerity. It showed enough that Apollo noticed without my dragon of order senses. "Yes, brother. Earth cannot afford our egos. Lord Enki, what is this solution of yours that you need our help with?"

He too lacked sincerity in granting Enki the honorific, "lord."

Enki placed a hand on the child statue. "My solution involves what you see here, only a hundred times over. I have placed these shrines of sorts in one hundred cities around the world."

Keith's eyes widened. "Shrines?"

Enki answered like a salesman. "Well, no, not really shrines. These are all the non-moving non-living parts of a powerful world-wide incantation. The statues are there to focus the participants' minds."

"On children?"

My indestructible assistant seemed to find some use of his curse to be the asker of awkward questions. I thought it a good find. Enki's words became sharp. "Yes, young man, on children. More to the desired point, the future of humanity."

Harold nodded. "Lord Enki, more to your point, what will this incantation do?"

"If all the mortal people alive in the world at a given time pass through these circles chanting a prepared incantation, they will create a powerful creature to fight Koseina."

Keith raised a hand as if to be called on by a teacher and spoke.

"But, how can you get all the mortal people of the world to pass through these circles? Not everyone will be able to. Not everybody will be willing to. You know. People are people."

Enki turned up his nose. "When the world sees the threat that Koseina is, the ones who can and are able will more than willingly kill the rest so as to fulfill the conditions."

I stopped Keith from replying with a reply of my own. "That's an awful solution, Enki."

"Can you defeat Koseina without my solution, dragon?"

Harold moved between us. "Lord Enki, if we are to agree to work with you, please pardon potential hubris, but may I see this incantation so I can confirm it will work?"

Enki snarled before pulling a parchment from his sleeve and handing it to Harold. "Be sure Wizard, not read it aloud. It is powerful, even outside the magnifying effects of the circle."

Harold's eyes moved back and forth before he looked up. "Lord Enki, this is most assuredly a very powerful spell. It will unite the minds of everyone who participates in the ritual."

"Yes, then you see that it will work."

"Yes, and like any proper practice of magic, even by evil dreaded wizards, as I once was, requires that there always be a counter-spell before one uses a spell. May I see the counterspell to this?"

"No, wizard. There is no counterspell. There are too many minds involved for that to be possible. But I don't see why one would ever be needed."

"Lord Enki, surely you must see, without a counterspell, all these minds will be imprisoned together in a common thread of thought."

"Imprisoned? More like liberated; free from the petty self-interests of different nations; free from having to compete for resources. It will be a world of total cooperation for the greater good."

I had hear enough. "Thumper, prepare to take us back."

Enki pleaded. "But we haven't discussed how you'll help the creature defeat Koseina."

Apollo grabbed my shoulder. "What are you doing?"

"My allies and I need to talk this through amongst ourselves. The world is at stake, I know, but you ask a lot of us. We have to think."

Enki's eyes shot about between us as we grasped the cat's fur. "Surely you know you have no choice. The world will die without you. You can't say no."

"Thumper, take us home now."

I needed to get away to talk and think it through without Enki around.

52

The routine of the city streets belied the crisis in the penthouse. Apollo updated Alexandra and Dogan as I watched clouds.

"It doesn't look like we'll have a clear sky tonight. Keith, what's the forecast?"

"Forecast? Oh yeah. Right boss. Just a moment."

Alexandra's grief continued to take a toll on her. She left Apollo for her room. "I know this matters but I need to rest."

My spatial awareness told me Dogan rushed toward me. "So, why did you leave before the meeting was over, Aiden?"

"I was too distracted by the awfulness of it all. We need to think up our response with great care."

"Oh, you poor thing. It's understandable how the intensity of the moment overwhelmed you. Harold, my old master, what would be your decision?"

"We are just wizards, you and I. Whatever we do we need to do it with the dragon. He's our leader."

Dogan grunted. "Uh huh."

Apollo's eyes dismissed Dogan and turned to me. "Son of Order, through all of this you've been working with my sister, Athena. Both Alexandra and I can tell you that while she is amazingly right about an amazing number of things, she has been wrong in the past. Toth, for example, once surprised her about something involving Siet."

"Do you think this is all about my faith in Athena?"

"Follow my reasoning. I'm pretty good at such things. If she was once wrong about an interaction between Toth and Siet, perhaps she was wrong about how things would go between Siet and Koseina. He is after all much more ancient than any of us."

A lump hit my throat. "He was."

"I think, and I think it's quite rational to think that if Athena were here she wouldn't be insisting that things were going all according to her preferred plan. Being her brother, I've known her longer than anyone else here and I believe she'd tell you to work with Enki's solution. She might even have a way to counter the spell we're just not seeing."

"There is so much more than reason involved here."

Dogan laughed. "What? Am I supposed to be the crazy one?"

"I have been told by multiple sources that I must be true to who and what I am. Why would that suddenly change?"

Dogan positioned himself as to eclipse me from the others. "The fate of the world is at stake and this dragon stands here contemplating clouds and telling us that he must be who and what he is. I for one can't accept the world dying for a dragon's conscience. Harold, can you?"

I let it go. They weren't about to follow Dogan and as for Harold, I wanted to know where he stood. My teacher's voice carried calm. "This dragon knows something about honor and respect for individual dignity, Dogan, that I doubt you will ever understand. This honor, as it were, is what keeps him from becoming a deadly tyrant."

Dogan's voice coarsened. "We don't have time for this, Harold. The world is at stake."

I thought out loud. "The world."

"What's that, my boy?"

"I can go anywhere now, and I have nothing better to do."

Dogan stepped away from me. "I am no longer the crazy one here."

"Keith, find me a relatively close place where at this moment there's a clear night sky."

"On it, boss."

"I see where this is going," said Harold.

"You've got me confused, dragon."

"I'm seeking wise counsel."

"Iceland, boss."

"Harold, take me to Iceland."

"Not me?"

"Thumper, there's something I keep from you for your own sake. The time for you to know will come soon, I suspect, but for now, you'll like me and everything better if I keep you out of this particular matter."

"I guess I don't have time to be curious."

"Harold, shall we?"

Apollo held his head in his hands. Dogan stomped off to his bedroom and we left.

HAROLD GAVE me some distance in the Icelandic night. We lost sight of each other in the black of things. I felt pulled into the field of stars and had to make sure my feet still touched the ground. The world took a slight turn. I called out. "Vedi?"

I met silence. I called out again. "Vedi, please, I need to talk."

"Aiden? What's wrong?"

"Do you and Nix know what Enki plans to do to stop Koseina?"

"Yes. Yes, we do. It's a terrible thing."

"It is; a thing I can't do, not and be who and what you married."

"Oh, I miss you and your commitments so much."

"And that is the only dragon you can return to, and oh, I want you back so much."

"But, my dear sweet dragon, which is more important, us or saving the world from destruction?"

I caught a lump in my throat. I couldn't deny her reason or her morality, yet I couldn't accept it either. "Vedi, you have reminded me to be true to who and what I am in order that you can return. I have dutifully headed that, and in so doing I discovered something."

"What, my pretty boy?"

"I don't believe I have ever really had a choice. I must be your husband and my father's son. If Athena placed me here to make this horrible decision, then she made a mistake. I simply cannot do it."

"Aiden?"

"Yes, my beloved Vedi?"

She raised her voice. *"But the world, Aiden, the world!"*

Her anger struck me as the last thing I wanted at that moment. "Vedi, please."

The wind moaned across the ground.

"Vedi, please talk to me."

I waited before calling on Harold. I needed to see things clearly. Loneliness embraced me. Could I destroy the world by inaction? Could I destroy its people to save them? My shoulders hurt. The air offered no advice, no comfort.

53

Harold returned us to the penthouse. I needed to take a seat. I wanted to watch the day fade over the city.

"So, boss, anything?"

"Did this thing I'm best off not knowing about have any help to offer us?"

I chose not to answer them because I didn't like the answer. Harold answered for me. "My former student is in a bind."

"Former student?" I asked.

"You have learned well, my boy, very well. Dare I say somehow you learned more from me than I had to teach. Now you're posed with a question for which there seems to be no right answer, but whatever the best answer may be, only you can know. That must be the one you give."

"If only I could stop being who and what I am. Harold, you stopped being Harold the Dread. Could there be one more lesson you could teach me from that?"

"Let us think about that. Shall we?"

"If I could somehow stop being the Son of Order—"

"Being the Son of Order isn't your problem. That part of you would have aligned with Enki's plan with ease. It's the being Aiden Ferris part that stands in the way."

"Being Aiden Ferris?"

"Your love of order doesn't keep you from this. It's your love of people."

"My love of people makes me willing to let them die?"

"You may recall there was once a moment when I was willing to die, and you refused to let me. Do you remember why?"

"Because it was the opposite of what you deserved."

"Justice, you called it."

"Yes. Yes, I did."

"Oh boy. I see where this is going," said Thumper.

"My problem here is that I believe the people of this world don't deserve to be entrapped into a common thought. That while still unjust, it would be more just that they die free."

Thumper's tail whipped about. *"And there we have it."*

I walked to the window. The city outside took on a new context. I wanted to save them but not at the cost Enki required of them. I whispered, "you'll die free at least."

Thumper joined me at the window, then Harold and Keith. The big cat leaned into my thigh. I knew the signal. He was saying without saying, "when you're ready to leave—"

The solemn moment lasted until Dogan came from his bedroom. "What's going on here?"

"We're paying our respects to Earth," said Keith.

"No, I mean to the portal. Why is it pitch black?"

I realized the implication and Harold did too. We spoke simultaneously. "Stay away from it."

Dogan stepped away. "What? Why?—Oh, but why would—"

I'd seen it before. "It's connected directly to the void."

"Yes, but who here made that happen?"

Harold looked at me. "No one here."

A hand with a diamond ring reached out of the blackness. I knew the hand and held up mine for all to see. "You see that ring; it goes with mine."

I grasped Vedi's hand and pulled her through. "Oh, my stars."

As we began to kiss, Harold spoke. "The answer to your question, Dogan, is that Nix herself probably made that happen, but you may need to wait a few moments before you can get a definitive answer."

NIX SENT Vedi back to me. Dogan got his definitive answer and he returned to his room. Thumper waited patiently for us to sit down before asking the questions all Children of Galinthius would want to ask. *"You're alive, chaos witch?"*

She smirked. "Yes, I'm not a zombie, lich, or vampire."

A ridge of fur formed along his back. *"You were with Nix?"*

Her muscles stiffened. I tried to calm things. "Vedi, this is Thumper, Rumbler's son. He's been helping me through most of this war. He saved my life at least once. Thumper, I'm sure you know this is my wife. She's been hiding from Enki's allies in the void."

He folded his ears. *"You were right. I was better off not knowing. If I had, I could never have helped you."*

Vedi spoke softly. "And I'm forever grateful that you did."

"You both have good reasons not to trust each other. Chaos magic is like poison to the Children of Galinthius and Vedi's family live with constant worry that they may someday be banished because of it. We all understand that, but despite that we're on the same side of this war."

Vedi grunted. Thumper's pupils enlarged.

"Oh, sorry," said Vedi. "If you're Aiden's friend, I will consider you mine."

"Then why did you grunt?"

"The war. Since Siet died it doesn't seem to be the same war it started as."

Thumper closed his eyes. *"I too can consider you my friend as you're the dragon's wife. I'll leave you two to talk."*

"Me too, boss."

Harold left with them. Vedi locked her eyes on me. "Aiden, now that I'm here, things are different."

"Much better, yes."

"Of course, that, but in other ways too; as to this war."

"Some of us guessed that Nix intends you to be her avatar. If that were so—"

"No. I see where your mind's going, and no, not as you might like."

"Nix isn't going to help us with this?"

Vedi pulled out a pendant; a clear diamond surrounded by several small black ones. "She believes direct help would be too dangerous. This was her solution to her end of the problem."

"What does it do?"

"It allows her to make me her avatar when the time is right, after Koseina is killed."

"Why not before?"

"Because she believes Koseina would do the same thing to me that she did to Siet and end up yet even more powerful."

"Okay. I can see that, but what does she expect us to do to kill Koseina?"

Vedi stepped back and locked her gaze on me. "Nix is confident that the combined efforts of you, Apollo, your allies, and Enki's solution will be enough to defeat her."

"If I help Enki."

Her voice stiffened. "Nix sent me early so that you'd no longer need to worry about getting me back. That frees you to do what's expedient."

"It doesn't free me to do what's wrong."

"Aiden, you're talking about the entire mortal population of Earth."

"As horrible a thing as it is, it's better they die free than be trapped into one common will."

"Aiden, you need to save them from dying."

"Not if it involves Enki's spell."

"Oh Aiden, have I been a fool all this time thinking I made any difference to you? You will be that dragon that you are even if it means the world ends, my world?"

"But Vedi, can't you see ..."

"Don't bother trying to explain. Unlike you, I'm human. Unlike you, I can't sit by and let the Earth be destroyed. I'm willing to die for it as I'm sure many others are. You're just willing to let it die."

"Better to die free."

Her shoulders raised. "Doesn't anyone really matter to you? If this Koseina killed me would you just say, 'better she dies free?'"

"I can't imagine what my state of mind would be if that happened. Please don't even mention it."

She swung her back to me. "Where can I be alone?"

I showed her to my room. Tears flew as she shut the door. She shouted through it. "Maybe Nix can save us from your stupidity, Aiden. Maybe she'll have a backup plan to you making sense."

"But ..."

"Leave me alone. I'll try to talk to her."

I SPENT our first night back together, alone on a couch.

54

I woke to a hand caressing my shoulder. Vedi, I hoped. Dogan spoke. “Aiden Ferris, you need to wake up.”

I pushed his hand away and sat. “What? What’s going on?”

“Vedi asked me to wake you and tell you where’s she’s gone and why.”

“Where did she go?”

“She said Nix had an idea for how to stop Koseina.”

“I asked where.”

“Vedi said it would put her life at great risk and she’d have to do it alone for it to work. That’s why she wanted me to delay telling you until after she left.”

I grabbed him by the top of his head and squeezed. “Dogan, where did she go?”

The pain I caused showed in his face. “Madeira, the nearest island to Koseina.”

“Did you take her there?”

“No, Nix changed the portal here to go there.”

“I’m going there now.”

“But, Aiden, it could be dangerous.”

“And that’s why I’m going. Tell the others where I’ve gone.”

A crackling came from the portal behind me. A ripple moved across the glowing opening.

I noticed a blue tint on the horizon to the south.

My nostrils filled with fresh earth. Rips and tears large enough to swallow houses surrounded me. I approached an anomalous turn in the cliff-edge. The amount of loose dirt in the air increased. The ground slid beneath me and pebbles tumbled beyond. I brought out my wings and hovered.

Dirty air highlighted where a new bay had been ripped from the island. Exposed roots reached in vain into the air for nutrients. Blue arcs, like fireflies, blinked in and out down the sides of loose dirt. High waves beat against an earthy beach. Amongst the blinking arcs, a white sparkle caught my eye. The diamond on the pendant Vedi received from Nix lay on rocks.

I swooped down. “Vedi?”

Tiny blue arcs, like worms, looped up and back into the soil. A dotted line of them led a few feet away.

“Vedi?”

The arcs clustered into the silhouette of a prone body. Altogether they formed a glowing shadow of a woman tethered to Nix’s pendant.

Harold yelled back by the portal. “Dogan, why didn’t you tell us all at the moment she left?”

I got beyond that question without and answer. Another question lay before me. I didn’t want its answer. Dirt and rocks tumbled behind me. Harold’s voice constrained. “Oh my. Aiden. My boy, Aiden.”

I turned to address him. He gazed at the silhouette. His hand to his face said what I couldn’t tell myself. I fell into the arcs. They scattered and left only the pendant. I dove to clutch it. I held it tightly enough to bleed.

As if my blood might answer I cried, “why.”

Dogan answered instead. “She wanted to save the Earth, dragon. Why do you think?”

Harold yanked Dogan. “Let’s go. Aiden will join us back in New York when he’s ready.”

My feet had roots. He squinted. "Oh, Aiden. I can't think of what to say. --- Only don't stay too long. Koseina's not far."

The time and space between where Vedi fell and the portal held no place in my memory. The next thing I recall was Harold, Dogan, and Keith talking to me at the penthouse.

"My boy, why would Vedi go off like that? She was smart enough to know that even if Nix gave her all her power, Koseina has all of Siet's power plus her own."

Dogan slithered into a chair. "Because, like the rest of us, she was desperate."

Keith took the pendant from my hand and pressed it against his chest. Harold patted his arm. "Even if that weren't broken, I doubt it would work on anyone but her."

Keith handed it back. "I thought it was worth a try. All the chaos magic running through me."

Dogan nudged me. "You see, dragon, we're all trying to do something. What about you?"

Harold raised his voice. "Dogan."

I muttered. "What can I do?"

Dogan got close enough that his breath hit my face. "Koseina just killed the one person in the whole universe you most love. If I were you, dragon, I'd have something to do."

Keith pulled him. "He can't work with Enki's solution."

Dogan shot a finger at Keith. "He couldn't, but now that his wife's nothing but a scorch mark on some remote island, maybe now he can, just maybe? Come on dragon, don't you think it's about time you saved the world? What are you made of?"

His efforts to goad me had nowhere to go. It seemed like I wasn't there. I looked at my hands and pondered the question. "What am I made of, Dogan? Tell me."

"Even in my insanity, even amid my lust for magical power, I once put the fate of this world ahead of that. That's why I first helped you back when. Now it seems this mad man that I am, even if I'm as pathetic as people say I am, I'm not as pathetic and useless as you, dragon."

A purple glow reflected off his pale skin. He backed up. I wished I knew where my anger was besides my eyes. I didn't feel it. I didn't feel anything. *How could Vedi be dead after all of this?*

Dogan tilted his face. "Are you finally going to do something, dragon?"

I turned away from my pale taunter. My spatial awareness told me he left the penthouse. Harold touched my shoulder. "My boy, he pushes you too soon after this tragedy. Get some rest."

"Do I have time?" I asked.

"Yes."

He spoke with high sincerity. Despite that reality, I didn't believe I had anything, let alone time.

55

I slept until nightfall and rose to a clear night sky. I wanted to go to the roof. Alexandra sat in the great room with her laptop open and her hands at her side. A tear glinted in the corner of her eye. Keith hunched in the kitchen and rattled pans. He mumbled, "everything has a place but me."

He mumbled again just as I exited the penthouse. "Soon there will be more places than things."

If he targeted me with those words, he aimed at a small target and missed. The roof gave me a good view of the stars. I stood a small dragon before an infinite sky.

Words rolled out without thought. "Vedi, can you hear me?"

Of course, she couldn't. A woman's voice did come, Alexandra's. "They're gone, Aiden. It's hard for us to accept but we must face it."

I tried to drill a hole in the firmament with my stare. Alexandra was right. The stars blurred into crosses and filled my vision. My eyes filled with tears.

Alexandra rubbed my shoulder. "Can we cry together?"

We did. We heaved and cried in each other's arms. Our throats needed clearing and we moved apart.

I cleared mine first. "Was this Athena's plan?"

"That the people we love die? I can at least see why she wouldn't have told us it would happen."

"Because we wouldn't have helped her if we knew."

Her eyes watered. "That's the way it goes, isn't it?"

"She keeps things from us to keep us from making wrong decisions."

"What kind of a price was this to keep us from knowing?"

I wiped away her tear. "She knew we needed to stay in place, to stay the course."

Alexandra embraced me again. This time she pounded my back. "Is it okay, Aiden, if I still hate her for it?"

"Yes. You and I can hate her together --- and yet stand by her."

"The wisest most intelligent woman in the universe. 'Not a goddess', my ass."

I found sleep again in my room until Harold cracked my door. "Aiden, my boy, I've got something you need to hear."

Could I accept any more? Harold persisted. "You need to come out here. Your action is needed."

I came to my door. "What is it, Harold? What more must I know?"

"You should sit down."

We sat in the great room. I prompted him to continue. "I assume this must be urgent."

"Prometheus and I went into the city to look for Dogan."

"Why does that matter so much?"

"I'll get to the point, but bear with me. I don't think you care about the details of how right now, but between the two of us we discovered he got a message to your father."

"He told my father about me?"

That would be the last of my major purposes in life gone.

Harold grabbed my shoulders. "No, Aiden, not that treacherous, but it's still quite serious."

"What did he tell him?"

"He told him about Koseina. As a result, he's now on his way to Earth to help Enki kill her."

"Not treacherous, you say?"

I yanked the coffee table off the floor.

"Calm yourself, my boy."

"If my father even so much as catches the scent of me, he will know he broke the biggest promise of his life and his dragon nature will probably kill him."

Thumper appeared. His eyes moved between us. *"Have you told him, Harold?"*

"Yes."

"When you're ready to leave Earth, dragon, I will take you. After this is over and your father has left, we'll come back."

"Wait. It's not that simple. Even if I leave, there will still be the impact of all the things I've done. The risk will still be grave for him."

"We have three days, dragon. Perhaps we can take some precautions."

"Three days to eliminate years of what I've done? All the remnants and Titans I've impacted? They can't be removed."

"Well, they could be, but Zeus wouldn't have it."

"And I wouldn't either."

"We'll just have to minimize the risks. It's all we can do."

"I only see one best way for me to minimize my father's risk and for me to at least do something to stop Koseina."

"My boy, you'll do plenty just to let your father take your place in this coming fight."

I put the table down. "Harold, I'm going to where Vedi died."

"To eliminate the evidence of her being there?"

"No. To launch what I hope will be a sneak attack on Koseina."

"Dragon, no. There's nothing to be gained."

Harold leaned over the table. "Sneak attacks achieve nothing if the surprise still leaves you hopelessly outmatched."

"I'll be outmatched if my goal is to kill her, but not if it's to hurt her."

"But she'll almost assuredly kill you."

"If I can hurt her, it will be that much less for my father and Enki's solution to deal with."

"It's likely that you'll achieve nothing significant against her at all."

"Even if that's true, at least in my dying I will potentially protect my father."

"How so?"

"If my father should become aware of my existence, me being dead and having died fighting for order will increase the chance that my father can survive the revelation."

Thumper turned his back. *"Even if that's so, I won't help you kill yourself, dragon."*

"I would never ask you to. You have been a good friend; a fine tribute to your father's legacy, Thumper."

His ears went back. I walked through the portal.

Laughter enveloped me. Blue invaded my eyes. The wind blew one way and then another and another. The darkness hung over the rip in the shore.

I could tell Koseina didn't laugh at me. Her core hovered over where Vedi's silhouette had been. She laughed at the hole in me.

I should have asked myself why she came back. Instead, I assumed the worst of her. She deserved such assumptions. She deserved the worst things I could muster. I took my largest form and filled my lungs with air.

"Dragon, you're back?" Again, she laughed, in all her many voices.

My tail twitched to the part of my anger I couldn't focus. The rest projected a purple glow to the air. I hoped she noticed.

In my determination to make my anger matter, I forgot for the moment about the island's inhabitants and let loose my sonic attack. The sound of brass and thunder combined. I split the darkness. The island shook. Koseina's voices put out shrieks.

"Yes, yes," I thought to myself.

The darkness reformed. "You mourn your precious wife?"

I inhaled and repeated. Again, the darkness split. Again, came the shrieks. Explosions scattered about the island. The ocean waves towered and plummeted. The darkness reformed; this time around me.

"I won't let you do that again, dragon."

A dozen hammer-blows struck me from all sides. The cracks of stone and scale and bone filled the air. A cascade washed the ground. Red filled my vision. Stone spires impaled. My blood flushed from me. I couldn't take another breath.

She laughed. "I watched your wife disappear."

She laughed again. "She and Nix were clever, but they failed. She faked her death to get you to help Enki. Instead you were a fool and came here to sacrifice yourself for nothing. She's alive and you're dead. You're both fools."

She lied about me being dead, but nothing else, and soon her one lie would be true. My blood spilled out and unlike the time of my beheading, this time had no moment to pull me back from. My body died.

56

Sandstone clung to an alpine slope. A chill wind met warm air with no swirling. One stopped where the other began in an impossible way; no way at all. I almost forgot my destruction amidst the spires. "This is wrong."

I found myself on the deck of what might have been called a villa, except for the architecture. An Egyptian desert palace of large pillars spread beyond and into the cliff. Tables displayed piles of fruit of all kinds I could imagine and more; all fresh.

Brisk mountain air and tropical fruit mixed in my nostrils. I asked with dread, "Is this heaven?"

I saw nothing wrong with any of my surroundings as they were. I saw something wrong with where they were in the context of me. "I just died, didn't I?"

"Son of Order, is that you?"

Siet? He approached from the shadows cast by archways. I answered. "Yes, it's me."

"My Alexandra made you wear my soul-stone."

"She wanted me to avenge your death."

"I see that you didn't."

I gestured to the temple and its view. "So, what is this?"

He came into the light. “This is what it’s like being trapped inside a soul-stone. Trust me, I never planned for you to be trapped here with me.”

I sensed his sincerity for the first time. He told the truth.

“It doesn’t seem so bad for being trapped,” I said.

“My Alexandra didn’t intend for you to end up here either. I didn’t think it would happen. It must have had something to do with that restorative magic in you.”

“If that’s the case then no one else is coming to join us.”

“No–no one.”

“I’ll never be with Vedi again.”

“Or I with Alexandra.”

I walked to the railing to absorb the situation. He took a seat at a table. “I’ll give you enough distance so that you don’t tire of me, and yet we can still talk when you want to.”

“How far do these mountains go?”

“This world is whatever you want it to be.”

“I can tell now when you’re not being completely honest. Not everything we want it to be.”

“Yes, sharing a soul-stone tends to expose the minds involved to each other. So, you think I’m lying?”

“No. You’re just not sure of your choice of words.”

“Ah, yes, of course. You can create whatever you want in this world within the stone, except another being with free will, and that’s what makes this place more like Hell than Heaven. That and the knowledge that nothing but your mind is real.”

I brushed some snow off the sandstone railing. “You could try harder to make it seem real.”

He shook his head. “You’ll see in a few days of this. You can’t intentionally make something that isn’t what you want it to be, and that very fact starts to yell it to you. Nothing’s real and you’re alone; all alone.”

“Things would be better if some things went against you?”

“Yes, much better I’d say. Life is a struggle against countering forces. Remove all challenges and how can anyone know they’re alive?"

"Are you suggesting that ending all suffering is not necessarily a good thing?"

"Not this side of the true end of the universe."

"Enki's solution involves making all humanity united in thought. He says it will both help defeat Koseina and end most of human suffering."

"Do you think it can defeat Koseina?"

"With my father's help."

"Of course. Now that they think you're dead, he's free to come and help. That should indeed work."

"But the mortals of Earth will all be trapped in a common thread of thought."

"And you and I hate that idea, don't we?"

He told the truth.

"Yes. Yes, we do."

He joined me at the rail. "At least now we'll have someone else with a free will to talk to now and then. That will make the long time here much easier to bear. Perhaps even better than Earth will be after Enki's done with it."

"Wait, I'm not quite ready to give up."

"What choice have we?"

"I just thought of something that could get us out of here. Someone who owes me a favor."

"You mean the Gray Wolf?"

"Yes, you think he can give Hana a new body, right? Why can't he do that for us?"

"He can."

"Then why are we assuming we'll be trapped in the stone for eternity?"

"I'll not give you a simple answer because it will only likely make you angry. Instead, please hear me out."

"You're the only person I have to listen to here. Go ahead."

"When Koseina defeated me, in that horrible moment, I saw many things clearly I didn't before."

"I hope that's not the core of your argument, Siet."

"No, no it's not. I realized at that moment that Enki would have to work with our side of the war to stop Koseina. I also knew enough about Enki to expect just the sort of horrible solution he would have, even if I didn't know exactly what it was. I expected it to be a solution I couldn't go along with. I'd prefer the world to be destroyed."

"And what does this have to do with the Gray Wolf not helping us?"

"I am known amongst the gods as the destroyer of worlds, and now I am the redeemed one who struggles to be seen as such. If I come back and oppose Enki's solution, as I would have to do, my redemption will seem no more real than the creations inside this stone."

"But you can't stop the Gray Wolf if he decides to restore us."

"I can't, but I am the master of deception. Even inside this stone, I can cast illusions to affect anyone observing what they think is in the stone. Thus, it looks empty and thus there is nothing to do."

"Then you plan to drop that illusion once you're sure Koseina is defeated?"

"Yes, but by then this stone may be locked away somewhere or buried. I wouldn't want to get your hopes up on us being discovered any time soon."

"Can you limit the illusion to only hide your mind and not mine?"

"I could, but you, like me, are likely to get in the way of saving the Earth."

"No. With my father on the way, I will be inclined to leave Earth and get out of his way. More importantly, my wife Vedi believes I died because of her own faked death. It's important I get to her before she does something rash."

He started to walk away. "Like you did."

"Siet, if she kills herself—"

He waved a hand. "Done. Your mind is now visible, but I must warn you, there's no guarantee they'll look now that it's done. If they don't, I can only say I'm sorry."

57

I watched the penthouse as if through a camera. Light abandoned the back of the penthouse's common area. Keith's hand slipped off the switch before falling to his side. "What is with Titans and leaving on unnecessary lights?"

"It could have been me for all I know," said Alexandra.

Epimetheus held up a finger. "It was me."

The tip of Thumper's tail appeared beyond the couch. Oliver and a thin old man appeared with him. Alexandra ran over and hugged Oliver. "I'm so sorry Oliver."

"I am too," he said.

Epimetheus rose. "You did the best you could with that dragon. He died nobly."

"And he did what he had to get his wife back from the void," said Keith.

Silence followed as Oliver and the older man filled more of my field of vision. Prometheus entered. He approached Alexandra. "The witch is still alive, at least there's that."

Keith bristled. "What do you mean by 'still'?"

Oliver's voice filled the room. "Let Prometheus be Prometheus I always say. That girl should be safe gathering reagents with Harold. For now, we have another one to take care of."

He gently patted the older man's back and pointed. "There, grandfather. That's Hana's soul-stone. Her body was destroyed."

"Huh?" he said.

"Hana, the kitsune."

"Yes, yes, of course."

The older man turned and smiled like a mischievous child. "I remember."

Oliver's finger tapped something just outside my view. His grandfather, the Gray Wolf as he's known, reached toward it and stopped. He sniffed. He cupped his ears.

"Grandfather, Hana's stone is right here."

The Gray Wolf jerked his hand from his ear. "What? Do you think I don't know anything anymore?"

Oliver's face turned red. "Okay. Yes, we discussed this before we came. We need to do what we came for before Koseina notices you."

"A mere kitsune? Really?"

"Grandfather, please. We don't have much time."

Again, a childish grin crossed the older man's face. He raised a finger didactically. "When time is short the rule is first things first."

"And we are here for only one thing and that is Hana."

His hand moved closer and stopped. "Then what is this?"

Keith answered. "That was Siet's soul-stone. Aiden wore that the day he died. It's empty."

He studied Keith. "Ivan, even you have lost faith in me? It's not empty."

"What, what do you mean?"

His hand blocked out the view. "Where's the dragon's body?"

My soul had been discovered.

Because of what I've been through, the void seemed reachable and I doubted if death frightened me anymore. Life did.

I opened my eyes to rock spires; each pointed a different way. My blood still stained them. Epimetheus loomed over me. "Good, Son of Order. Take your time."

Alexandra stood behind him with a void of emotion. The world spun. The Titan caught my head. "The old Gray Wolf needed to keep enough energy to leave. You're going to need time to recover most of yours on your own."

Alexandra choked out words. "Was there anyone — no, of course not. I'm torturing myself with hope."

She ran off. Epimetheus helped me to my feet. "Let me know when you can walk. I know I said to take your time, but that blue monster is closer than I'd like her to be."

"Where's Vedi? I need to let her know I'm alive. Where's Keith?"

"You're not all back yet upstairs, I see. Their chaos energy would likely attract Koseina. Why else do you think they forced me to play escort?"

I took a step and then another. "Is Vedi still gathering reagents with Harold?"

"Um, how do you --- well of course."

He cringed. "Yes."

"I need to let her know I'm alive before I do anything else. What about my father?"

"Two days out."

I reached for and didn't find the torch amulet. "I need Thumper."

"He's waiting for you in New York."

We passed through the portal to dry air. Thumper sat at the window. The torch amulet hung around his neck. *"Welcome back, dragon. I'd be grateful if you would take this amulet off me"*

Keith hugged me briefly. "Death doesn't seem to be a thing for you, boss."

I wasted no time in getting the amulet. "Can you take me to Vedi?"

"There will be a transition."

"Fine, just take me to her."

"The transition will be in Morocco. My superiors want me to get a read on Koseina's position."

"Can't you do that after you take me to Vedi?"

"Not and maintain the proximity to you they want me to."

"So, I'm getting the Olympian treatment, like Athena often gets?"

"She may be the most intelligent mind, but she hasn't seemed to die and come back twice, let alone once."

"They're not sure they trust me, right?"

"The other explanation sounds better, but yours is probably more accurate."

"Okay, then let's get going. I want her to know her attempted deception didn't get me killed, and sooner, rather than later."

Another rocky shoreline appeared, or rather we appeared at it. A ridge grew on Thumper's fur. I studied the horizon. "There's no sign of Koseina being near here."

"She's beyond the horizon as she should be."

"Well then, I don't want to be pushy but why haven't you set out for your reading yet?"

"I need to rest it seems. You, dragon, took too much effort to teleport."

"I wore you out?"

"No. I can handle teleporting much more than just you normally; several times in fact. You just took much more effort than you did before for some unknown reason."

"What, I've gained weight or something?"

"No. Those with a lot of chaos magic are difficult to teleport. You as a dragon of order are relatively easy. There has been some chaos magic in you before; a residual as it were; Probably from your union with your wife. Now, based on the effort it took me to get you here, I'd say you have much more than that now, like a chaos god's worth of chaos magic inside you."

"Epimetheus told me the Gray Wolf held back when he restored me, so he could leave quickly. If he's right, then it's not that."

Thumper's eyes grew black. *"Hang onto your pendant, dragon. I better get this reading done quickly. Whatever the reason for the energy inside you, you're a beacon to Koseina. She's probably already on her way here."*

58

Thumper vanished. I pulled the torch pendant's chain to lift it off my chest. "Siet?"

His voice roared in my head. He screamed and then used words. *"You tricked me dragon and I am not happy."*

"I didn't trick you. How could I?"

"When that demented Gray Wolf returned you to your body, he returned me to it too. Now I'm where I'm likely to nag you to stop Enki's solution. I may yet doom all the mortals on Earth; again."

"Once I get to Vedi, we're leaving Earth, so you have nothing to worry about."

"Perhaps so, but I still hate this."

"At least now you're likely to get help from the Gray Wolf without having to wait an indefinite amount of time."

"No offense, dragon, but I hate being stuck inside your body especially."

"Oceanids and Dryads seem to find me pleasant enough to look at."

"It's nothing like that. It's that you're an order magic shell around my chaos. Any other sort of person or creature and I might be able to —hold on."

"What?"

I saw what in the west. A darker blue than the rest of the sky grew. With the pendant off my chest, Thumper couldn't hear me, but he could still speak to me. *"Oh my."*

"That doesn't sound good, Siet."

"Hold on," Siet repeated with emphasis. The sky flashed white as if an arc welder worked behind us.

"What was that?" I asked.

"Well, how about that. I can use my magic from within your body, dragon."

"What did you do?"

"I cast a confusion that should hide my chaos magic from Koseina."

The darker blue on the horizon continued to grow. Thumper spoke. *"Whatever that flash was, Koseina's heading your way even faster now."*

I pressed the pendant to me. "We're where you left us and waiting for you to pick us up."

I pulled it off.

"I can't deceive myself and she's got my power, I must remember," said Siet.

Thumper spoke quickly. *"She's closer to me than I want. I'm coming in."*

White streaked down with a thud. Thumper hit the ground and didn't land on his feet. Blood flowed from his head onto the rocks. I rushed to him and touched him. Healing moved through my hands. His eyes opened. *"Thank you, dragon. Her chaos aura is making it hard for me to aim my teleportation."*

"Aim high and get us out of here."

"We could end up moving too quickly too high. Too dangerous."

"Staying to fight her is even more dangerous."

"You fly, I run. We have a chance to lose her."

"You can ride my back."

"I run faster than you, dragon, can fly."

He leaped into a dash. I took wing. We moved east. A plume-ridge of dirt and sand crossed the ground.

"You do move fast, Thumper."

"One hundred and twenty miles per hour, I'm told."

"Only forty or fifty here. Thanks for not running ahead."

"I'm not holding back."

Siet laughed. *"Well, well, well. I am able to speed you up, and quite a bit."*

"Is that a spell, Siet?"

"Siet?" asked Thumper.

Siet answered my question. *"No, dragon. Your flight is managing to augment itself with my magic energy. Imagine that."*

"Are you okay, dragon? You sounded like you called me Siet."

"No, not you, Thumper. I found out why I seem to be carrying around the chaos magic of a chaos god. Guess whose mind came out of the soul-stone with mine?"

"Oh, not good, dragon. Siet's going to get us killed. Koseina's aura has gotten stronger. She's catching up with us."

I pondered and came up with a plan. "Thumper, we don't need to keep running together. If you veer off at ninety degrees, you should eventually get away."

"And leave you to die?"

Siet shared my concern, *"If he stays with us, Koseina will most certainly kill him. She'll kill him first. She hates his kind."*

"Siet and I don't have to die. Between the two of us, even if in an awkward way, we could find a way to evade her. You, on the other hand, would stand no chance. Now go."

"I'd rather die beside you."

"Like when your father died trying to save an Olympian from his foolishness? Now, who's being more foolish, you or me? Veer off, Thumper. Go. Fight another day."

He gave me a look over his shoulder and veered south. *"Don't lose the pendant, friend."*

"Any ideas, Siet?"

"Maybe we can catch her in weather dual, like last time."

"But she's much more powerful than last time."

"Yes, but this time our goal isn't to defeat her. If we throw up enough

wind and sand, and I play it right, we might get her lost in it all and get away."

"You've got eons of experience on anyone in such things. Sounds like a reasonable shot to me."

"Pick a good sandy place."

"That shouldn't be hard in the Sahara."

I found a place with no people in sight for miles, and just in time. All turned black. The blue darkness of Koseina's core eclipsed the sun. We could no longer run. Cold air danced with hot. "Shall we begin?"

"I'm pretty sure I can protect you from projectiles, dragon. Max out your size to confuse her."

"What?"

"A good non-magical deception is best built on a distraction. Trust me."

I grew to maximum size and past it. Instead of like Rocky Top I rivaled Everest. Koseina started to laugh and stopped mid-way. Siet then laughed instead.

"Now that's a distraction and then some. Now for some of my stuff."

Nothing happened. *"Uh, dragon, I need a hand wave here, or rather a claw wave. Raise your front right foot for me and hold it there until I get some storm magic going."*

A loose circle of a half dozen tornados rose from the sands around Koseina. Her voices cacophonied, "You have certainly become a god dragon since I last killed you, but your storm magic is pathetic."

"I'm afraid she's right. I can only do a fraction of what I hoped through your orderly hide."

59

I tried to ask if we needed another plan or if I should despair for another way to escape. A low rumble came out instead. Words formed everywhere except where they could leave my maw.

Koseina's shattered voices spoke with perfect diction. "There's no point in standing in my way."

A new tornado dropped from the sky; larger than the others. It collided with one. The smaller one disappeared into its midst. The larger one grew larger and moved to another. The same result followed, and it repeated this for the rest until it approached me in size.

"I'm not going to feed it any more of those," said Siet.

As Siet pondered what to do I acted. I recalled my Earth Science lessons about tornado life cycles. They're fed by rising warm air; abundant in the Sahara. If I could somehow remove the warm air, the tornado would fade out of existence. I needed cool air and I knew where to find some fast; about the altitude of my head. I just needed to fly my wings up there.

Koseina used my delay to direct her monster tornado at me. It met my chest and yanked. I attempted to fly. Instead, my hind feet smacked the ground. I flexed and pushed off. That worked. I rolled across the desert floor. Clouds of sand towered in my wake. I pushed some down as I finally flew.

Siet spoke. *"I just trained your motor functions to allow you to speak in dragon form."*

"I don't see the value of that."

My voice, like a giant Russian bass, rumbled. Koseina's voices answered. "Oh my. The voice of a god too—now get out of my way."

The tornado grew taller. I guessed she didn't know her Earth Science. I flew over it and hovered. My wings pushed large amounts of cold air to the desert floor. The tornado still reached with growing height. I had to dodge away and return over it higher. The new position gave me even colder air. The tornado reached again.

Siet laughed. *"Well, at least, dragon, you've got her busy trying to win a pointless contest. But do you plan to win?"*

"Yes."

Unless her tornado fed on pure magic, I knew its stretch into cold levels of the atmosphere only helped me. I flew up an extra height and dove at the funnel. My wings drove an extra-large amount of cold air down to the desert floor. The funnel cloud quivered and evaporated.

"Very good, dragon. Now as for me training your voice. I'm hoping to help you cast spells."

As he spoke, her core rushed me. I recognized the move to envelop me so she could deal instant death like before. In despair, I swung a claw at the darkest core of her being. With more thought I increased my distance from potential spire-making matter. She moved away. I deflected her somehow.

Seeing as she just attempted her killing blow, I let loose with mine. My sonic attack of brass and thunder made giant dunes dance. She screamed in agony. We had to be heard over the horizon.

"Confusion," I said. I hoped Siet could prevent what had to sound like Heaven's wrath and Hell's anguish filling Mauritania.

"I've got nothing to spare, dragon if I'm to protect you from her."

Concentric circles spread across the sands until they flattened. The rumbling of distant earthquakes came from all directions.

Koseina's core split for a moment and then came back together. My sonic blast could not deal much more than pain to her noncorporeal body. Her voices followed the settling of my attack. "Again, dragon, I've had enough of you."

A mountain's worth of sand jumped. The air cracked from its velocity. Pitch dark pounced. The tips of my wings stung and then burned.

"Sorry, dragon. I've got you now," said Siet.

The pitch dark became a red glow. The sand burned against an invisible shield. A wall of molten glass formed against it. I could see Koseina's blue core closing. I stepped back; too late.

She crashed through the shield. I attempted to move away. I didn't expect to be able to push off. Still, I reflexively reached out. My claws met heat. Smoke rose from them. I couldn't pull them out of the heat. I pushed in vain, or rather I thought it in vain.

The smoke stopped. Despite my worst fears, my claws remained. I clutched fur. A hillside's worth of fur-covered flank pressed against me. I used its momentum to push it past me. Koseina's blue glow mixed with black fur hit the sand and rolled.

I spoke under my breath. "What did you do?"

"I did nothing. Your restoration, that thing you got from marrying the chaos witch, acted on her."

Koseina rose from the sand, part flopping black fur and half incorporeal blue energy. She cried, "No."

I sensed an advantage and flew at her. I aimed to take the fight to her for a change. She cackled and a dozen of her appeared. I kept at the one I started. My claw swung out and met nothing.

"Foolish dragon. All that power has been wasted on you."

Darkness invaded my peripheral vision just before it enveloped me, and completely. She caught me from behind and I hovered too close to her deadly toolbox; the ground.

"Too bad I didn't finish you sooner," she said.

Stone spires like skyscrapers sprung into existence and broke my flesh. Something differed this time though. Instead of hammer blows and cascades of blood, I felt gouges and the warmth of slow bleeds. My efforts to turn succeeded.

Her spires blocked her attempted exit. I grabbed the part of her core still dark and blue. The flank of flesh riled against me. I held firm. Smoke rose. Heat singed me. The air filled with smoke from my burning flesh. The spires retreated into the ground.

"Let go of her, dragon. You'll burn yourself to death."

I held on as long as I could bear the pain. When I let go she bounded away. There in the desert, we towered. We stared at each other. My claws healed from their burns. She lowered the shoulders of her fox form and growled. Her eyes glowed red. Her many tails whipped about like Scylla's heads.

"By the time you heal she'll ..."

I let loose a second sonic attack. This time it didn't split her. This time it broke her bones. They sounded like the cracking of redwoods. I saw her jaw open. Her eyes bulge. I couldn't hear her screams over my blast. She collapsed to the ground, the last of her life draining. So much power turned pathetic, almost pitiable.

"Tell her I'm so sorry that I failed her so as a teacher."

"Siet says he's sorry he failed you—"

She projected words into my head. *"Siet. You taught me everything I wanted to know. I did what I wanted to from your last lesson on."*

Siet could give no answer. She died.

60

I returned to human form. The prone fox corpse towered over me.

"I don't want to just leave this literal mountain of flesh here."

"Hold up your left hand."

I did as Siet said. The desert crawled up and around her body.

"Now speak these words. 'Mit fe Siet.'"

"Mit fe Siet."

The sand hardened into an amorphous stone shroud.

"No one's going to notice a new mountain here?"

A white flash filled the sky.

"No one's going to realize it hasn't always been here."

I didn't want to think too much about the deception involved. It would make me sick and more importantly, I had a more important thing to do than consider my complicities just then. I grasped the torch amulet. "Thumper. Koseina's dead. Come back to me."

Thumper's voice in my head carried doubt. *"Really, dragon? How?"*

"I'm not sure I have time to tell you the story right now. I need to get to Vedi to let her know I'm not dead."

"How do I know this isn't Siet pulling a deception?"

"Thumper, please. Even if this were Siet, wouldn't it mean we're still alive?"

"Don't bother convincing me. I've confirmed that her chaos aura isn't there. I'm coming now."

Thumper appeared. He studied the new mountain. *"You fought her here?"*

"Yes, Thumper. Please take me to Vedi."

"The mountain shows no signs of the sort of damage I'd expect from her chaos magic."

"That's because her corpse is hidden in it."

His ears shot back. *"Convenient that it was here."*

"It's not convenient that I'm here."

He leaned into my thigh and evergreens surrounded us. People didn't.

"Where are we? Where's Vedi?"

"The Taiga in east Siberia. This is where I last talked to them, just a couple hours before the Gray Wolf brought you back."

"Are you sure they're still near here? Harold could teleport them anywhere on Earth."

"Harold told me they expected to be gathering reagents here for most of a day. Stay here. I'll look around."

He vanished. I stopped myself from shaking.

"This is almost more than I can take. She may do something rash if she still thinks I died because of her faked death."

"Don't take full size right now. That last illusion wore me out too much to do it again any time soon."

Moments before, I towered like a mountain over one who could destroy the world. At this moment I found myself helpless to stop my own world's destruction.

"It's a classic tale of tragedy," said Siet.

"What?"

"One lover fakes their death to be with the other, only to have it backfire and cause the other to truly kill themselves."

"I didn't fake death, not intentionally anyway."

"Dragon, dragon, I didn't mean you were the one."

"She faked her death to inspire me to help Enki, not to—"

"Nuhah now, friend, if I may call you that, just like you, everything

she's done since she first discovered the cabal has been so she could be with you."

"You can't lie to me while inside me, but how can what you say be true? How could it be said that she faked her death to be with me."

"You can see it if you try. To be with you she needed the world saved. She did what she hoped would change your mind about the thing that I must say, both of us refused to do."

It came to me quickly.

"Yes. I can see it now, but now I need to get to her before she tries in error to join me yet again in death."

"Aiden?" said Harold behind me.

I turned to see only him and Thumper. "Where's Vedi?"

"I wish I could tell you I know, but she has lost me."

Thumper vanished again. *"Looking about."*

"Does she know I'm alive?'

"No, my boy. I've only learned of that moments ago myself when Rumbler's son told me. I am most pleased and relieved to see you, but I fear Vedi remains dangerously distraught."

"Why did you take her out here if she's so distraught? You know she's mortal."

"I thought it best to give her things to do, helping us to prepare for the fight with Koseina."

"Well, Siet and I have left her dead body in the Sahara. Do you have any idea where Vedi could have gone?"

"Siet's alive too?"

I pointed at my head. "It's a story for a time after I find Vedi."

Harold bowed his head and shook it. "Oh dear. Oh dear."

"If she's in this forest, Thumper should find her soon."

He continued in the same way. "I should have known better. Oh dear."

"Harold? Is there something more I should know?"

"She had me cast a cloaking spell on her to help avoid detection by Koseina. That's what she told me."

"Will it hide her from Thumper?"

"I'm afraid so."

"Vedi," I shouted.

"I heard that, dragon," said Thumper in my head.

I noticed the torch amulet had been in my grip for a while.

"What will hide her from me?"

"Harold's cloaking spell that he cast on her."

"The wizard is helping us?"

"She tricked him."

"Cloaked or not, if she's in this forest I can find her."

"He says he can find her anyway."

"I'm happy about that, though I'm not sure how."

"How is it you can find her even if cloaked?"

"Just between you, me, and that refugee inside you, I can find her even if she's cloaked because of the one thing she can't hide, the space she takes up that no other object can at the same time. It takes a lot longer than for someone not cloaked, but if she's in this Taiga I can find her within the hour."

"Well?" said Harold.

"It's maddening, but we wait. It could take hours, but he's sure he can find her—as long as she hasn't left this Taiga."

"I'm so sorry I contributed to this situation."

"She tricked you. Her reasoning might have made sense to me too."

Harold put his hand on my shoulder. "Whatever happens, my boy, I know you have the strength to get through it."

I hated his choice of words.

61

I ran about the woods calling out, "Vedi, it's Aiden. I'm alive."

I wanted so much to hear her voice respond that I first mistook Siet's for hers.

"Dragon."

"Vedi?"

"Dragon, stop for a moment and listen to me."

"Do you have an idea for finding her?"

"As a matter of fact, yes, but I'll admit it's self-serving. Nonetheless, I believe it could be the best course of action for both of us."

"Please then. I'm listening."

"Instead of you running around, I can cast multiple illusions of you doing the same thing. They'll respond to whoever interacts with them as they expect the real thing to, just incorporeally, and if anyone attempts to touch one, I'll know so we can check it out."

"You have the magical energy for that?"

"Yes. Just enough."

"Great. Which hand do you need me to raise? What do you need me to say?"

"It's a miner enough a spell that I shouldn't need you to do anything, but I will beg one thing of you."

"And that is?'

"You have Harold take you back to my New York penthouse so you can tell my wife that I'm alive."

"Oh, wow, Siet, I should have thought about you too."

"And I can't blame you. Your wife is mortal and perhaps more impulsive, but still, I worry about Alexandra."

"Cast your illusions and I'll let Thumper know what we're doing."

KEITH JUMPED out of his chair when he saw me. "Boss, you're in the news."

"That can't be good."

Alexandra looked up. They both had been watching the same computer screen.

"Alexandra, I've got some good news for you," I said.

"I know, Aiden. You've got my husband inside of you."

"Smart girl," said Siet.

"How did you figure that out?"

"Someone managed to get a video of your fight with Koseina."

"So sorry, dragon. I thought we were well out of sight."

"I thought nobody could see us in such a remote area."

Alexandra pointed. "I could tell from the spells you cast and your god-like size you have to have Siet inside you."

"The Gray Wolf mistakenly put us both in my body."

"But how could we not see his mind in the soul-stone?"

"Go ahead, dragon, tell her. She'll save her wrath for me after I'm in a body of my own."

"Siet used magic to hide himself, hoping to not be rescued from the stone until after Koseina was defeated."

She rubbed her forehead. "I guess I'll ask him why later."

Keith fidgeted. "Boss, this video is a big problem."

"My father can't see it, right?"

"I'm not sure that's even a problem," said Alexandra.

"What? Why?"

"Those distributing this video have identified you as the rebirth of Tiamat. You have been sent by the planet to punish humanity for their sins against the planet and their wickedness and injustices against themselves."

"People are believing this?"

"Yes, boss."

"Well, what happens when I leave having not carried out these punishments?"

Alexandra pointed at the screen. "That will keep you from being discovered by your father, but the video includes an appeal for people to do what Enki wanted to be done all along."

"Who's going along with it?"

"Athena's allies inside world governments and news services have tried their hardest to get the videos dismissed as a hoax, but Enki's cabal has many such connections of their own."

"And so far, how goes it?"

"We're losing. Violent mobs are starting to form around the world. In the streets below us, cars have been sitting still. I dread what may be about to happen."

"By tomorrow I can make people forget this as long as millions of them don't become of one mind and will," said Siet.

I stepped to the window. "We need to break all one hundred of Enki's circles. Keith, get me a phone."

"Right boss."

He handed me his. I dialed my only human contact with the Children of Galinthius. "Zeke, are your employers ready to help me?"

"Damnit, son, what have you been up to? Tell me you're not possessed?"

"Not by Tiamat anyway."

"I didn't ask by who. Shit, son, I don't need this god-damned game of yours right now. What the shit in Hell is going on?"

"I killed Koseina with Siet's help. Long story, we don't have time."

"Siet's help? You don't have time?"

"Enki's using a video showing the combination of our powers to frighten Earth's mortals into participating in a ritual that will unite them in mind and will."

"That's a damned way to make yourself useful. You're not helping him intentionally, are you?"

"No. There are two really bad things about this ritual. One is that all the mortals on Earth who won't participate will be killed. Two is that once all the survivors are of one mind, they can't get back out."

"Okay, that's bad, I think."

"Think about how powerful that one mind made of many would be and think about how well others with that much power have done with it."

"Okay, it's bad. What do you want from us?"

"There are one hundred ritual circles around the world. Your cats should be able to make short work of them."

"Yeah, they can and they will. What are you going to do?"

"I don't have time on my side, but we'll do what we have to."

"You know I hate it when you don't give me simple direct answers, and I think I'm going need one here. What are you going to do?"

"We'll stop as much mayhem as we can within time restraints."

"What are your time restraints?"

"I need to find my wife before she kills herself and then get away from Earth before my father arrives."

"That last part should be unnecessary. With Koseina dead, we're already working on turning him around. Now as for your wife, damn it all Aiden, how many things have you kept from me? How's she even alive? She died the day of your wedding."

"She is, and unlike her last apparent deaths, one of which you know about, this next one will be real, and you know I can't lie to you. I need to find her and stop her."

"Once we're done destroying those circles, we could find her for you."

"There may not be time for that. She's already taken measures to disappear and not be easy to find."

"Okay, son. I'm just going to have to trust you. Holy shit. I'm on the circles. Just know I'm going to demand a lot of explaining and apologies from you after this."

"Will do."

I hung up. After months of keeping things from him, the secrets didn't seem to matter anymore. I wanted Vedi.

"Blast," I said.

"What's wrong, boss?"

"In my rush to get their help, I made Zeke a couple promises."

"Big ones?"

"One's small." I tapped the window. "The other is near and urgent."

The streets filled with people on foot, carrying things to hit each other.

62

I returned Keith's phone. "Call Gabe and get any of our allies, our past allies, our potential allies from amongst the remnants to do whatever they can to quell what's going on."

"Here?"

"It's probably any place that could have seen that video. Tell them, we've got New York city from here. Harold, take me to the roof."

Harold waved a hand and we stood on the roof.

"Now return to Keith and give him any help he could use to getting our allies to act."

"Right."

He waved his hand and vanished.

"Can we get a closer look at those crowds down there?" asked Siet.

I moved to the edge. "What are you thinking?"

"I make people think or perceive things that aren't so. I need to know some details of what they're doing to do that."

"What about them seeing me flying?"

Waves of light moved from my head across the rest of my body. *"Now, only those you intend to hurt will see or hear you, and then they'll forget you the next day if they're still alive."*

"Good enough for me."

I took to dragon form and dove to just above their heads. I hovered. "Well, Siet?"

"Good. No cars are running. Awe it is."

People filled the streets as far as I could see. "Can you cast that as I fly along?"

"Yes. Go."

I flew down the middle of Manhattan. I glowed. Wherever I passed people fell over backward.

"What are they seeing?"

"A very few may see you, but most don't know why they've suddenly been overwhelmed with awe. Just that they have."

"So they won't fight today?"

"Tomorrow will be another thing as it usually is for them."

"In the meantime, we're playing with their emotions."

"Only fighting fire with fire, so to speak."

Everywhere I flew, people intent on causing harm fell to the ground and wondered. That is until I reached a certain street corner. An angry crowd pressed against a barricade of cars. Another crowd rushed to enter a steepled church. A small group of men and women in red berets pulled wounded from the cars and up the church steps. Just outside the barricade a large group of people in black masks also drug people from the cars, only they were beating them with bats.

"Too late for awe on this group."

Which side favored Enki's solution and which side considered refusing seemed apparent. The masks made no sense, yet the beatings made it clear enough. I decided to test Siet's confusion spell and flew to the steeple. I clung to it and roared at the black masks.

Most of them moved back. Those caught up in the bloodlust of beating their victims continued in it. Some of the runners, to my amazement, rallied and brought out rifles. A clatter of weak thunder accompanied the kick of their guns. Bullets ripped through the crowd of people trying to escape.

I launched at them and landed on some. The others implausibly reloaded. I threw the bloody mess of flesh that had been some of their fellow shooters at them. They still fired. I spun around with my tail. The crunching of bones and popping of flesh sickened my ears. My spin placed the bat wielders in front of me.

I hoped to save as many of their victims as I could. I swung my claws at the level of the average clavicle. I lost all sense of mercy. The earlier retreat left room for me to pile my targets' split bodies away from the barricade.

Once no more bats swung or guns fired, I took my human form and saved those I could. As none of those I helped could see me, they just moved to the church.

"They're going to give Jesus credit, you know."

"I don't think they shouldn't."

A large black cat bounded onto the barricade and looked around.

"That's a Child of Galinthius. Can he see me, Siet?"

"You want him to?"

"Yes."

"Will do, but keep in mind that everyone will be able to."

"Do it."

The cat's eyes came to rest on me. *"Aiden Ferris?"*

"Yes, I am."

"I see that your quelling is done on this island and I'm afraid I need your help."

"I told Zeke I needed to concentrate on finding my wife after this."

"Dragon, the circle I was assigned is being guarded by much more than I can deal with."

"None of the people I've dealt with are going to think to use it until tomorrow. By that time you guys should be able to attack this circle enforce."

"Not this one, dragon. This one is guarded by Enki himself."

I squeezed together the skin on my forehead. Harold taught me to do that whenever I feared to lose my temper.

"I only promised to do what I could within the time restrictions of finding my wife."

The big cat walked to my thigh. *"Thumper says he hasn't found her yet."*

"But I can't leave in the middle of a fight with Enki, but I will have to if he finds her."

"Until then, brave dragon."

He brought me to the United Nations ruins. Enki towered over his child statue. Imhullu covered his right arm. He pointed to me with his left. "The Children of Galinthius disappointed me greatly when they took your side over mine. I guess there's not much of a chance left for me and my goals; all except one; a new one. To make sure you don't get to your suicidal wife in time. --- That way we both lose."

"How do you know about Vedi?"

"There, behind his ankle, dragon," said Siet.

Dogan peered around, expressionless, true to his life's pattern, the betrayer.

63

Dogan's lips moved and his hands spread. A translucent dome appeared over the area. He stepped behind Enki and my spatial awareness told me he left. Enki stepped aside and I saw a small portal vanish. Enki smirked. "No need for him to stick around. I can't grant you the pleasure, however small, of killing the man who betrayed you. I want your suffering to be as great as possible."

I wanted to defy his confidence. "We don't know that Vedi will kill herself."

"I'd like to say that I'm afraid we do, dragon, but the afraid part would be a lie. You see, Dogan ran into Vedi in the Taiga and found her very distraught. She as much as told him she intended to kill herself since she believed you to be dead."

"And I suppose you won't tell me anything to even hint as to where she's gone?"

A small crowd of people approached the dome. They walked in unison but without cadence. Their eyes focused as one. Enki chortled. "Seeing her despair, Dogan opened a portal with which she could leave the Taiga, and also gave her a one charge wand she could use for one more teleport; once she gathered her means and decided where she wished to do the deed. Oh, dragon, she very much intends to kill herself."

I hoped he'd lie so I could logic something out. Instead, he told a truth that gave him a perverse pleasure to tell. I grabbed my torch pendant. Enki pointed at it and grinned. "This dome he summoned not only blocks teleportation in and out but telepathy as well. Dogan really is the talented little traitor, isn't he?"

"I know he's prone to betrayal, but he always has had a noble reason before. This treachery makes no sense to me."

"You think anything he does makes sense? Maybe there's hope for his secret obsession after all. He wants your wife out of his way so he can get to you. Insane, right? Ah, but for him to get you, you must be the winner of this fight and I've killed more powerful dragons than you."

I flew at the dome. I met it with a sudden stop and a familiar sound from behind; Imhullu. The gauntlet he used to kill Tiamat, he let loose with it. My dodge came a tad late. A blast of air that could puncture steel screamed by my head. The disruption of the air where it passed caught me and sent me tumbling through the air.

The force of the disruption vectored off the dome and spun me like a wobbly football. I struggled to break out of the trajectory while two more shots from Imhullu followed. Animal reflexes and perhaps panicked calculations were all that allowed me to dodge them. One of the shots struck the ground and the other the dome. Both created holes. The one in the dome closed within a second.

The Child of Galinthius broadcasted his telepathy within the dome. *"The dragon is not alone, Enki. I will do whatever I can to aid him."*

"Too bad he hadn't left before the dome got cast. He could have fetched Thumper for us," said Siet.

"Don't think that puny animal can help you, dragon. This fight is just you and me and no matter who wins—you lose."

I pulled out of the wobble and landed on my feet. I spoke under my breath for Siet's sake. "If I try to close, I won't be able to dodge. Any misdirection we can use?"

"Yes, the one Koseina used on us."

Enki tried to surprise me by lowering his gauntlet before popping it up. I read the deception in his face and dodged. He followed it with a second shot as I moved. That one confirmed my theory. Any closer and I wouldn't have dodged it in time.

"Take a large form," said Siet.

I no longer doubted him. I shifted to a dragon the size of a house. The crowd chanted in unison, "bring him down. Bring him down—"

Then they gasped in unison. Six illusions of me surrounded Enki. Three more hovered over him.

"Now take a smaller form."

I returned to the winged human form. I knew the game from there. I flew back and around. Enki sent a shot of air at my last position. It screamed through and illusionary flesh and blood billowed out the back.

Enki raised an eyebrow and grinned. He knew the game too. He turned and shot at one and then another illusion. He changed aim and turned with super-human speed. My chances of reaching him alive dropped from near-certain to about fifty-fifty. I hated the odds.

The big black cat screeched. His rear dropped to the floor and yanked himself free from something. He faked getting his tail stepped on and did it well; well enough to deceive Enki. The god of learning fired Imhullu at the illusion next to the cat. As the fake gore flew, I dove to Enki's arm and grabbed Imhullu.

He struggled in vain. My strength enhanced by Siet's energy pulled the gauntlet off and I tossed him against the dome. He regained his feet. I put on Imhullu and closed. The crowd silenced. Enki screwed his face. "Stupid dragon. Why would you close when you've got Imhullu?"

"Because you're in my way."

I unleashed wind weapon on him. Only a magic device could launch such force with no knockback. All the force struck Enki's chest. He turned into a pinata of blood and thick cloth. I dove at the hole where his chest had been and through a hole in the dome right behind. It closed just as I cleared it.

The observers fell to their knees and in unison scowled. One spoke for the rest. “Dragon, how dare you try to stop us.”

“You’re not going to fight me now, are you?”

"We don’t need to fight you. Change is coming and you can’t stop it. We will rise. The world will change and when that happens expect no mercy from us."

“For saving you from yourselves? I will not be the only dragon you face.”

“We are beyond fearing your kind.”

“You can't slay dragons you refuse to see.”

“We will beat you.”

“I'm not the one before you. That one wants to kill you. See her before she does.”

As if a troop of actors called from the stage, they left in the same uniform motions they came. Thumper’s voice entered my head as I watched them. *“Aiden, I’ve found one of Dogan’s portals in the Taiga.”*

“Enki told me about that before he died. Vedi took that portal.”

“I’ll come to get you.”

“Take me to where that portal goes.”

Enki proved not much of a fight. I only hoped he hadn’t delayed me too long. Something in my gut told me he had.

64

Thumper appeared just outside the dome. The black cat inside meandered his tail. Thumper closed his eyes. *"Shall we be going, dragon?"*

"Yes. Hurry."

We re-appeared in his favorite field. I glanced at the sky where I once spoke to her. "I think I can take a little less decompression if it will speed this up."

"I know. I'll not make us wait here any longer than we need."

Thumper scanned the field. *"Just so you know, dragon, we'll get Harold to dispel that dome for us."*

"I wouldn't want your fellow Child of Galinthius to languish there long. He did an admirable job aiding me in that fight."

"He'll last long enough for you to deal with this. In the meantime, you'll probably need Harold, yourself."

"For what? I've got you to teleport me."

"You'll have both of us. Now brace yourself. We're moving fast."

My ears popped and a ring like the inside of a huge bell brought my hands to my ears. It subsided and Harold came into focus.

"Where's Vedi?" I said.

"My boy, we're still looking. Follow me."

I recognized the plastic walls of the refuge. Harold led us through a door. A man in his fifties sat and clutched a piece of paper. He raised his head. "Aiden, you're finally here."

I recognized him. "Mr. Asta? Did Vedi visit you here?"

He nodded. "Less than an hour ago. Oh, son, she's intent on killing herself and is doing everything she can to not be found. But surely you can find her, Aiden. Surely you can."

"Enki told me Dogan gave her a one charge wand to teleport her wherever she wants."

"What a hideous fool Dogan is!" Harold waved it off.

"Mr. Asta, do you have any clue as to where she might have gone."

His eyes welled up. "Hunter is on his way to Milpitas and has the coven searching the area, but I don't think she's there. I was hoping you might have an idea."

"We need to both think on this, sir, the two men she loves the most."

He started to wring his hands. He had to recover the paper. He unfolded it and handed it to me. "Perhaps you may see a clue in this note she left me."

I clutched it as if I grasped her hand and could pull her to safety in my arms. It read:

"Woe is me and all around me for I accepted an impossible task. I chose as chaos to try and satisfy order. I have been a fool. I failed. Daddy, forgive me for I am out of strength. I will go to the place I first started to try, and there I will join my beloved dragon in death."

I HAD to stop the world from spinning in order to think. I reacted more than responded. I needed to act lest I freeze. "Harold, take me to the place where she faked her death."

"You mean the island?"

He mumbled an incantation. Mr. Asta said, "Find her son."

The island's rocks swapped for the floor at our feet.

"I'm with you," said Thumper.

"Start searching the island."

"Already, friend."

"So, my boy, what makes you think she'd come here?"

"She tried and failed to make me help Enki here."

"There's the spot on the shore where she faked her death."

The ground there possessed nothing. My mind cleared.

"No, wait. She's not here."

"You sound so certain."

I pulled out the note. "What she says she failed to do was to satisfy order. That's me. She wasn't trying to satisfy me here, and it certainly wouldn't have been her first effort if she did. She tried to force my hand here. She tried to satisfy me and first much earlier."

"So, before your wedding, my boy?"

I clutched the torch pendant. "Yes. Harold. I remember when she first kissed me. Antarctica, you know the caverns. Take us there."

As he mumbled his incantation, Thumper spoke. *"Antarctica, right, I'll find you there."*

White enveloped us. Frost covered Harold.

"Where are the caverns, Harold?"

"They've caved in, it seems. Good thing you've got someone of my skill teleporting you, otherwise we'd be buried in ice."

"You think she could be buried there?"

"No. Dogan was my understudy after all, and he would never short-quality his work, even to save his life or kill someone he hates."

I scanned the horizon in all directions. "There's nothing to obscure my vision here. She can't hide from us out here."

Harold shivered. "Just being here reminds me of how tired I became teleporting us out of here because of that dark blade."

"Yeah, because of that dark blade. Wait, of course, Harold, that's it, hexagons."

"What, my boy? Are you okay?"

"Her first attempt to satisfy me was when she carved those hexagons into a tree in Terra Del Fuego. Take us there."

"I hope we find Vedi and warmth there," said Thumper.

Harold finished his incantation and shrub-like trees surrounded us. Harold walked ahead and pointed out the tree with the pattern burned into it. "They are indeed perfect, aren't they, Aiden?"

I answered by reflex, "perfect vandalism if such a thing can be called perfect."

"So, she really did fail to satisfy order that day, didn't she?"

A lump plummeted down my throat and tore at my heart. "I am the monster that I am."

Something glimmered on the ground and then two other things. They formed a rough line, at the end of which I saw Vedi's hand. I'm not sure I got there from standing. I just joined her body on the edge of the underbrush. I took her wrist into my hand.

"Well, my boy?" asked Harold.

"Is she—" asked Thumper.

I felt less warmth than I hoped for. I felt no pulse. She didn't breathe.

"Dead."

65

I placed my hand under her head. I closed my eyes and waited. Nothing happened. I waited some more for my healing. "Her body's not cold yet."

"Can't you heal her?"

I waited on. *What else could I do?* The three glinting objects, her class ring, Nix's amulet, her wedding ring, they mocked me. "She hasn't bled out. There's no blood anywhere to be seen. Why can't I heal her?"

Harold squeezed my shoulder. "I hate to suggest, perhaps you can't."

"What? But why?"

He pointed out a small black bottle. "She took a poison. Knowing her it's magical in some way that prevents healing."

"No."

I picked up the bottle. The smell of almonds wafted from it. "Does cyanide lend itself to such magic spells?" I asked.

"No."

He tore away the underbrush from her body. She looked as if she convulsed before succumbing. "Cyanide is horrible enough without adding magic spells to it."

"Why would she kill herself this way?"

"She was always the sort of spirit to do things others wouldn't dare. Most who commit suicide want it to be as painless as possible."

I cleared my eyes. "She wanted to punish herself."

"And there was no need for magic to achieve that."

I picked up Nix's amulet and Vedi's wedding ring. "Then why can't I heal her?"

Siet spoke inside me. "*Your restoration power has left you for some reason. You can't heal anyone.*"

Harold put his arm around me. "My boy, you have always been what you've had no choice but to be. This just didn't have to happen. Such a tragedy."

I studied the gems in the two pieces of jewelry. The glimmer from Vedi's diamond duplicated in a tear in my eye. All the panic left me. Like a complex lock, my thoughts tumbled in place. "You did this, Harold."

He stepped back. "I did, didn't I. It's a shame there isn't enough of that poison left for me; for justice. I thought I could better Shakespeare and have my star-crossed lovers live. I am truly the greatest and most dreadful fool of all."

"No, Harold, just shut up."

I grabbed her twisted hand and slid the ring onto her finger. Thumper appeared. *"What's going on?"*

I whispered, "with this ring, I am wed, as it has been and still is."

I reached under her stiffened shoulders and lifted her head under my chin. Tears rolled down Harold's cheeks. "What a horrible thing I've done to you two. I'm so sorry my boy."

Where my hands touched her, they burned.

Harold's tears stopped. "Oh my."

Vedi's body shook in my arms. Her limbs flailed. I struggled to hold onto her without breaking any of her bones. "This is what you did, Harold. You made it possible for me to save her."

I almost lost hold of her as she convulsed.

"Stay with it, my boy. Her healing may be as painful as her poisoning was."

Her body calmed and she let out a shriek of agony. She breathed rapidly, and finally she opened her eyes to see me. She simpered. "Am I in Heaven?"

"No, Vedi, you and I are on Earth."

"But how are you alive?"

"Siet's soul-stone."

She sighed. "Heaven would have been better, you know?"

"We're right where we belong for now."

She got up and stumbled. "You think I can stand?"

As no more heat came from my hands I answered, "yes, just be careful and let me help you."

She walked over to the tree and ran her fingers in the singed marks. "I just can't seem to do what's right by you."

I held her. "You are with me. That is right by me."

"Yeah."

I brushed her hand away from the bark. As I did, my restoration acted. The burn marks vanished, replaced with healthy bark. I tried to kiss her. She started and pulled away. "The bark, Aiden, what's wrong with the bark?"

"I fixed it without thinking about it. It just happened. I didn't mean anything."

"I know, Aiden. It's just that my carving is still there."

"What?"

The tree, though covered in uncarved and unsinged bark, still had hexagons on its surface. The bark itself formed in hexagon shapes just like the ones Vedi carved there. They were perfect.

"There's nothing wrong with it, Vedi."

"But the hexagons."

"They're perfect, aren't they, and now they're no longer vandalism; just a sign that we were here."

"But how can you, a dragon of order—"

"Make order from chaos?—with you I guess."

I could tell my answer satisfied her. We kissed. Harold mumbled something. I think he said, "Eat your heart out friar Laurence."

Vedi's eyes caught mine in a way that didn't need telepathy. I held up a finger. She nodded. “Harold, Thumper has one of Dogan’s magic domes for you to dispel in New York. Vedi and I will wait here until you’re done.”

“Ah yes, of course. Thumper, shall we?”

“Oh and no hurry.”

66

None of my abilities could speed up Vedi's complete recovery. I healed her body and I could calm her mind, yet one part of her needed time, her soul. I let her cling to me in silence. At other times she wanted solitude. Even in the void she was never alone. Nix was always there.

I believed I could identify. The last few days I shared my skull with Siet, an inescapable presence. Ending that proved less intrusive than I feared. Alexandra took Siet's soul-stone and pressed it against my chest. "Stay still until we're done."

Siet's voice filled my head. *"The next time we speak, dragon, I will be in a body of my own."*

Alexandra put her weight into her push. "Are you coming out?"

"He's wishing me a fair well."

"Yes, dragon, fair well indeed. Until we meet again."

The core of the stone lit like a filament. Alexandra bent her knees like the recipient of an egg toss and pulled the stone to herself. "Now to wait for the Gray Wolf."

"And now for me to return to my wife. Harold, are you ready?"

"Yes, my boy. We're just a short incantation away from Milpitas."

We appeared in my sitting room. Goth metal whined through the bedroom door, My Immortal. Harold padded my back. "I think that's a good sign. I'll take a walk through the park."

"Should I ..."

"No, I think your place is here. I think the clouds are clearing."

I approached the bedroom door. "I'm back, Vedi. Siet is finally out of me."

Her answer choked. "Enter."

My dragon advantages told me the coast was clear. There'd be no passive aggressive ambushes. I entered. She sat with tears in her eyes. I rushed to her. "Are you okay?"

She smiled. "Any time I actually listen to this song's lyrics, they make me cry."

"You know it's not about me? I think it's someone who's actually dead."

"Yes."

She sniffled and turned off the music.

I caressed her shoulder. "How are you feeling?"

She threw her arms around me and whispered in my ear. "Finally."

"You're happy Siet's out of me?"

"I'm happy I'm finally through all the things that kept us apart."

"Olympus has forced us to do so much for them."

"I want to forget them for now."

I gripped her. "I think we can."

She pulled my forehead to hers. "It hurt me so to leave you, but it was the only way I could see to save you."

"I understand. Harold told me."

New tears welled up. "All that time in the void away from you, it could have killed me if hurt could kill."

"It hurt me too."

She stroked my hair. "Through much of it you thought I was dead. You mourned my passing. I cried in pain to think you might move on without me."

I had to close my eyes. "I didn't mourn well. I might not have ever moved on."

She embraced me. Her words vibrated through my chest. "No matter now. We're together. We're finally together."

I clutched her and wished I could never let go. She brushed my face. "Aiden, a tear? An iron dragon cries?"

I kissed her. After a time, I let her up for air. "As long as you live, Vedi, I will be yours and probably for an eternity after."

Her eyes welled. "Have I trapped you?"

"No. Have I you?"

"No. I love you."

"And I love you too. That puts us both exactly where we belong and free."

She buried her head deeper in my chest. "Finally."

67

We appeared inside a tunnel, Thumper, Keith, Vedi, and me.

Vedi touched my wrist. "You know Harold would probably have liked to bring us here?"

"He's still a wanted war criminal here."

"No one would recognize him in these caves full of homeless people, and he still feels responsible for me almost dying. I think we should give him more opportunities to see we forgive him."

"You mean that he ultimately did a good thing?"

She looked at Keith as if to apologize for my nature. I wanted to change the subject. "Keith, you got me cloth armor to wear and Vedi a robe. And you got yourself a robe too?"

He lit a kerosene lantern. The light emphasized his grin. "I think robes are more comfortable."

Vedi laughed. "It becomes you, Keith. Very Keltic-druid-like."

"Thank you, Ms. Ferris."

"I'll look around for any potential trouble while you three chat," said Thumper.

A voice approached with another lantern. "There you are, dragon. I hope I didn't keep your party waiting here too long?"

"No, Lewin, we just got here."

"Ah, and this must be your improbable wife, the chaos witch?"

"Yes, Vedi, this is Lewin, a physician formerly of Toth's court."

"Pleased to meet you, sir."

Lewin looked askance.

"Problem, Lewin?"

"Please forgive me, dragon but I didn't expect a chaos witch to speak so politely. And oh yes. I'm pleased to meet you too milady."

"Married to Aiden, I have to try harder about such things."

"We both have to try harder but it's worth it."

Lewin led us down the tunnel. "I'm just in awe at the both of you in this."

Vedi smirked. "And what may I ask, my husband, makes it worth it for you?"

"Without you, I'm only order. I'm not good. Likewise, without me, I think you'll admit, you were chaos but not good. Together we are good."

Lewin led us into a domed chamber occupied by bats on the ceiling and people on the floor. A woman squinted as he walked up. They exchanged quiet words in the native tongue, and she stood. Lewin took her by the hand and brought her to me. "This the thief's aunt. She's the head of his family. Most of them are in this chamber."

"Is the thief here?" I asked.

"No. He's out scavenging. Do you want someone to fetch him?"

"No. That won't be necessary. Seeing me would probably frighten him. Let's get this deed done."

I turned. "Keith?"

Keith reached into his backpack and handed me a satchel full of coins. I hefted them. "These are lighter than the gold bars we traded for these coins."

Lewin lay his hand on the satchel. "As it should be, dragon. The currency here is worth more than the material it is made of."

"I see trouble in your future," said Keith.

Lewin seemed disturbed. I smiled. "He's not a seer, just a student of a certain set of historians."

Lewin gave Keith a stare, took the satchel and handed it to the woman. I patted Lewin on the back. "I trust she'll be well advised on buying a good farming homestead for all her family?"

"Yes, noble dragon. You are most generous. Between you and your polite chaos witch, this has truly been a remarkable day."

Thumper's voice interrupted the moment. *"I'm waiting where I dropped you off."*

I grabbed the torch pendant. "Is there a reason to hurry?"

"Yes, or at least I'm being told there is. Zeus and Athena may be returning earlier than expected."

"Did everyone hear that?"

Vedi's voiced oozed with sarcasm. "Ooh, Zeus and Athena, we better all put on our Sunday best and crawl to them on our knees with grateful smiles."

Lewin's eyebrows raised. I smacked his shoulder. "You see there, she's the genuine article."

SIET STOOD in his favorite spot by the window, Alexandra under his arm. She turned when we appeared. "Welcome back."

Keith ran to his room. His voice muffled down the hall. "We better get changed out of this anachronistic gear."

Alexandra yelled back, "no need to hurry."

"What? I thought we were expecting Zeus and Athena back early?"

"So sorry if you were enjoying yourself in that other world, but it seems that while they have returned, they're not ready to see any of us yet."

"Athena hasn't even wanted to see you yet?"

"No, not me, not Gabe, not Marcus, not anyone."

Vedi leaned into my side. "This mysterious teacher they went off to see worries me."

Alexandra pointed at Vedi's chest. "Does he worry Nix?"

"She's giving me time off before becoming her avatar. You know, until after Aiden and I's honeymoon."

I gave her a squeeze and addressed the chaos god in the room, Siet. "You haven't taken your eyes off the city since we've gotten here. I'd expect you to be cheerier after the Gray Wolf recovered your body for you and got you out of my head."

He let his words bounce off the glass. "You and I saved the world and yet still in the minds of most Olympians, I am still the destroyer."

Alexandra rubbed his back. Harold entered the room. "I will always be to an entire world, Harold the Dread."

Vedi moved into the middle of the room and held out her arms. "Such gloom in the face of victory. Talk about killjoys. Harold, you may have acted out of selfishness and despair when you brought Aiden and me together, but you made us both better and you may even have saved this world in doing it."

"So, all's well that ends well?" said Harold.

His words lacked sincerity. I took him by the shoulders. "Teacher, what if we put it this way? If Vedi and I could go back in time, we wouldn't have wanted you to do anything different than what you did as far as us. Yes, you caused us struggle and pain, but it's the past that we want."

He grabbed my arms and started to speak but stopped. His smile and the water in his eyes said all that needed said.

A rainbow showed through the window. Thumper announced, *"I think Zeus and Athena are ready to see us."*

68

Nereids and men in dark suits moved to kettle drums. Santa Cruz probably had probably never seen a party that weird; yes, even in California. Between the setting sun, the nimble nymphs, and awkward Empusa, passersby were distracted from the string of guests, us included, disappearing where the serf met the shore; on our way to Elektra's throne room.

Keith dodged a surge in the water's edge. "Why not hold the meeting in Olympus?"

Alexandra paused before the portal. "Knowing Athena, there must be a good reason."

"Well, wanderer, you see, they can't let one such as me enter Olympus."

"After you and I pulled them from the brink, I think they'd change their minds, my friend."

"About you in some way? Perhaps, but you have always been something they like, dragon."

Two Oceanids stood guard by the exit from the transition tunnel into the throne room. One of them held a finger to her lips. We heeded her warning and entered in silence. Unlike the fake party on the beach, silence and earnestness filled the place.

Over a crowd of Oceanids and their blue-tinted blonde hair towered Apollo, and two other Olympians I guessed were Hades and Poseidon. Elektra stood on the dais. Behind her throne the two reasons for the meeting discussed something. They glanced at Apollo and then in the direction of my allies and me. They didn't look at the other Olympians, the ones complicit in all this trouble. That worried me.

They stared at each other and I sensed discomfort like perhaps they disliked some decisions they were about to make. Zeus nodded to Elektra and she turned. "Oceanids, other welcome remnants, and those invited by the throne of Olympus give us your attention. The king of Olympus is about to speak."

Zeus stepped in front of the throne. His eyes bounced off Apollo to nowhere. "Apollo, some of your actions have displeased me and forced me to make decisions I should never have to make."

Apollo answered him as only his son dared. "I opposed Enki in the end. I defended what I believed to be your will."

Zeus raised his hand. "Shush. None of that is where you offended me or Olympus, but you did indeed offend both with another action of yours."

Apollo's face stiffened in what I recognized as resolve. Vedi squeezed my hand for she knew as well as me what Zeus spoke of.

"You committed one of the most serious crimes an Olympian can commit. You stole a golden apple from Hera's grove and fed it to the dryad Ylera. Do you know the penalty for that?"

"I will gladly accept banishment."

Zeus turned to Athena and they exchanged a few words.

"Banishment, Apollo? You do know there are worse punishments than that I could assign; many worse than banishment, but I suspect the worst would be to have Ylera executed or even just sent to Tartarus."

Apollo gulped. "Better to kill me instead, I beg of you, father."

Zeus pointed and nodded. "Ah, now that would be a punishment to discourage future such crimes."

Apollo moved forward. Athena grabbed Zeus's arm. He grimaced and held a hand up to his son. "Now, let us stop right there, Apollo. Athena and I have already agreed upon a punishment for you and we think it's wisest."

"But father, I cannot allow Ylera to die for my own actions."

Zeus took a long breath. "Apollo, as punishment for this I banish you to Earth where you will be assigned tasks in the service of Olympus. There, you and Ylera will stay until such time that no Olympian envies you."

Vedi nudged me. "Poor Apollo." Her sarcasm blared in my dragon senses.

"That is settled. Now I turn my attention to Siet."

Siet let go of Alexandra and stepped away from her. For a moment I thought he might speak. Instead, he waited for Zeus to continue.

"To you, Siet, I must ask you, you caused the end of many an age, but this one you preserved. What was different about this age of iron that you would preserve it? What appeals to you about it?"

"I cannot tell you if this age is special or not. It could even be worse for all I know, but I helped save it for two reasons."

"And what sort of reasons should stop the destroyer of worlds from doing what he has done so many times until now?"

"The first is that I am not what used to be. That alone is enough."

"So says a master of lies, but please tell me the second reason. Perhaps it carries enough plausibility to counter your reputation."

"The second is, that unlike all those previous ages, I am part of this one. The rage that used to rule me and alienate me is behind me thanks to my wife, thanks to your daughter Athena, and thanks to—"

"Stop. The next name frightens me so don't say it."

Athena spoke again in private to her father. This time I could read her lips. "Perhaps in time father."

He closed his eyes and turned back. "Siet, I take it you no longer wish to be called a god?"

"While I'm too used to it to object as often as I should, yes."

"Then as you are this way, I no longer consider you the destroyer either. I will let it be known throughout Olympus that the throne no longer sees you as the destroyer. Live on Earth with your wife, my daughter's chief researcher, in peace as long as you can keep it."

Siet showed no sign of anything. His wife, Alexandra, embraced him. "I think you're going to have to stay at home."

Zeus waved. "Elektra, as of now, I am making you matriarch of the land remnants as well as that of the sea. I am counting on your continued fine judgment. This relieves Siet of any responsibilities other than his, up until now, neglected wife."

Zeus smiled for a second and then squeezed his eyes shut. Athena couldn't look at me.

"Oh no," whispered Vedi, "how could we be about to become the unfortunate ones in this?"

69

"Aiden and Vedi Ferris, we Olympians have worked for thousands of years to keep a delicate balance of power in the universe. We knew that allowing the descendants of Dakk and a dragon like Aiden to live on Earth came with huge risks, but these risks were still tolerable compared to all other humane alternatives. That was until Harold the Dread abused his assigned position as Aiden's teacher to magically manipulate the two of you into marrying."

Vedi reached a hand to Harold.

I defended my teacher. "Now hold on."

"Silence, dragon," shouted Zeus.

I approached him.

"Aiden, no," said Vedi.

The glow of my eyes reflected off those around me. My hands stiffened. Zeus, for his part, his eyes also glowed and white arcs danced on his clenched fist.

"Father," said Athena. She tugged on his arm.

He turned. "He challenges me, Athena. I can't have that."

"Can't you see, father, he's displaying exactly what we talked about."

"Yes, daughter. You are right."

He held up his hand and the arcs vanished. "Stand down, dragon, and listen before you choose to fight the king of Olympus."

Athena nodded, and I did as he asked. Zeus finished. "Harold the Dread, you are both one of the most unfortunate and fortunate men I've ever heard of. Your curse of being a small animal for decades is hard to exceed and the crimes against Olympus you committed in your despair to lift it? Truly no one would want to be you. However, it was this very crime that led to this dragon being able to deal with Enki's errors. And through it all, you demonstrated a sincere love for your student and his wife."

Harold bowed his head. Zeus cleared his throat. "I only hope, Harold, that you have left your days of recklessness behind you."

"I'd like to think I have, Lord Zeus."

"We had to decide what to do with you. A wizard on Earth is less than ideal but we certainly can't send you back to your homeland. You're a hated war criminal. Fortunately for you, Athena came up with a strong solution. I'll let her explain it."

Athena placed her hand on Zeus' back. "Harold, I believe it will be a wise use of our resources if we consider you one of ours."

"At your service, milady."

"More directly, Harold, you will be at the service of Aiden and Vedi. You will officially be a refugee under our protection, and you will be under their custody. You are expected to provide them with teleportation services while under their custody. This will free up resources they've, up until now, been burdening the Children of Galinthius for."

Vedi hugged Harold. "I guess that makes you part of the family, Friar Laurence."

Athena paused to glare at Vedi. "Vedi Asta Ferris, I fear that Nix has chosen her future avatar unwisely. You seem incapable of taking things seriously."

Vedi returned her glare. I took my turn encouraging her to restrain herself by placing a hand on her shoulder. Athena shared her own glare with me. "We have not yet gotten to how we intend to deal with the power balance issues you two present us with. Until then and during then I will be needing both of you to seriously attend to my words."

She gestured to a corner of the room. "Bring the prisoner forward."

"The what?" whispered Vedi.

Two Oceanids prodded a man along wrapped in twine. A cloth bag covered his head. The twine held his arms against his body and even bound his fingers; two together here; three there; two to two or two to three.

"Remove the head-covering," she commanded.

The reason for the bindings became clear when they pulled away the bag and revealed Dogan's face. Their precautions had been thorough. A wad of cloth had been stuffed in his mouth. I had no doubt they wanted to be sure he couldn't cast a spell.

"This one showed up looking for my brother in a dryad refuge. He seemed to have sorely misjudged the shifting tides."

Her eyes moved to the other Olympians and then to Vedi and me. "He put your father's life at risk and tried most intentionally to kill your wife. So, we put his fate in your hands, Aiden Ferris. What do you wish to be done with him?"

I gave Vedi half a hug. I feared she might misunderstand what I was about to do. I stared at Dogan and he stared back. I saw fear in him. It seemed new and to some satisfaction.

"This man has managed to betray everyone he's ever worked for, except possibly Dakk, the one, my wife should forgive me for saying, most deserved betrayal. He owes his pathetic life to his talent with magic. It's proven valuable enough for people to thus far overlook his amazing lack of character."

"Do you think the time has finally come for him to receive justice?"

"If I may ask you, Athena, being the wisest amongst us by far, what would you do with such a man."

A wide smile came across her face. She turned to her father and then back. "I would give him a task that requires his skill; a task he cannot abandon."

“Then, if you can think of such a task, I will place him with you.”

“Are you granting me his custody?” she asked.

I gave Vedi another squeeze. “Yes.”

Athena turned to Zeus.

He nodded. “So, you think that corroborates what we’ve discussed earlier?”

“Yes, father, I do.”

Vedi put her mouth near my ear. “What have you gotten us into this time, pretty boy?”

70

Zeus placed his hand on the throne's arm and looked to Elektra. She nodded and he sat and leaned forward. "We Olympians left Earth because we knew daily direct interaction between us and mortals caused strife. We asked the dragons to leave for the same reason and they did, and they were highly cooperative in this, I must say, of all natures even."

He stopped to stare at me. No one spoke and no one shuffled their feet. The silence tugged at me until I spoke. "Have I outgrown my stay here on Earth?"

He turned to Athena. She shook her head. He sighed. "Uh, yes, very well. What we decided."

"I am willing, but my wife has a promise to keep that would require we stay at least some time more."

He cleared his throat. "Uh, no. I wasn't saying yes to you. I was saying yes to Athena. Quite to the contrary, dragon, your actions in this crisis have taught me something I wish I'd known before I convinced your kind to leave. Unlike the mere consciences of we Olympians, dragon natures and more importantly, dragon honor is steady."

He stopped again and swallowed. Again, a long silence. Athena patted his shoulder and he returned to speaking. "We believe Earth will actually be a better place with a few more dragons about. For this reason, we will begin to allow dragons to request to immigrate to Earth. The application and process and the supervision of their assimilation will be amongst Apollo's duties while he's on Earth."

"Certainly, you won't allow chaos dragons to come?"

"Of course not. We will use reasonable discernment to only bring those who we believe can contribute in a positive way."

"Then surely you'll want me to leave so none of them discover me, and my father gets the word that I'm there?"

"No, Son of Order, you will stay. Athena assures me it's workable."

"Can I know how, Athena?"

She nodded in my direction. "Only those we can trust to keep your secret will be allowed to come."

"That's going to be a small group."

"Yes. As it should be. Any dragon we can trust to keep your secret will be the very kind we want. Just as we want you here most of all."

I realized I had no choice but to trust them in this. I returned her nod. Zeus raised his hand. "Now as for you and your wife, we're not done telling you what's been decided."

I spoke under my breath, "please tell."

"We believe you will have plenty to do over the next few years between whatever promises to Nix Vedi has to keep and keeping her brother out of trouble. Because of that, my daughter has promised not to ask anything of you until you decide you're bored."

Laughter rose from the crowd.

Free at last.

I THINK Horseshoe Falls is the most beautiful of the Niagara Falls. That's why we got a honeymoon suite with a view of it. I turned a chair to appreciate them. The cascade I heard came from the shower. Vedi turned it off and curtain rungs slid.

"I'm not sure why you bothered with the shower."

"You want me to be clean, don't you?"

"Yes, but you know my aura will clean you. You don't need soap when I'm around."

"No offense, pretty boy, but your clean doesn't smell like lilacs."

"Point taken."

Her voice drew closer. "Not to mention, I like a little water on my skin now and then. What's this?"

I turned. "What's what?"

"This little white box on the table."

"Oh that. I think it was placed there by the hotel. You know, complimentary."

She read a note stuck to it. "No, Aiden. It's not from the hotel."

"Then who?"

"Athena."

"She better not be asking me to do anything. Zeus has me on sabbatical."

"You call it a sabbatical, Aiden? I don't recall you becoming anyone's scholar."

"Okay, so maybe not the most accurate way of putting it. See, I'm loosening up—so, what's in the box?"

Vedi put the box down and stepped away from it. "You don't think—"

"like Pandora?"

"Yeah. Oh my. That would be awful, wouldn't it?"

I jumped up and grabbed the box. "I know the author of that story, and unlike most myths, that one is just a story."

I opened it. An object lay under another note. I couldn't read what it was written in. I handed the note to Vedi. She read it to herself and then out loud. "The choice of immortality is not one to be taken rashly. Keep this in the box until you are sure of your decision and whatever you do, don't let anyone but yourself use it."

The object in the box looked like a few peddles of a golden pinecone. Vedi retrieved the box. "So, that's what a golden apple looks like?"

She returned the note inside and closed it.

"So, do you plan to use it?"

She put the box back on the table. "I'll take her advice and think carefully about it."

"It sure would solve the problem of me having to spend thousands of years without you."

She placed her hands on my waist. "For right now, pretty boy, let's think about the two of us together."

"Yes, of course. The long-overdue honeymoon."

I reached back and pulled the drapes.

As for Vedi's promise to Nix and her time as her avatar, that's Vedi's story to tell, not mine. Mine is the story of how I created a wake into which many other noble dragons could follow and make wakes of their own; good, bad, or otherwise.

ABOUT THE AUTHOR

K. D. Menzies has a varied education ranging from Bachelors degrees in psychology, computer science, a lot of ancient writings, oral traditions, and a Masters of Divinity.

He loves cats. One currently provides him with daily hair care and acupuncture services. He also loves writing despite being dyslexic. Unlike many other dyslexics, he chose to avoid most assistance and tough it through to a masters level of reading. It hurts some times but it gets done. Fortunately, writing doesn't hurt.

The symbolism of dragons along with his unique dyslexic perception inspire his writing. Just as 'd' and 'b' interchange in his mind so do the roles of dragons as both villains and champions; monsters and fellow humans. Unlike those letters swapping, the dragon interchange works. His dragons demonstrate the duality within us all.

www.ingramcontent.com/pod-product-compliance
Lightning Source LLC
LaVergne TN
LVHW010053110826
845155LV00028B/316

* 9 7 8 1 9 4 6 6 7 5 6 0 6 *